Praise for *Th*

"Sorensen has a knack for cliffhangers that make you want to start reading the next chapter immediately."
— *Frank Errington, Cemetery Dance Online*

"...a perfectly paced, well-plotted, and compelling haunted house tale filled with oppressive atmosphere, sympathetic and detailed characters, and only a touch of gore."
— *Becky Spratford, Library Journal*

"Chilling and forceful, Sorensen's story of family, emotional pain, and suspense will maintain listeners' rapt attention."
— *AudioFile Magazine*

"*The Nightmare Room* is one creepy little gem...I highly recommend this fantastic 5 star read!"
— *Horror Maiden's Book Reviews*

"...a really well written haunted house story that's easy to follow and scary enough to leave the light on or read during the day. I loved it! This is a must have for your horror collection!"
— *Mother Horror*

"*The Nightmare Room* is one of the best debuts I've ever read. It's one of the best haunted house stories I've ever experienced."
— *Cedar Hollow Horror Reviews*

"I think it's one of the strongest horror novels I've read in quite awhile."
— *The Shades of Orange*

"Holy hell it's been awhile since I whipped through a book so fast. And not because I was eager to be done with it but because it was just so good."

—*GracieKat, Sci-Fi & Scary*

"Simply put, *The Nightmare Room* is a surprisingly strong haunted house story and a heck of a horror debut for Sorensen."

—*Michael Patrick Hicks, author of BROKEN SHELLS*

"...I enjoyed the hell out of this book. I cannot remember a book that enthralled me like *The Nightmare Room* did."

—*Brian's Book Blog*

"*The Nightmare Room* is a very well written haunted house story packed with genuine scares, heart wrenching emotion and strong characters you care about."

—*Kendall Reviews*

"...I was blown away by a killer twist in the story and I didn't see the ending coming! This is hands down the scariest book I have read so far this year."

— *O. D. Book Reviews*

"This is one haunted house that had me running for the door. A must read!"

—*Hunter Shea, author of CREATURE*

"*The Nightmare Room* lives up to its title."

—*Laurie, Horror After Dark*

THE HUNGRY ONES

BOOK TWO OF THE MESSY MAN SERIES

CHRIS SORENSEN

Harmful Monkey Press / Sparta, NJ

Chris Sorensen — First Edition

ISBN 978-0-9983424-2-9

For My Triumvirate

CHAPTER 1

Flashing red lights appeared in Butch's rearview mirror, and he bit down reflexively, his back molars cutting into the side of his tongue. The taste of copper filled his mouth.

"Shit!"

Butch eased up on the gas and guided the old pickup to the side of the road. So, this is where it ended. A DWI stop. He'd refuse the breathalyzer; they'd take his blood. He already knew what the result would be. He'd cracked his first can of beer just after sun up and polished off his last ten minutes ago. The truck was littered with dead soldiers. Impossible to miss. Legal limit? That was for amateurs, and Butch Long was no amateur.

His front tire grazed the curb as he slowed to a stop.

How could he have been so stupid? Instead of driving up and down the strip all night, he should have parked in the lot at Heinz's Grocery or, better still, lain low along some side street. Waited out the last few minutes until midnight.

But no…his hands had already begun to shake, his throat—down which a trickle of blood from his tongue now ran—itched like mad, like it had sprouted spines.

Like I swallowed a dead porcupine.

A night behind bars at the Warren County Jail would do him in. Of that he was certain. There was no way he'd see the next morning. He'd hang himself in his cell before letting his hunger bloom. For that's what the thing inside was, wasn't it? A dark flower dwelling deep within him. Waiting for the dead of night before opening. A dark, carnivorous thing that would eat him from the inside out. He would die screaming, pleading until it swallowed him whole. Until it...

The cop car passed him by, letting loose a deep bleep as it rushed off toward the south side of town.

Butch exploded with laughter.

Not tonight, you sonofabitch! Not tonight!

His violent guffaws caught in his throat, giving way to a hacking cough. The tang of blood was back, and he reached for the rearview mirror and twisted it his way.

He barely recognized the fat man who stared back at him. Eyes drowning in a flabby face. The patches of facial hair were due to neglect, not design, and the sour sweat that beaded on his pasty brow made him look like what he was— a middle-aged drunk.

His lips were wet and crimson with blood. Gingerly moving his tongue from side to side, he could feel the ragged edge where he'd taken a chunk of flesh. He reached a finger inside his mouth and touched the angry spot. Nerves lit up from jaw to ear.

Butch reached for a discarded beer can, then another, hoping for a last mouthful of brew to swish his mouth clean. No such luck. The cans were bone-dry. Further evidence of his drinking proficiency.

Fuck this.

Butch gunned the engine and threw the pickup into gear. It lurched, upset with his rough touch as he steered it back onto the road.

Fibber's Liquors closed at midnight, but old man Fibber would sell him something after hours. Liquor laws were bendy for Fibber. Once, Butch had rolled up around three in the morning and found the old fellow in his office, two bottles into a case of wine. Fibber would hook him up.

He'd better.

The shakes were back with a vengeance, so much so that Butch grabbed the wheel at ten and two like a student driver.

In an hour or so, he'd be right as rain. Floating on air. Dancing the hokey-pokey. But getting from here to there would be tough. There was no getting around it. He imagined himself splayed out in the truck bed, staring upward, all his worries washed away in the Church of the Summer Sky.

But not if I'm shaking like a goddamn pussy.

The scent of approaching rain was heavy in the air as he rolled down Main Street, passing Ecklund's Pharmacy and the burned-out remains of Charburger Castle. The humidity was high, warning of an impending downpour. Butch hoped it held off until he had finished his business.

The flickering Fibber's sign blinked out as he approached.

"Oh, come on," Butch spat. He pulled over in front of the store, cut the engine and jumped from the truck, clipping the side of his tongue with his teeth in the process. "Shit!"

Fibber's sported big glass windows in front and on one side, allowing for better viewing of its liquid treasures. The overhead lights were dimmed to about one-quarter of their usual brightness—a level at which they would remain until Fibber opened up the next day.

Butch gave the door a yank and was surprised when it swung open. A loud bling sounded from within followed by a yelp. "We're closed!"

A scrawny, young man in a Corona t-shirt bounded out of the darkness and stalked toward the door. He waved both hands in front of him as he approached as if warding off evil spirits.

"Where's Fibber?" Butch asked.

"Hospital. Broke his ankle." The young man grabbed the door handle opposite the one Butch feverishly clutched. "You mind?"

Butch licked his lips. "See, he usually lets me…I'm a regular, comprende?"

"Then you know we close at twelve."

"Oh, come on!" Butch felt heat rise up from his gut, felt his face go flush. He rattled the door, rattling the young man's arm as well. "Come on!"

The young man took a step back. "Dude, I'm just part-time. I don't need this hassle."

"Okay."

"I don't wanna call the cops."

"I said okay!" Butch let go of the door and raised one hand while reaching into his pocket with the other. The young man tensed until Butch pulled out a wad of tens and twenties. Pilfered from Grammy Long's dresser—her bingo money. "You sure we can't work something out? Like I said, I'm a regular. Fibber and I go way back. How'd he break his ankle, by the way?"

"He was mowing and stepped in a gopher hole." The guy's eyes never left the wad of cash.

"That's tough." Butch peeled off a ten, paused and peeled off another. His hands had suddenly become remarkably steady. "What'll twenty bucks get me?"

"Lot less than thirty."

"Thirty?"

"You don't like it? Go on down to the Blind Rock and get yourself a twenty dollar six-pack."

"Fine. Thirty," Butch grumbled and added another ten.

The young man deliberated a moment, loosed a deep breath and gingerly took the money. "Gonna have to be a bottle from the bargain bin. Fibber don't keep track of those."

"Sounds good. Lemme just take a peek—"

The guy in the Corona shirt held up a hand, ordering Butch to stand his ground. He stepped to a large galvanized tub with a hand-printed sign that read Bargain Booze, grabbed a bottle and handed it to Butch.

"Knock yourself out."

With that, the man pulled the door closed. Butch heard the metallic click of the lock.

He looked down at the bottle in his hands. Root beer schnapps.

Little prick.

By the time he turned the key in the ignition, Butch had already downed three large mouthfuls of the sickly sweet stuff. It burned his wounded tongue something fierce, but it made the itch in his throat stand down. It would do. It would get him through.

Emboldened by the booze, Butch pulled a U-turn rather than take the loop around the square and was soon heading north on Main Street, the lights of downtown receding behind him.

He took another long draw of schnapps and swallowed fast, willing himself to empty the bottle before he reached the traffic light, seven or eight blocks ahead. He polished it off in two.

Butch pulled off Main into the asphalted area in front of the Crossroads Motel. The place was a throwback to the 1950s when a motel was an oasis to weary traveling salesmen. Now, it was a glorified flophouse. Work clothes hung from makeshift clotheslines strung along the railings of the second floor. A sedan missing both its rear tires took up two parking spots. And the whole place, every sprawling inch of it, was painted a dirty, Band-aid beige.

It sat at the crossroads of highways 34 and 67, hence its truly original name. Main Street became 67 once you crossed 34, and Main/67 split Maple City in two, halving the town into east and west. East was where all the action was—most businesses, most stores, the college; west was all schools and parks and homes.

The small, two-bedroom house Butch shared with Grammy sat in the southwestern quadrant of town, squatting alongside Sudso's Laundromat next to the tracks.

A Mickey-D's had sprung up across the street from the motel, and cattycorner was the Gas-4-U where he'd won a hundred bucks on a scratcher. He'd dumped the hundred back into the till and come away with a case of PBR, cigarillos for Grammy Long and a stack of lotto tickets. The beer was gone by the next day, the house stank of cheap tobacco and he'd won a whopping fifteen bucks on the tickets. Story of his life.

Set apart from the block of motel rooms was the office. A broken neon sign kept secret whether or not the Crossroads had a vacancy. Beyond the office but attached was what had at one time been a steakhouse, as evidenced by a large, plexiglass steer propped up on the roof. Held fast by cables, it stared down on the scene in dumb disapproval of the place's dilapidated state.

Butch pulled up parallel to the old restaurant, switched off the headlights but let the engine idle. If all went well, he'd be in and out before he knew it.

He turned back to the shotgun in the rack and froze the instant his hand touched the stock.

What am I doing?

It would be easy, he'd been told. A walk in the park. Over before you know it.

Easy. No big deal. A piece of cake.

The words rolled around in his head like balls in a bingo cage.

B4!

He had stolen money from Grammy Long.

G56!

She had caught him.

N45!

Caught him rooting around in her drawer. Searching through her underwear. Looking for the cash.

I27!

She had slapped him. He had hit her.

N35!

7

Again and again and again.

O63!

And now, here he was. Shotgun no longer in its rack, but in his grip. Extra shells in his pocket.

N31!

Striding toward the office because he'd been told to. Ordered to. Kicking in the door.

O68!

Greeting the night clerk with a blast. Decorating the wall with his guts. Exiting the office and heading straight for the first room on the first floor. Catching a glimpse of QVC on the television and spotting the steam curling up from under the bathroom door.

BINGO!

Barreling into the room. Pumping to reload. Determined to claim his prize.

* * *

Butch stood in front of his pickup in a fog. Blood trickled from his nose. The shotgun felt hot in his hands.

Heat lightning lit up the night, punctuated by the wail of an approaching siren—a mournful, accusatory sound.

"What...what...?" he stammered, a million miles from forming a coherent question.

A floodlight flickered overhead, and he glanced up. The plexiglass steer on the roof blinked on, off, on, off in the staccato of the faulty spotlight, a cloud of mosquitoes swarming around it.

The cow's painted eyes were locked on his, and Butch felt anger welling up inside. Anger at being tricked, for well and truly tricked he had been. He'd gone from door to door, firing away, snuffing out life one room at a time. And for what? Nothing! He saw that now. No prize, no reward. Tricked!

"But...you promised..."

Butcher, they'll call you in the papers, the cow crooned. *The Butcher of Maple City.*

"Shut up!" Butch screamed as the dark flower bloomed inside him and began to feed.

It practically writes itself. Moo-oo!

He raised the shotgun, eager to blast the cow's damn head off.

At the last second, he settled for his own.

CHAPTER 2

Jessie Voss stood at the edge of the empty pool and stared down into the deep end. A swirl of snow scooped up a cluster of dead leaves and whirled them about, fall and winter caught in a wild waltz.

The wind rattled a metal sign attached to the chain-link fence that surrounded the pool area. The sign had once read *Swim at Your Own Risk*, but thanks to some graffiti genius it now read *Swim at Your Own Dick*. The base for a diving board remained, but no board was in sight. Off to the side sat a shallow kiddie pool in which a soiled mattress lounged.

In all, it had the makings of the saddest pool party ever.

Jessie pulled her flannel coat tighter about herself, drawing her chin deeper into the collar. The chill brought a throbbing ache to her hip, and she shifted from foot to foot to relieve her discomfort. The metal always got cold before the Jessie surrounding it. Oh, the joys of sporting surgical steel at thirty-five.

"Jess!"

She turned back to the parking lot where Steph in her long, purple puffer coat stood waving next to the motel office. A bumper crop of weeds sprouted from the stretch of cracked asphalt that divided them, dead and shivering in the November breeze.

Jessie turned into the wind and made her way toward her friend. Steph was older than Jessie by a good twenty years and sported a somber disposition that kept strangers at bay. But the woman's friends knew better—they knew beneath the stony demeanor lay the heart of a prankster, of someone who could throw back tequila with the best of them and come away on top. Steph was a woman of few words, and the fact that Jessie counted her as a friend was a testament to the lack of bullshit Steph brought to the table. Jessie had had enough bullshit in her life recently, enough to last a lifetime. But it was time she changed that, by God.

The plexiglass cow on the roof of the office leaned precariously to one side, tethered by a single cable and rocking with each gust. Wired about its neck was a *For Sale* sign—the thing that had originally drawn her to the property in the first place. Driving by a month ago, she'd seen the sign and jumped to the conclusion that it was the *cow* that was for sale, not the motel. She'd always had an eye for the unusual, and a rooftop Angus certainly fit the bill. When she learned that the Crossroads was up for grabs, the gears in her head started turning. Leading her here.

As she approached, a flurry of snow whipped down from the office roof as if conjured by the cow, temporarily hiding Steph from view. When the woman emerged, Jessie had a vision of some pioneer woman stoically crossing the plains of nineteenth-century Illinois, wisps of greying hair fluttering about her stern face. There was definitely something *Little House on the Prairie* about Stephanie Hoyle.

"I jiggered the lock," her friend said with a smirk.

Jessie pulled a ring of keys from her coat pocket and jangled them. "They gave me these."

Steph shrugged. "Good to stay in practice. Let's check it out."

Jessie followed Steph into the office, grateful for a break from the wind. The floor was covered in dirt, rocks, cellophane wrappers and, oddly enough, dozens of sugar packets. Jessie gave one of the packets a kick.

"Coffee station." Steph pointed to a pile of powdered creamers. "Damn. I could sure use a cup right about now."

"I'm sorry."

"Said you were going to bring me a coffee. Didn't bring me a coffee."

"Steph…"

"Would've been nice."

Jessie socked Steph in the arm, not hard but hard enough to make her point. "I'll get you a triple, half-caf, mocha whatever you want when we're done."

"Don't wanna put you out." The woman loved yanking her chain.

Steph pointed to the back wall which had been stripped down to the studs. "Looks like the cleaners chucked the drywall."

"Why?"

Steph cocked her head. "It was probably a hell of a mess. Blood. Bone. This is where he started, you know. Here in the office. June 5th. Must've been standing right about where you are now."

Jessie suppressed the urge to step back. She might as well get back in her Honda and bid farewell forever to the Crossroads Motel if she couldn't stand her ground.

The murders occurred over two years ago. June, as Steph had so helpfully pointed out. The same time she was laid up in the Maple City hospital bed pressing her morphine button like a fiend. Time to step up. Time to cut the crap.

"I want to see the rooms," Jessie said.

As the two crossed the parking lot toward the two-story row of rooms, the wind saw fit to give them a respite, and the sun almost dared to show its face.

"If you take this on, you're gonna have to learn a lot real fast," Steph said, a full stride ahead of Jessie. "Laundry, security, payroll. You ever managed employees?"

"I ran a scene shop with twenty students under me."

Steph snorted. "Students. Wait'll you gotta wrangle moms who can't come to work because their brat is having his tonsils out. For the *third* time in two months."

"Not a problem."

"You have first aid training? You know CPR? When I was working at the Sandburg Inn over in Galesburg, I had five—count 'em—five ODs. Was able to bring two back, but the other three? Adios. Kind of made retirement all that more attractive, you know what I mean?"

"Are you trying to scare the shit out of me?" Jessie asked.

Steph shook her head. "Just want you to know what you'd be getting yourself into."

The door to the first of the ground floor rooms was missing.

"Might wanna get a new door," said Steph.

Jessie elbowed past her and stepped into the room. The place was empty save for a mangled ironing board. There were hooks on the walls where bad motel art had once lived, and a frayed cable snaked from the wall.

Jessie did her little trick and the room populated with furniture in a snap. It was her gift, one she'd never been able to explain. Not even to Donovan, though she credited him with having a healthy imagination. Perhaps it was the hours spent designing sets for various summer stock and college productions. She could look at a space, reduce it to its bare essentials and then decorate it in her mind's eye. She could shuffle pieces around, swap them out, change the color of the walls, settling on a finished design in the space of two heartbeats.

If only I could stick a cable in my head and print out the finished product.

"Or not," Steph grumbled.

"Huh?"

"I said you could use my cousin Eric if you decide to pull the trigger. He's a damn fine drywaller, and if you hired him, I could stop lending him money."

"How many cousins do you have?"

"Here in Maple City or statewide?"

"Here in town."

Steph thought about it a second, doing the tally in her head. "Twenty-two. Give or take."

"Sheesh. You Hoyles breed like rabbits."

"It's part of our charm," Steph said without cracking a grin.

Jessie headed for the bathroom. Like the front door, the bathroom door was missing.

Is there a black market for motel room doors?

The toilet was cracked and the bowl filled with trash. There was a small shower stall, the cheap plastic type that afforded the bather little room to maneuver.

A large chunk of the stall's back wall was missing. Blasted away. The two-by-four frame visible through the opening was pitted with small holes.

Steph leaned in behind her. "Jesus," was all she said.

Jessie put her hands on her friend's shoulders.

"Are you still on board if I do this?"

"It's a risky move. A settlement like yours doesn't come along every day."

"Well?"

"If it were me, I'd buy some land. Something that doesn't need months and months of work. Something that just *is*. Set. Done."

"Are you on board?"

Steph fixed her eyes on Jessie's. "Aw, crap. You already did it, didn't you? You bought the damn place."

Jessie tried to grin, but it felt more like a grimace. Steph saved the day by laughing for possibly the first time in her entire life.

"Your man is in for a big surprise!" Steph hooted. "I'm in. JR's gonna kill me, but I'm in. You can tell me the particulars over coffee. I'm freezing my ass off."

Steph slipped past Jessie and headed for the doorway. Jessie stood alone for a moment in the filthy motel bathroom. Steph was right. Donovan was in for a *big* surprise. She'd tell him tonight. She wasn't sure how, but delaying it wasn't an option.

She was about to follow after Steph when she heard a faint squeak. Not a mouse squeak. Not an animal. But the drawn-out sound of skin on a smooth surface. Like a hand wiping down a fogged mirror.

Jessie quick-stepped it out of the room and into the parking lot. The purchase of the Crossroads Motel was frightening enough. No need to add imaginary ghosts to the mix.

CHAPTER 3

The sun beat down hard, as it had for the past week. Thankful for the lack of rain but still wary of sunstroke, Jessie could almost see the finish line. September was a month away and brought the promise of Homecoming crowds. And after that, the holidays were close behind. The reservation line had already started to buzz.

As she watched her workers replacing gutters, spray-washing the pool area, putting the final coat of sage paint on the office exterior, Jessie breathed a sigh of relief.

The past six months had been a whirlwind. Winter took its own sweet time shoving off, so work was relegated to inside. The motel rooms were clean, if sparse. The office was presentable, although the little room she'd be calling home until she lined up more front desk staff was still unfinished.

The same was true for the restaurant section. Steph had royally pissed her off by telling her to do the work in stages. Save the restaurant for another day.

"Don't worry," Steph had said. "Eric and his boys will rough the whole space out. But trying to launch a motel *and* do food service at the same time? Don't make me slap you."

So, the restaurant had become a catch-all. It was loaded with rolls of linoleum, paint cans, light fixtures, bags of cement and, of course, the plexiglass cow. During the second of two sleepless nights, Jessie had named the cow. Elmer. Like the glue.

He was her watchcow, keeping an eye over all of the construction materials piled up in what had once been the Crossroad's Steak and Suds.

Of course, the motel needed a new name as well. The night she'd bought Donovan the most expensive bottle of scotch Maple City had to offer and revealed her purchase of the motel, she offered up the name as a kind of olive branch. Donovan had been equal parts confused and upset that she had gone behind his back. But the money was hers, and if buying the Crossroads Motel was her last act as a single woman, so be it. Since they had met working in the theater department of Maple City College—the school where he still worked—she suggested the name. Intermission Motor Lodge. Theatrical, vintage-sounding, fun. Three things that got Donovan's motor running.

It had taken a good week before he warmed to the idea. He was about to open his production of *The Tempest*, and things were not going well. When the show had a miraculous recovery, and Donovan received a handwritten letter from the president of the college praising his work, he had given his blessing to the project.

"Let's do this," he'd said.

Let's do this turned out to mean *Go ahead and do it, and I'll concentrate on my theater program*. Not that Jessie minded. Once she had Steph's cousin Eric lined up, she found she had a knack for project management. Eric begat Dino the electrician, Dino begat Carlos the painter and so on. Even as she watched her settlement tick downward, she never once looked back. "Let's do this," she'd say to herself. And do it she did.

Laundry room finished? Check. Satellite TV set up? Check. Security cameras installed? Check. Pool filled and ready to go?

Well…one thing at a time. Although the pool was another item Steph had told her to sideline for her next season—what was the point of filling the pool only to empty it again when the weather turned cold—Jessie had insisted on having it ready for her soft open. How hard could it be, she'd asked herself.

The filtration system was serviced, and all safety codes were followed. Those were bullet points she'd checked off early on. The holdup was the water itself. In her infinite wisdom, she'd forgotten to schedule the water delivery, and now the Pool King was giving her the runaround.

Breathe, Jessie. Breathe. At least you've got the internet guy scheduled.

Carlos, in his paint-spattered white shirt and shorts, interrupted her reverie.

"Miss Voss! Delivery."

The man was pointing frantically toward the flatbed truck turning into the parking lot with a car-sized payload strapped to its back.

It was the sign. The Intermission Motor Lodge's neon sign she had designed herself, complete with comedy/tragedy masks signifying vacancy/no vacancy. Sheer brilliance.

She waved down the driver before he could exit the truck.

"If I give you fifty bucks, can you give me a lift?"

* * *

Jessie guided the driver to the rear bay of the Van Ausdall Theater. She couldn't wait to show off her masterpiece.

"Wait here," she said as she clambered out of the truck and lit out for the steps up to the backstage entrance. Stairs were no problem—she'd been the star of stairs in rehab. While the rest of her maimed companions were content to put in the minimum effort required, eager for the painkillers at the end of their workout, she was busy getting on with getting on.

Still, she felt a twinge of pain as she hit the top step.

She'd stayed away from the theater since the accident except to support Donovan on premiere nights, sitting through two-plus hours of mediocre acting and bad lighting so she could smile at faculty members and sip Chardonnay out of a plastic wine glass. This had been her world too, for a time. Before her life had tilted.

As she stepped into the wings, she caught sight of Donovan center stage, locked in an embrace with a willowy girl. She recognized her from various play openings—Terebeth, the girl with the odd name. Her mind muscled in to protect her.

It's Dramafest. Happens every summer. It's a scene. He's acting in a scene.

When the kiss continued past the point of any dramatic value, the truth hit home, and the bottom dropped out.

She turned and left him there, in the arms of the ingénue. She returned to the truck and told the driver to head back to the motel.

Jessie Voss took a deep breath.

Well, that's that.

*   *   *

Despite the fact that Friday's soft open was for friends only, Jessie was starting to get nervous. Although the big and scary *grand* opening wouldn't happen for another week—just in time for the influx of college families returning for Homecoming—the fact that the soft open was only two days away kept her busy.

Jessie was determined to have the office painted by Friday. She was okay with her friends seeing the Aerobed sprawled out in the back office, okay that the dumpster company had missed its pickup, but she'd be damned if she was going to greet her guests in an unpainted office.

She could already imagine the awful, pitying smiles as her friends carefully avoided any mention of Donovan and his young student, who had apparently moved into his studio apartment.

Enough. Back to work.

She was busy loading up the roller with Persian red paint—her final choice after sorting through dozens of options in her head—when she heard the door open behind her. She turned to find a woman about her age sporting a Def Leppard t-shirt and a determined look.

"I need a room with a queen-sized bed and a rollaway, and I'm too tired to haggle," the woman said.

"I'm sorry," Jessie said, pushing the hair out of her eyes with her forearm. "We're not open yet."

The woman gestured to the neon sign in the window. It was glowing orange. *Open.* One of Steph's little tricks. She'd been pushing Jessie to open her doors early.

"Tear the seal off the sucker," Steph had said. "Make a few bucks."

Jessie glanced past the woman to where a Ryder truck sat parked next to an old Prius. She could make out a slender man standing at the car in the light drizzle, leaning through the window to talk to a young child. A thin boy in a baseball cap, half-wrapped in a blanket. Jessie could make out the logo on the kid's cap, as could any good Midwesterner—the good ole Cubbies.

A father. A son. And a mother who could obviously use a break.

"Our restaurant is being renovated, there are no quarters in the change machine. The internet is acting up, and the rooms smell like paint. But if you need a room, you need a room."

"Thank you." The woman's relief was palpable as she fished her driver's license from her purse and handed it over. Hannah Larson—New York State.

Jessie set down the roller, nudged aside the can of paint she'd set on the desktop and entered the woman's info into the computer. "Welcome to the Intermission Motor Lodge, Ms. Larson. How many nights will you be staying with us?"

After letting the woman use the restroom in the hallway that attached the office to the once and future restaurant, Jessie handed over the keycards to room 201 and realized that, ready or not, the Intermission Motor Lodge was now open for business.

She peered after the woman as she rejoined her family, reconnoitering before splitting up, moving truck and car into place outside their room. The boy in the blue cap pointed out the pool to his mom.

I'm glad I got it filled. That kid looks like he could use a little fun.

A loud thud startled her, and she cried out. Turning, she found that the paint can had fallen behind the desk. Its contents were splattered across the back wall as if shot from a cannon. Or a gun. A violent bloom of Persian red.

CHAPTER 4

"Spider!"

Michael Larson raced for the bathroom, abandoning his half-unpacked suitcase.

"Don't hurt it, Mom!" he cried.

His mother *hated* spiders. Even more than mice. But mice, she'd leave for Dad to handle. Spiders she'd dispatch herself.

Michael burst into the bathroom and caught his mother with tissue in hand, ready to smash the little black intruder that sat poised on the edge of the sink. Ready to smash and flush.

"I'll get rid of it!"

Michael swiped the wad from her hand and gently scooped up the spider. It danced about on its tissue perch.

"Go, go, go!" his mother said, waving him off.

Michael dashed past his father, out the door and to the railing overlooking the parking lot where he shook the wad of tissue vigorously. The spider held on valiantly for a few shakes and then relinquished its hold, dropping delicately to the pavement below.

"You done saving the world, Sport?" Peter Larson asked, holding the door open. "If so, I could use some help unpacking."

"Thank you!" his mother called, unseen from the bathroom. "You're my hero!"

He placed his clothes in the dresser which was brand new and smelled like it. Curious, he opened the door to the adjoining room and found a second door staring him in the face. He tested it. Locked.

Michael pulled the ViddyBox from his backpack and deftly hooked the device to the TV.

"How'd you know how to do that?" his father asked.

"Dad. Even a monkey could do it."

"Oh, really?" Peter gave his best monkey hoot and commenced scratching his armpits. "Even a monkey?"

"Da-ad," Michael moaned.

"Monkey no know how to make picture box work. Monkey no smart."

Michael's father grabbed for his belly, fingers wiggling wildly. The boy's body tensed.

"No!" Michael squealed, laughing despite himself. "No more tickling!"

"No? More tickling?" Peter twittered. "Okay, monkey tickle more. Monkey thought you no like tickle. But Michael want more, monkey tickle more."

Michael's chest tightened and a gurgle came from his throat. Hannah bolted from the bathroom, instantly alert.

"Peter, stop," she ordered.

"You okay, sport?" Peter asked.

Michael's breath came in pants and he squeezed his eyes shut to calm his racing heart.

Hannah guided Michael to the bed and made him sit, hovering over him as Peter launched into a story—a proven method to ease his seizing chest.

"How about this one? A long time ago in the mythical land of New Jersey, there lived a terrible beast known as the Jersey Devil."

Hannah shot him a look. "Really, Dad?"

"More," Michael croaked. He tuned out everything but his dad's voice and his mom's hand on the nape of his neck—the story, the fingers stroking his newly-grown hair.

And then, like that, the spasms were over.

Hannah turned to the mini-fridge and pulled out a small can. "Here, drink your Ensure." Her remedy for all his ills.

"Aw, Mom..."

"Drink."

Michael did as he was told.

Peter picked up a menu lying next to the phone. "Shall we dine in tonight? Who's up for a pizza from Tommaso's? Best pie in town, it says."

"Mushrooms!" Michael said, spurting out a spray of protein shake.

"Not tonight," Hannah said, grabbing the keys to the Prius. "We've had nothing but junk food for the past two days. I'm going to the store and picking us up some salad, fruit and a rotisserie chicken. What do you boys want to drink?"

"I guess root beer wouldn't be part of this fun and healthy meal you've got planned for us," Peter said.

"Actually, root beer calms his stomach."

Peter raised his palm to Michael, who gave him five. "Score one for the guys."

Hannah headed for the door. "Where am I going?"

"There used to be a Giant's over on North Eleventh and a bargain place downtown. Hurtz's or Heinz's or something."

"I'll ask the woman at the front desk." Then, pointedly to Peter, "Don't get him riled up."

"Aye-aye, Cap'n," Peter said and gave her a little salute. The square dad nature of it made her smile. She returned his salute and disappeared out the door.

"How long are we staying here, Dad?"

"This motel or this town?"

"Town."

Peter sighed. "We're gonna have to play that by ear, Sport. Grandpa—"

"Big Bear."

"Big Bear needs us. Could be we stick around for a while. Think you can roll with that?"

"Are we going to be poor?"

"What makes you say that?"

Michael shrugged. "You're not working. Mom's not working."

Peter laid his hands on his son's shoulders. "Once I know the lay of the land, I can have my booth up and running in no time. And you know your mom—she could sell a glass of water to a drowning man."

"So, we're going to be okay?"

"I promise." Peter beckoned for the ViddyBox remote. "Let's find a movie Mom would absolutely *hate*."

* * *

Michael's stomach rumbled so loud it woke him up. The salad his mother had made him eat was fighting back. Carrots, cucumbers, peas and those disgusting sprouts.

Maybe I'm allergic to sprouts.

He rolled to his side and adjusted his pillow. He liked the rollaway bed, liked how it opened like a book. He had to kick the covers off to undo the most tucked-in sheets he'd encountered in his eight years on earth. Even the covers on his hospital bed were easier to negotiate.

He stared across the dark room to where his mother lay sprawled next to his father. Dad had a tendency to curl up into a ball when he slept, clutching a pillow to his head. Maybe that was because Mom talked in her sleep. A lot. But not tonight. Maybe she was too wiped out from the drive to chat.

He toured the room with his eyes, getting a sense of it. The popcorn ceilings, the extra thick drapes, the gentle click-click of the ceiling fan. The clock radio that read 2:11.

His stomach rumbled again, and he knew he wasn't going to be able to get back to sleep.

He thought about the new game he'd downloaded for the trip, Chompmaster II, but his phone was charging on his dad's nightstand.

Dang it.

An idea popped into his mind, and he instantly knew that he would need to employ all of his skills to pull it off. Mom's purse lay on the table next to the door. A crumpled receipt and her change from her grocery run lay beside it.

It was time to make a vending machine run.

He'd seen the thing when they came up the stairs, sitting inside the laundry room. He had a kid's ability to locate any access to candy within a square mile. He could see the vending machine standing next to a soda machine—they called it pop out here—and a couple of stacked dryers, their doors open in a wide-mouthed O.

He would slip out of bed, snag the money, sneak out the door and be back with a chocolate bar safely stashed away in his belly. Easy-peasy.

Michael made his first move and his first mistake. As he swung his legs around and set his feet on the floor, the bedsprings complained loudly. He had been psyching himself up to tiptoe as quietly as he could across the room, imagining how stealthy he'd be as he collected the money and opened the door ever so slowly that he hadn't contemplated the possibility that the rollaway bed would betray him.

His mother stirred. "Take the day," she mumbled to the room.

Michael waited it out, and eventually Hannah quieted down. Resuming his move to the table—slower this time, much slower—he rose, padded across the carpet and swiped one of the bills. He did it quickly, figuring one short sound wouldn't wake anyone. He was right. Michael slipped the bill into the waistband of his pajamas.

As he turned toward the door, he saw movement in the corner of his eye and was certain he'd been caught. He froze in place, eyes and ears on alert, ready to blurt out either a denial or a confession. Whatever the mood in the room demanded.

But all was silent. And although he was certain—yes, certain—that he'd been spotted sneaking out, he proceeded to the door, turned the handle ever so slowly and slipped out of the room.

It was then that Michael almost made mistake number two. Elated at having gotten this far, he moved to pull the door shut.

No! It'll lock behind you.

Stupid, stupid, stupid. He was done with chemo but sometimes the fogginess returned, especially at night. He'd almost lost the game right then and there.

Easing the door back open, he reached inside. The door had a security latch that swung on a hinge. Twisting the latch outward would keep the door from closing completely. It would let a bit of sound in, like the distant rush of long-haul truckers tooling down the highway, but he'd have to risk it if he was going to continue.

As his fingers touched the latch, something touched his fingers.

Cold!

It wasn't a hand but a close approximation. A tangible chill gripped him, interlaced with his fingers and squeezed.

Michael jerked back and the door closed with a click. He hadn't been quick enough; the door was locked.

He shook his hand, willing away the tingle of the touch. Much like his on again/off again brain farts, his nerves still loved to play tricks on him. Phantom itches, crawling skin, twitching toes. The price of pumping his system full of foreign liquids.

Those were fingers.

But of course they weren't. Couldn't have been. It was just part of the damage left behind by the big C.

I know what I felt.

Michael had two options. He could knock on the door and give himself up right now. That would lead to a world of questioning from his mom. Why was he up? Was he okay? Had he overdone it again?

Or he could go with plan B—go get his chocolate on and figure out the rest as he went. A rippling rumble in his stomach made the decision for him, and he turned for the stairs.

The night was cool without being cold. *Brisk*, he thought. A word from his vocabulary list. Homeschooling sucked. He'd only gotten halfway through third grade before the cancer had come a knockin', and he missed being around other kids. But then came the diagnosis, the medicines and the bed. Always the bed. At least that part of the whole mess was over, but his mother hadn't yet made the transition. He had the distinct impression that she'd prefer to have him safely tucked away in bed for the rest of his life.

The thought prompted him to take the last of the stairs two at a time. He paid for it by almost taking a tumble, but it was worth it.

As he approached the laundry room with its vending machine full of wonders, his radar went off. He whipped around, fully expecting to find someone—another guest, a motel worker—coming up behind him. But there was no one. Just the empty courtyard awash in halogen light and the wavering blue of the pool. Another prank of chemo brain.

He decided to double-time it, and he made a beeline for the vending machine, spotted the chocolate-covered peanut butter cups he'd been salivating over in his mind and fed the bill into the slot.

The machine spat it back.

He tried again, turning the bill around this time; it was rejected again. It was then that he spied the instructions printed above the money slot.

Insert Bills Here. Accepts $1, $2 & $5.

First of all, he had never seen a two-dollar bill. Second, he couldn't believe his dumb luck. He could have swiped any of the bills from the table, but no—he had to snatch a ten.

A change machine hung on the wall next to the washers and dryers along with a handwritten sign that said, *Go to Office for Change.*

Did he dare? Offices meant adults, and adults meant questions. But if there was one thing he was good at, one thing that he had picked up from his dear old dad, it was how to spin a story. His stomach hurt and he needed a soda. His blood sugar was low and he needed something sweet. He'd come up with something.

* * *

The office was brightly lit but empty. Michael walked up to the front desk and stood on tiptoe to get a better look. There was a small room beyond the desk with a floor lamp and an inflatable bed covered in rumpled sheets.

He heard a voice off to his left and spotted a half-opened door at the side of the room. The sound was coming from behind that door. A distant voice speaking at full volume. A woman's voice.

Michael slipped through the door and found himself standing in a long hallway. This part of the motel was different from the rest. It was unfinished and cluttered. There was no carpet on the floor, only bare plywood. Two open doorways led to his and her restrooms, and Michael peeked inside both.

Urinals; no urinals. It was a fact of life that still made him shake his head.

As he proceeded down the hall, he found that it opened up into a larger space lit by haphazardly-strung work lights. The place brought to mind a junk shop his dad had taken him to on a trip up to Ithaca. No, not a shop. It had been more like a junk warehouse. This room was much the same. It was filled with boxes and stacks of building material.

And a woman. A woman talking to a cow.

CHAPTER 5

Jessie finished painting the office around ten and was surprised to find that she had worked well into the night. Too exhausted to clean the roller, she instead wrapped it in aluminum foil—a trick Carlos had taught her.

A light flickered on the newly-installed landline phone, and Jessie picked it up the moment it began to warble.

"Intermission Motor Lod—"

A burst of static interrupted, followed by a garbled, complaining voice.

"I'm sorry, I think we have a bad connection. Could you try calling back?"

The line popped and went dead. Jessie waited a moment for the possibility of a second ring but no such luck. Perhaps the caller had moved on to the reservation line at the Collegiate Inn. Ah well—win some, lose some.

Jessie decided to take a loop around the buildings, walking her property. Checking in on her first and only guests.

This must be how new mothers feel.

The lights were still on in Room 201. If her guests were of a mind to look out the window, they'd catch their host peeking up at them. Snooping.

Jessie took in the expanse of the place. Twelve people in all had lost their lives that night at the then-named Crossroads Motel. People said it was thirteen because it sounded more ominous, but it was twelve. Evidence of the crime had popped up constantly during the renovation.

The most disturbing had been the tooth. One of Dino's electricians had discovered it embedded in the wall when he was wiring the rooms and lit off to find himself a bottle. She had saved the tooth and given the thing a proper burial, if proper meant digging a shallow hole at the Eventide Cemetery, dropping the tooth inside and covering it before anyone could see.

Jessie understood why the electrician needed a stiff drink. The tooth was too small to be an adult's.

As she finished her circle heading back to the office, her leg buckled and gave way. She hit the pavement with a groan. Damn knee. As if the shattered hip weren't enough, the doctors had put her in traction while she awaited surgery. And that meant drilling a hole straight through her knee. She was awake for the whole thing. She was amazed that not only had they employed a real-life drill to do the deed, but that she could *smell* the process. A burnt smell. Meaty. Hell, she actually saw smoke.

Then the traction. With the metal pin in place, two bolts of metal sticking out either side of her knee like Frankenstein's monster's famous electrodes, a young physician had attached the pulley and weight system.

"Sorry," the doctor had said when she screamed in white-hot pain. "The ball of your hip shattered your pelvis. I'm trying to pull it back out." It took the young physician two tries to get it right and achieved a level of pain that bordered on mythological.

Jessie rose, shaking off the memory. Pain was fake, a trick of the mind. She'd learned that. But still sometimes it was a real bitch.

She hobbled back to the office and arrived in a sweat. She'd been overdoing it for about a month now and it was no surprise to her that she was paying the price.

Perhaps it was time to break the safety glass.

Jessie rounded the front desk and stepped into the back room. It had a sink, but the water pressure to it was down to a trickle. She was showering in room 109—the unfinished room she'd designated as her future home—and using the restroom down the hall to the old restaurant. No worries. She could muddle through for a while, camping out here in the back.

A collection of toiletries sat on a small shelf above the sink. A box of tampons, her favorite moisturizer, her second-favorite moisturizer and stash of prescription bottles.

Two of the bottles contained antibiotics, a third was the anti-inflammatory she'd insisted upon after she had weaned herself off of the Rexaphine, or as she had taken to calling the monster opiate, the T-Rex.

The final bottle contained the last of the bad boys. One pill. She'd saved one pill in case of an emergency. As she unscrewed the cap and poured the white tablet into her palm, she weighed if this, indeed, was the occasion.

"Donovan is history," she said to the pill. "I hurt like hell. I sunk my settlement into a murder motel and there's no going back." She turned the pill over and over in her hand. "Whaddya think?"

The pill remained silent, and so she popped it back into its bottle and tucked it away underneath a pile of scrunchies.

Jessie sat on the Aerobed and her ass practically touched the floor. The absurdity of it made her laugh, even though it hurt her hip.

Bleep.

She wiped away tears.

Bleep.

Laughing and bouncing on the deflated bed.

Bleep.

It was absurd.

"Afterword," a voice said.

Jessie looked up. The office was gone.

"If you have read this far, perhaps you will journey a bit farther." It was a man's baritone, whispering in her ears.

Her left leg was wrapped in a foam cast and hoisted upward, held fast by cables. Dark iodine stains adorned either side of her knee, through which a steel bolt ran.

The rhythmic bleep of her heart monitor sped up.

Jessie tried to speak but could not. The hospital room in which she found herself spun as if floating on the high seas. Her stomach swirled, moaning and morphined, threatening to empty its contents.

She turned her head, and there was Donovan, asleep in the chair next to her bed, a People magazine draped across his chest. The railing was down on this side and his hand rested on the sheet next to her.

Honey? She reached out to the man in the chair. *Donovan!*

"So, listen closely and hear my closing words…"

Jessie's hands went to her head to stop the sound of the voice and discovered a pair of headphones clapped to her ears. She ripped them off and tossed them aside. As soon as she did, the room began to move even more violently. The air began to pulse, the pressure of it crushing her ribs. She was inside a subwoofer with the volume turned all the way up. Each bass beat of the room made it harder and harder for her to catch her breath.

She gritted her teeth, prepared to throw herself from the bed, into Donovan's lap if that was what it took to end this assault. She rolled first in the opposite direction, dislodging her leg with a sickening wave of agony. With kamikaze abandon, she rolled toward the edge of the bed.

She hit the floor with a shout.

It wasn't the fall she was expecting. In fact, it was hardly a fall at all. When she lifted herself up, Jessie saw that she had done no more than roll off the Aerobed onto the carpet.

Damn.

She'd actually fallen asleep sitting up. That's something doctors pulling double shifts did. The stress of getting this place open must be finally catching up to her.

Jessie grabbed the bottle out from under the scrunchies and turned on the faucet. It only gurgled and sputtered.

"Shit."

Her nerves buzzing, Jessie headed for the bathroom down the hall and some water to swallow the damn pill down.

* * *

The boy found her in mid-conversation with Elmer. The cow was a good listener, and over the past few months had become her faithful confidant on top of pulling double-duty as a security guard.

When the boy walked into the room in his shorty pajamas and wide-eyed expression, Jessie leaned into Elmer and said, "We'll circle back to this later."

"Are you talking to that cow?" the son of Hannah Larson from New York asked.

"No," Jessie replied. "I'm talking to that *plexiglass* cow. Big difference."

The boy seemed to seriously consider this for a moment before breaking into a grin, and it made Jessie like the boy immediately.

"What's it saying?" the boy asked.

"Very little. I'm doing most of the talking. What are you doing up?"

"What are *you* doing up?" the boy countered.

Jessie nodded toward a darkened corner of the room where a large, wooden box lay. "I'm trying to figure out whether or not to smash that to bits."

"What is it?"

"Tell me your name and why you're prowling around, and I'll show you."

"Michael."

"Hi, Michael. I'm Jessie." She raised her eyebrows for him to continue.

"I couldn't sleep. I wanted some chocolate. I locked myself out of my room," Michael said in a rush.

"Well, I think I can help you with two out of three. Getting back to sleep? You're going to have to take care of that yourself."

The boy's tension level dropped two notches and he looked toward the thing in the corner.

"Let's have a look, shall we?" Jessie said.

She passed Michael on the way to the corner and gave him a quick pat on the back. Kids had never been her thing and so the instinctive gesture surprised her.

Jessie grabbed the sheet of wood that made up the side of the box and let it fall with a whoosh, kicking up sawdust. Packed away safe inside, held firm by wooden cross braces was an oval neon sign. It didn't look like much without its luminous gas buzzing and snapping through it, but still the boy drew nearer.

"Whoa," the kid said.

"Ya think?"

"Yeah."

Jessie gave it another look. Intermission Motor Lodge. It had turned out perfectly. But perfect no longer matched her life.

"Why isn't it outside? Don't you want to put it up?"

Jessie sighed. "Not really. I made it to make my fiancé happy, only someone else was already making him happy. Long story that would bore you to tears."

Michael touched the glass tubing. "If you made it, you should put it up. I think it would look really cool."

"Really?"

"Yeah. I like the emojis."

"The what?"

The boy pointed to the tragedy and comedy masks.

"Ah…"

"Yeah," the boy said. "It needs to go up."

And that was that. She would call the guy tomorrow and get it mounted and wired. She would save the pill stuffed in her pocket for another day. She would get on with it.

"Thanks, kid," Jessie said. "Lemme go make you another keycard."

* * *

Michael approached the plexiglass cow with caution. Elmer, she had called him. Another cool thing locked away where no one could see it. Adults were so weird.

"Moo-oo!" Michael called, his voice echoing in the large space. The cow just stared. Michael fidgeted. How long did it take to make a keycard anyway?

A chill went up his spine and the feeling of being watched was back, multiplied a hundredfold. He caught his breath as he heard a distinct *buzz* behind him, low and threatening.

If he turned around, what would he see? A giant bee? A giant, electric, buzzing bee? Because that's what his ears told him he'd find if he dared to look behind him.

The work lights stuttered and went out, one by one, plunging the room into inky blackness. No...not blackness. The walls pulsed a deep red, a warning red—the red of police car lights and fire alarms.

Michael turned slowly into the source of the glow. He felt himself being drawn closer and closer to the wooden box, to the neon sign the woman had made but hadn't put up. He felt drawn and yet fought against it. Partly out of fear, but mostly because the sign itself told him not to.

So, instead he backed away as the tragedy mask portion of the Intermission Motor Lodge sign blinked on and off, on and off.

No Vacancy. No Vacancy. No. No. No.

* * *

Jessie was in the process of swiping the new card when the kid came racing down the hall.

"I gotta go!" the boy said as he tore past.

"Slow up," Jessie said, holding out the card. Michael snatched it away. "I've got the keys to the vending machine. I could snag you a free treat."

"Maybe later." The boy raced off across the parking lot. "Thank you," he cried back.

Jessie shook her head. Yup, kids were a mystery. She went to close the hallway door and paused as a red glow was suddenly extinguished. Something electrical? She'd call Dino tomorrow.

"Goodnight, Elmer," she called.

The cow responded with a reassuring silence. Trusty Elmer.

She set the *Ring Bell for Service* sign on the desk and double-checked the security system.

Shoving aside all thoughts of her accident, the hospital and the stressful days ahead, Jessie tumbled into the under-inflated bed. As she drifted off, she could have sworn she caught the scent of burning bone.

CHAPTER 6

The dark figure followed Michael back to the room. As he bedded down, it retreated to the corner where it watched the boy and his family.

But it seemed the Messy Man was no longer content to simply watch. The blinking *No. No. No.* of the sign was proof of that.

Deep within the shadowy figure, where Peter and Whisper intertwined, dwelling together as one, a civil war was taking place. When Peter forced himself upon the shadow in that basement, forced them to become *one,* he'd allowed his younger self to be free of the nightmare he himself had had to live with.

And that had been his curse: being forced to watch another version of himself grow up happier than he had, without the dark baggage of taking the Old Man's life on the stairs, of taking his own son's life as well. It was self-preservation in the first case, mercy in the second, but they were twin blots that he still carried with him. Stains of which the Peter who now lay in the bed across the room, his arm around Hannah, had grown up blissfully free.

The price? It was heavy and it was his own to bear— becoming half of a dark conjoining, melding with the maniacal spirit that prided itself on its names: Whisper, Mr. Tell. They were Jekyll and Hyde both awake and kicking at the same time, minds overlapping and feuding for control.

Oblivion would be better than this hell. But try as he might, he could not break free. He was tethered not only to the people in this room, but to his demonic companion who only snickered at his pain.

This was a bad place, or at least bad things had been done here. In either case, this was no place for Michael. And so, he had caused the neon sign to flash its warning. And now that he had pierced the veil between his world and Michael's, he knew he would pay for it.

The attack was instantaneous.

Back! Back! Away! Away!

The coal black darkness enshrouded him, digging its claws deep. There were rules to staying alive, rules negotiated over what seemed to be eons of nights, and he had broken a big one. The thing he shared this dark womb with was furious and looking to strike back.

Do your worst, you bastard, Peter thought.

Its worst was pretty damn bad.

Peter had no body to speak of. Not anymore. Not since he'd forced himself upon the shadow in that basement. Forced them to become *one*. The wounds the thing inflicted were not physical. No. They were a hundred times worse.

Wrong! You did wrong! Whisper hates.

A searing streak of pain cut through a memory from his childhood—fishing with Big Bear along the banks of the Mississippi River—rupturing it. Causing it to bleed. The memory burned bright before fading. Gone forever.

"That's enough," Peter hissed.

A midnight talon slashed out at another memory. His lips on Hannah's. Not their first kiss, but the first one that mattered.

The one he had stolen during their train trip to Boston. The one that made her sit back in her seat, eyes locked on his as if she were seeing him for the first time.

"Wow," she'd said. "Just wow."

That wide-eyed stare was the beginning of it all. The beginning of Peter and Hannah. And later, Michael as well.

And this devil was about to burst the moment, drain it, let it dissipate into nothingness.

"Hands off!" Peter shouted, the force of the thought causing the boundaries of this world to quiver. He wrapped himself around the memory, protecting it with sheer force of will.

The thing shrieked, its prize denied.

Wrong!

It ripped at him, clawed at him, bit. As Peter endured the onslaught, he could sense the raw anger coming off the thing like steam. He didn't know much about the frantic being that called itself Whisper, Mr. Tell and a handful of other pet names—the majority of his new life trapped in this inky hell was spent simply holding the thing at bay—but of one thing he was certain.

It was stark, raving mad.

And in its madness, it was cruel. They were not equal partners in this symbiotic relationship. Far from it. The demon was in the driver's seat, and all Peter could do was occasionally hit the brakes. Keep it from interfering. Hold it back. Each time he did so, he paid for the intervention. It was at times like these that ol' Whisper would pull back the curtain and give him a peek. And it broke his heart every time.

45

Through the window Peter saw an alternate life playing out in devastating detail. For not only did he *see* the scene before him, he *felt* it as well. Sometimes Whisper punished him by forcing him to watch as Peter curled up in bed alongside Hannah. Sometimes the thing was more blunt about it, like the time he'd shoved the moment of Michael's birth in his face. His own memory of the boy's birth was charged with joy and fear and excitement. Seeing it anew from afar gave rise to anger and jealousy—yes, jealousy!—toward the other Peter. The Peter of the stolen life.

Perhaps that's why he had eased his foot off the brake momentarily, allowing Whisper, allowing Mr. Tell to lurch forward and *appear*.

The shocked look on the other Peter's face startled him, and he wrestled the darkness back through the window.

The other Peter, the Peter who was becoming a father that very second turned pale and stumbled. A nurse passed him a water bottle, and Hannah—*breathe, Hannah, breathe!*—snorted, her husband's apparent wooziness at the messiness of the birth giving her a much-needed laugh.

Messy! Yes! We're messy! Hahahahaha!

Hannah pushed. And Peter pulled away, taking the jabbering, gnashing darkness with him.

Whisper retreated and fumed. Peter lowered his guard, content that his memories were safe. For now.

A thought dawned on him. The thing had followed Michael down to the office, hadn't remained behind to keep watch over the other Peter. That was a first. That was something new. Was it good or bad or simply different? He'd have to pay close attention. Not that he wasn't already on alert. They were back in Maple City—Peter, Hannah and the boy. Back where he'd left off. Where he'd handed the reins over to his younger self and stepped out of the story.

Out of the story and into the abyss. With Whisper. With Mr. Tell.

Not alone...

The thing wasn't speaking to him. There was no trace of malice in the words. More surprise than anything else. And— was it possible—hope?

Not alone. That was for damn sure. It was apparent the minute they arrived at the Intermission Motor Lodge. The motel was...loud. There were others here. Unseen. Hiding. But still...

Loud.

"Then we'd better whisper," Peter said to the darkness. And wonder of wonders, the darkness chuckled in reply.

CHAPTER 7

The sign guy grumbled on the phone, but after admitting he had a cancellation, he agreed to swing by around noon. Jessie's second call was to Steph. The woman had sent her an exceedingly long text message.

"What's naloxone?" Jessie asked.

"It's a nasal spray. One spritz and you can make an OD turn a u-ey."

"Keeping meds in stock? I don't know. Couldn't that open me up for legal trouble?"

"So could a dead body in the pool. Just get it."

Jessie scrolled through the text. "And why do you want me to buy a box of condoms?"

"The upcharge you can add is ridiculous, believe me. You aren't opening a Sunday School, dear."

"And what about—"

"Are you going to go through the whole damn list? See you in fifteen. I've got your next employee in the car with me."

"What next employee?"

When Steph arrived in her old Chevy Impala, she had a slight young woman in tow.

"This is Lin. She's my cousin's neighbor. Knows her way around hospitality. Figure she could help you keep things rolling."

Jessie smiled at the girl. "Where was your last job, Lin?"

The girl looked to Steph, who nodded encouragingly. "The Donut Mill." Her answer sounded more like a question.

Steph jumped in. "Selling donuts is all about hospitality. Donuts *are* hospitality. Go on into the office, Lin."

* * *

Jessie and Steph rode in silence for a few blocks before Jessie blurted out, "Donuts are hospitality?"

"Okay, so sue me. The kid needs a job and she used to schedule everything over at the Mill. Flour deliveries, counter help. If Jerry Pride hadn't gotten handsy, she'd still be there."

"You think she can handle it?"

"Wouldn't have brought her if I didn't. Turn right. Band practice."

Jessie steered the Honda away from the approaching MCHS marching band, flag twirlers in front, and cut through the back way to Ecklund's Pharmacy's side lot. As she walked through the door, the entrance bell sounded an electric *bing* and she caught a glimpse of a familiar white sedan with the Maple City College logo on the side.

Shit.

Don't sweat it, Voss. Could be anyone from the school.

But as she headed down the row of hair products toward the back of the pharmacy, she spotted the tousled mop of hair she had once played stylist to, snipping away in the kitchen, making sure to leave enough to cover the premature bald spot.

Donovan. Wearing his trademark cable knit, coal tar shampoo in hand.

Steph dove in feet first. "Dandruff sure is a bitch, isn't it, Professor?"

Startled, Donovan looked up. He grinned momentarily, recognizing Steph. Before he could reply, he spied Jessie, and his demeanor switched gears.

"Jess," he said, gripping the bottle tightly. "It's good to…" What a rarity—Prof. Donovan Haig at a loss for words.

Jessie remained silent. She steeled herself and walked right past him, intent on making it to the pharmacy counter without showing a shred of emotion.

She was foiled by the appearance of a thin young woman with long black hair and a Maple City sweatshirt who turned the corner into the aisle ahead of her, shopping basket in hand.

Terebeth.

The girl's eyes went wide. "Donny?" she managed to squeak.

Jessie was trapped—ingénue ahead, deceiver behind.

"How's the motel?" Donovan was grasping but it gave Jessie an escape from the death stare she had locked on Little Miss Maple City College.

"Good," she said sharply. "Soft open is Friday. You should check it out." Now that she was speaking, the shock had abated. "Both of you."

Donovan shook his head. "I'm hosting a visiting playwright this weekend, otherwise…" He abandoned his thought and surprised Jessie by taking her arm. "Can we chat?"

Steph stepped in, ready to throw down if the situation demanded it, but Jessie waved her off. "You've got one minute." She extracted herself from his grip and strode down the aisle into the seasonal section, forcing Donovan to follow. Flanked by Halloween masks and decorations, she turned about. "So? Chat."

"I never got a chance to say I'm sorry."

"Do it now."

"I'm sorry."

"Okay. Is that it?"

Donovan looked at her with a pained expression that made him look more constipated than concerned. Jessie thought this *chat* might better suited to the laxative aisle and the idea made her snort.

"I'm glad you find this amusing." It was his patronizing professor voice that had always gotten her hackles up. "I thought I owed you an apology."

"For what, Donovan?" she asked, her temper flaring. "What are you hoping I'll forgive?"

This caught him off guard. "Why…" he stammered, waving in the general direction of the girl.

"Oh, please. So you wanted a younger model? Fine. You wanted your ring back? No problem. Better for me to know sooner than later. What I'm pissed about, what I'm *really* pissed about is that we were a team. And you let me down."

"You sued one of the school's biggest donors."

"Damn straight."

"Who do you think paid for the new Agriculture Center?"

"That truck could have killed me."

"Do you know what kind of position that put me in?"

Jessie laughed. "Were you going to pay my medical bills? Six figures—were you going to pay that, Donovan?"

"Keep your voice down."

"No. You don't get to tell me anything, you hear? Not one goddamn thing. Out of my way. I've got shopping to do." Jessie brushed past Donovan and toward the eavesdropping Steph.

Donovan followed. "I don't think we're finished."

"Oh, we're finished." Jessie turned to stare at the girl. "Wouldn't you say we're finished?"

"I still think we should have a coffee," Donovan offered. "And talk."

Steph muscled in between Jessie and her ex. "She's too busy. Reservations are rolling in, and it's one chore after another."

"I see."

"Take this shopping list Jess sent me, for instance," Steph said, pulling up the list she had sent Jessie and waving it in front of Donovan's face. "Kleenex, Lysol, a jumbo box of condoms. Imagine that—a jumbo box of condoms. What's that all about?"

"Excuse me," Jessie said as she turned and slipped past the young woman, extracting herself from the situation.

"You'll take care of her?" Donovan asked.

"Better than you did." Steph switched off her phone with a flourish and brushed past Terebeth, stopping to whisper, "As the one woman here who didn't sleep with that asshole, I count myself lucky."

Jessie rang the bell and the ancient Mr. Ecklund appeared. "Ah, little Jessica!"

"Good morning, Mr. Ecklund, I was wondering if you had this in stock." She scrolled through Steph's list and pointed out the naloxone.

"I seem to recall I've got a few spray bottles left. Sadly popular, that stuff. Oh, and don't forget your meds."

"What meds?" Jessie asked.

"No more refills, I'm afraid. You'll have to check in with Dr. Bhattacharya. Is that how you pronounce it? Bhattacharya?" The elderly pharmacist retrieved a white bag from the back.

Eager to get this part of the day over with, to put Donovan and his chippie behind her, she took the proffered bag. Thirty pills. The bad boy. The T-Rex.

"No, Mr. Ecklund, I don't need any—"

A *bling* sounding from the front of the store interrupted her, and Jessie watched as Donovan ushered the girl in the sweatshirt out the door.

She checked her feelings, expecting a wave of loneliness. But instead, she found—*was it possible?*—relief. As she stood there with her prescriptions in hand, Jessie Voss knew she wouldn't give Donovan another thought. And as she rode back to the motel with Steph, she actually caught herself humming.

CHAPTER 8

By the time Jessie returned to the motel, the sign guy was already well under way.

"He was getting impatient so I told him he could start," Lin said. "I hope that's okay." She then proceeded to show Jessie a preliminary housekeeping schedule, an emergency contact list she'd made in Word and her suggestions for snacks for the soft open. "Everyone loves donuts."

"Thank you," Jessie whispered in Steph's ear as Lin launched into her ideas to improve the website.

"Don't mention it. I'm going to steal her after this to make a Shopmor run. Anything new for the list?"

"Always."

After Steph and Lin departed, Jessie ambled over to where the men of The Neon Company were finishing up securing The Intermission Motor Lodge's new sign atop twin supports.

"You've got a bad tube," the owner, a stubby man working the crane, said. "Your little frowny face won't light. It's fried."

"Can you fix it? I've got people coming Friday."

"Yes, I can. But not by Friday."

"When, then?"

The stubby man scowled down at her. "Not by Friday."

Jessie was steaming by the time she entered the office, and so, when she found the man setting up a wire brochure stand, she was in no mood to play nice.

"Excuse me?" she snapped.

"Ah! You caught me." The man stepped back, and in so doing dropped the still unassembled stand with a clang. "I came by earlier, but—"

Jessie set the plastic bags from the pharmacy on the desk. "What do you think you're doing?"

The man stared, silenced. She figured he was about her age but he dressed like her father. He wore suit pants, a dress shirt but no coat. His shoes were shined but old.

Salesman.

"I didn't order that," Jessie said, pointing at the stand, the open boxes of brochures.

The man gave her a sideways grin. "Well, actually you did."

"Pardon?"

He pulled a paper from his pocket and read. "Jessica Voss, Intermission Motor Lodge, Maple City. I've got you right here."

"Let me see that."

Jessie grabbed the paper as the man continued. "When you join the Midwest Independent Lodging Association, you get me. And a free brochure rack."

"There's no price listed here."

"That's usually what free means."

A Prius zipped past the office, and Jessie watched as the Larsons, all three of them, headed off downtown. The boy in the cap gave her a little wave from the backseat.

"Woodrow," the man said, hand out. "Wood to my friends. I'm your rep." Again with that cockeyed grin.

"What's all this?" Jessie asked, waving toward the cardboard boxes.

"A little bit of everything, really." The man extracted a number of brochures and leafed through them. "I got your Bender's Snake Farm, Kandles of Kirkwood, Noah's Petting Zoo. All of central Illinois' finest attractions."

"Sounds...exciting."

"Yeah, well, most of these places suck. But they help to pay the bills. Mind if I finish setting it up?"

Jessie stepped behind the counter and proceeded to check her email.

"Oh, and could you book me a room for tonight?"

"Tonight?"

"On top of dropping off brochures for Rader's Rifle Range and the like, I dabble in reviews. The MILA links to my blog which helps me get advertising. Figured since I was in town, I might as well hit you up." The man snapped the final piece of the stand into place. "I'll pay full price, of course. I'm not looking for special favors."

"If you want a room tonight you'll be getting special favors. We're not officially open until next week."

"Oh? Your sign says different," the man said, gesturing with his thumb toward the glowing *Open* sign.

Damn it, Steph.

Jessie switched over to the reservations screen. "Just tonight, then?"

"Maybe longer. I don't have any more appointments until Tuesday. Thought I might see what Maple City has to offer."

Jessie flashed a wan smile. Turning away a reviewer a stone's throw from when she opened was asking for bad karma.

"Let's set up that reservation for you, mister...?"

"McKay."

"May I see your driver's license?"

Wood approached the desk and pulled his wallet from his back pocket. As he handed over his ID, Jessie caught a whiff of something. Strawberries? Watermelon?

She looked from the license to the man. Iowa. "Could you write down the make of your vehicle and license number?" She nodded to a stack of scrap paper. The check-in forms were still en route. The man scribbled *Lincoln Town Car* followed by a Minnesota license plate number.

The man chuckled. "I thought you said you were having a *soft* open this weekend."

Jessie didn't catch the man's meaning until she followed his eyes to the box of lubricated condoms sticking out of its plastic bag. Thirty-six count. The pleasure pack.

Blushing, she locked her eyes on the screen and tapped the man's info into the system.

* * *

By the time Steph and Lin returned from their errands, Jessie had made sure she was well-versed in the neon sign's operation. The sign guy had helped her set the timer, showed her the toggle between vacancy and no vacancy.

"I'll be back this weekend to do your repair. Supposed to go see the wife's family in Waukegan, but I'll swing by first."

Jessie thanked the man and tipped him one hundred dollars. The guy simply stuffed the bill in his pocket and hopped into his truck without so much as a word.

When Steph rolled up with Lin, Jessie waved them down.

"Looks good," Steph said.

"Really good," Lin agreed.

"Wait until I turn it on!"

"Dark but good." Steph didn't even crack a smile.

"Jeez, give a gal a chance to show off, will you?"

As Jessie was about to slip back into the office to ignite the sign, the Larsons pulled into the lot in their Prius. Pumped from the moment, Jessie flagged them down. The boy was the first to roll down his window.

"You did it," Michael said, beaming.

"I did it."

The boy cocked his head. "I thought it would be brighter."

"Comedians. I'm surrounded by comedians. Hold on." She turned to leave and realized she was keeping the Larsons from their room. "Do you mind? It'll only take a second."

Hannah shooed her on. "Go on. We'd love to see it."

Jessie darted into the office and opened the newly-mounted electrical box. She flicked the switch.

"Oooo!" crooned Steph from outside.

"Ahhh!" echoed Lin.

The Prius's horn tooted a couple times.

Jessie rejoined the group in the parking lot and stared upward. The neon sign that had once been a flicker in her mind now buzzed bright above her head. Announcing her intentions to the world. Heralding a new beginning.

"You got a bad tube," Steph said.

Jessie would have expected nothing less of the woman.

* * *

THE HUNGRY ONES

Wood's watch said seven, but the streetlights were already flickering on in uneven succession along the road in front of the Intermission Motor Lodge. He had the sense of stage lights going up at the beginning of a performance.

Echoing his sentiments, the neon sign came to life, lording over the place in a mix of greens and blues and reds. A small group applauded it like it was a Fourth of July fireworks finale. At the center was the woman he recognized as the new owner of the place.

Jessie.

She sure cleaned up the joint. Used to be a shithole.

He took another hit off the vaporizer, and the car filled with a cloud of strawberry.

A steady stream of burger-hungry people passed him by as he sat parked on the side of the Mickey-Ds. Sat watching as a lone car turned in to the drive to the motel. Sat enjoying the last of his smoke.

He held the vape pen up to the light and guessed he had six, maybe seven good hits left before the cartridge was dry. The sickly pink strawberry liquid was the best flavor he'd found to mask the other taste—the flecks of black that danced in the liquid. Bitter and sweet at the same time. And rotten.

He had a few hours to kill. And he wasn't about to sequester himself in his motel room. Not yet. The witching hour would come soon enough.

Perhaps he'd take a drive around town. Maybe treat himself to a pork chop or a Maid-rite. Who knew? The sky was the limit.

Throwing caution to the wind, Wood took the end of the pen into his mouth, pressed the button and took a long, warm toke of berry mist and rot.

CHAPTER 9

*C*ody floated alone in the pool on the inflatable raft he'd found abandoned next to a pile of wet towels. He had stripped down to his boxer shorts, relishing the last hits of Missouri marijuana.

He wasn't registered at the Crossroads. Hell, he wasn't registered for anything. Over the course of his young adulthood, he'd neglected to register for the draft, register to vote, take a driving test or buy insurance for his car. The only thing that Cody was caught up on was his dental health as his sister Rachel, the studious one, used his mouth for practice. In a couple years, she'd be a full-fledged dentist, and he'd probably be right where he was now—lying back and watching planes pass overhead in the night sky. If anyone from the motel asked, he'd tell them he was waiting for his folks to check in.

He ran his fingers through his long, greasy hair. That was another thing he had neglected—a haircut. He'd gotten his last from the deaf barber near the high school, but since the old dude kicked it he'd have to find another joint. He wasn't above cutting his own hair. He liked the looks he got when he walked through town after going at it with a pair of scissors. His sister called what he did with his hair a massacre, and he liked that description quite a bit.

He took another hit and felt the paper burn down to his fingertips. His cousin Case was his supplier. Case was a recluse *who spent most of his time fishing, hunting and growing weed. The guy was growing more and more reluctant to answer Cody's calls, and he knew that someday soon he'd call and find the number disconnected.*

No matter. Legalized pot was sweeping the nation. Its ubiquity took a bit of fun out of things, but it did raise tantalizing opportunities. Dispensaries. In Cody's mind's eye, he saw himself walking into a pot shop, offering his services and bam! Full-time employment and a hefty employee discount. And why not? Who knew more about the skunky stuff than he?

A loud crack scattered his thoughts. He sat up on the floating mat and almost lost his equilibrium. Damn, the stuff had really kicked in.

He peered out across the parking lot, half expecting to see an accident tying up traffic on Main Street—the sound was sharp enough to be a late night fender bender. But the street was empty, as was the parking lot itself.

No. That wasn't quite true. There was a man lumbering across the lot away from the office. A fat man with a shotgun in his hands. And he was reloading.

Cody toppled into the water, the resulting waves spreading out across the pool. He gripped the mat, peering over it at the approaching man, his mouth riding the surface of the water. The scent of the over-chlorinated pool stung his nose.

At first it seemed like the man with the gun was heading straight for him, but as he came nearer his trajectory shifted, veering off toward the rows of motel rooms.

Cody would wait it out. Wait until the nutjob passed and then hightail it outta there. Across the field and to the highway where he'd wave someone down. Get the hell out while the getting was good.

The inflatable mat began to lose air. Why now? He'd been lying on it for the better part of an hour, stretched out and smoking his joint...

Jesus...the joint!

Cody spotted the smoldering remains a second before they melted through the vinyl with a puff and a hiss. The mat folded in half, giving its best impression of the Titanic.

Alarmed, Cody compensated by giving the slightest kicks he could to remain above water. The last thing he wanted was to attract attention.

Unfortunately, he was unsuccessful.

The man announced his presence by clearing his throat. When he raised the shotgun, Cody responded by diving straight down.

As he sank, his arms and legs working overtime to go deeper, deeper, Cody flinched as shot ripped the crippled mat to shreds above his head. Buckshot blasted the water but was instantly slowed, dropping slowly downward after him. When Cody's back hit the bottom of the pool, a manic sense of joy overtook him.

Can't get me down here! Water's too dense. I saw it on Mythbusters, asshat! You can't get me!

He remained there for as long as he could, kicking upward to hold himself below. But soon his lungs began to complain. Then they begged. Then they screamed. He let loose a column of weed-kissed bubbles that rose to the surface. A moment later, he followed them, the hunger for air driving him upward. When he broke the surface, the fat man was waiting. And smiling.

CHAPTER 10

"Cannonball!"

Michael hit the end of the diving board hard and sprang into the air. He was so thrilled his mom was finally allowing him to do something fun that he forgot to pull in his arms and legs. The result was a monster of a belly flop that dowsed his mother who lay poolside and caused his swim goggles to pop off.

"Thanks a lot!" Hannah cried.

"Sorry!" Michael called back, his stomach still smarting. He kicked to the middle of the pool to tread water and stare up at the ruddy sky. This was his idea of a good time. Twilight swimming in a chlorinated kingdom all his own.

His father had intervened in the tug-of-war between him and his mother. The doctors had cleared him to get back in the water two months before they'd made their cross-country journey. No risk of infection, they'd said. His white cell count was solid. But still, his mother had objected.

"Let the kid swim, Hannah. It'll be good for him."

"Can we not discuss this in front of the child?"

In the end, Dad had won.

"More coins! More coins!" Michael shouted.

"It's almost bedtime. Aren't you getting tired?"

"No!"

Hannah rose in her chair and set her tablet aside. She picked a few coins out of a puddle on the cement and held them aloft. "Ready?"

"Ready!"

In went the coins and down went Michael. His descent was steady and sure. His mother had been a lifeguard during her college years and had insisted her son know his way around the water.

The quarter was easy to spot in the soft glow of the underwater lights. It was lying to the side of the tiled line dividing the deep and shallow ends. Michael returned to the surface with his treasure in tow, tossed it in the general direction of his mom and dove back down.

The penny was nowhere in sight, but he caught a glint of silver in the deep end. The dime sat on the bottom, down by the rectangular drain. Almost on top of it.

Michael psyched himself up and swam deeper, his legs—not strong but stronger each day—propelling him in small, downward bursts.

It felt good to work his body while giving his mind a rest. There'd been plenty to think about during the day. First, there was breakfast with the lawyer—a man called Moots. He'd snickered at the name and caught a frown from his father.

"I'd try a skillet if I were you," the chubby lawyer had suggested before launching into legal speak with his parents. Michael tuned out most of the conversation, opting instead to eavesdrop on the booth behind them where a minister in a flannel coat and Carhartt cap was offering advice to an elderly farmer with red eyes.

After breakfast, during which Michael had wolfed down his French toast—*see Mom? No lack of appetite for me*—the Larsons took a trip out to the nursing home. During the ride, he'd caught the gist of the meeting with Moots. Due to some legal mumbo jumbo, they couldn't stay at his grandparents' house, but Moots had said there might be another option. Michael grew sullen at this bit of news. He was perfectly content living at the motel. He had his own folding bed. The owner talked to a plexiglass cow. And there was the pool.

His goggles fogged up as he reached the bottom, but no matter. He had the coin in his sights.

Dad had cried on the ride back from visiting Big Bear and Grandma in the nursing home.

"Where did my father go?" his father said, and Michael didn't understand. His grandfolks seemed the same to him. They were still old, still cheek-pinchers. True, they were in a nursing home instead of their own house, but Michael liked the home. He'd spied balloons strung up for someone's birthday, a man leading a karaoke sing-along and glittery posters on the walls announcing Movie Night. To him, the nursing home was a happening place.

Before donning his swimsuit, he'd tried to cheer his father up by finding a movie on the ViddyBox, but the darn thing was acting up. Every time he slipped his thumb about on the remote's little trackpad, the cursor on the TV would fly around the alphabet, typing a garbled mess of nonsense.

"The woman at the office said the internet was acting up," his mother sighed.

Jessie. The woman's name was Jessie. Her cow was Elmer, and her sign said NO-NO-NO. Maybe the sign was acting up too.

No. It was like the sign *knew* he was there.

Shaking off the memory, Michael had made a game of the misbehaving ViddyBox by pressing the voice control and babbling into the remote.

"Nikso-blah-blah!"

The ViddyBox did its best to interpret, and the movie *Nixon* appeared on the screen.

"Bunsy-tiger-murky-moe!"

The box offered up *Once Upon a Time in America*.

"Gerkin-wellbo-teeshee—"

"Give it a rest, will you, Sport?" His dad was squeezing his temples while his mom squeezed his dad. Michael gave it a rest.

He locked in on the dime. With a slow motion grab, he reached out and snatched the coin.

As he did so, something pressed against his mouth. *Around* his mouth. Michael's brain couldn't process the sensation and instead spat out the closest approximation from his memories. It was the moment he'd woken in an ambulance en route to the hospital with an oxygen mask pressed against his face.

But this time, the air wasn't going in—it was going out. Something was drawing the breath from his lungs.

No, not a mask. A mouth.

Smoke! I taste smoke.

Panicked, Michael kicked backwards. The pressure lifted, and without thinking, he took in a mouthful of chlorinated water. Choking, he dropped the dime and quickly shot upward. When he broke the surface, he let loose with a great spray, coughing and gasping.

Hannah was at the pool's edge in a second.

"Michael?"

Still gulping air, he pulled himself out of the water and clung to the ladder, panting. He spat. The smell and taste of smoke lingered in his nose and mouth. What happened down there? Was it simply more chemo brain shenanigans or…what?

"I think I need a break," he said, anticipating his mother's next words. "I'm okay, but I think I need a break."

"You *definitely* need a break."

"I know, Mom. I just said."

She reached to help him up, but he shrugged her off, ascending the ladder on his own. When she threw a towel around his shoulders, he winced.

"I don't want you to catch cold."

"Okay, okay." He was over being babied.

His mother caught wind of his disapproval and scrunched up her mouth. "Until we get a few more scans under our belt, better safe than sorry."

Michael sighed. Mom had *scanxiety* and she had it bad. It was the word cancer families used to describe the buildup of worry that accompanied each new scan. Michael thought Hannah Larson had scanxiety 24/7.

Still, she was letting him swim. One thing at a time.

A burst of bubbles broke the surface of the water, and Michael turned.

"Huh. Something must be wrong with the filter," Hannah remarked.

Michael remained frozen in place, water dripping down his back and pooling at his feet. For a split second, a slick of beet red water spread across the pool's surface.

The next moment, all was back to normal—the crystal-clear water undulating and inviting.

Michael exhaled, unaware that he had been holding his breath.

Yes. He *definitely* needed a break.

CHAPTER 11

*T*he Crossroads Motel wasn't fancy like the Holiday Inn over in Rock Island, but it would do. And Marybeth didn't seem to mind. In fact, she practically dragged him into the room without a second look at the place.

Luke was certain of it—tonight was the night.

He'd been trying to get MB in the sack for the better part of the year, ever since they'd made out at the ShopMor Christmas party. The party proper had been relegated to the stockroom, but he and MB had made a run for it, ending up lip-locked in the home goods section. They might have done it then and there amongst the hand towels and comforters if it hadn't been for that damn nosy Tandy.

"Get up, y'all," the big man had told them. "Get up and get back to the party. Don't need no cleanup on aisle three, know what I'm sayin'?"

They'd returned to the party but for months after, Marybeth was a ghost. She quit her cashier's job at ShopMor, and at first Luke thought she had gotten back with her ex-boyfriend, a cop out of eastern Iowa, and he wasn't going to go messing around in that kind of situation. All he needed was a jealous police officer causing him grief.

But his buddies down at the Blind Rock told him otherwise. After buying the boys a round, they revealed that MB was going through some sort of family situation—something about a fire and a troubled younger brother. Whatever the matter was, she seemed to have put it behind her when they'd met up last week at the Memorial Day BBQ at the Y.

"Save me," she'd said as a volunteer piled a massive dollop of potato salad on her plate. Luke wasn't sure if he was meant to save her from the picnic or from her life in general, but in any case she found him at the end of the evening and planted one on him. "Take me out on a date, Luke Locke."

That date was tonight. Here, at the Crossroads Motel. And Luke was itching to get to it.

As MB flopped onto one of the twin beds, her shirt pulled up in front revealing her pale belly and her pierced navel—a single turquoise bead on a silver loop.

"I'm sorry I made you wait," she whispered, but Luke was too busy kicking off his shoes and unbuckling his belt to respond.

As he was pulling his shirt up over his head—buttons were too damn slow—he heard two sounds in rapid succession. First, a loud pop from outside; then, a frightened cry from Marybeth.

"When's hunting season start?" she asked, a hitch in her voice.

Luke wrestled off his shirt and turned toward the door.

"Not 'til November."

At that, the door flew open, kicked inward by a hulking figure silhouetted in the night.

That's not fair. I was just about to get some.

The figure raised a shotgun, pointed it Luke's way and the world awoke with a blast of orange-white light.

CHAPTER 12

Wood closed the door to his room and set the security latch in place.

Dropping the green duffel bag on the bed, he surveyed the room. The dueling scents of fresh paint and potpourri filled the air.

His stomach rumbled, unaccustomed to the massive dinner he'd fed it. His evening meal had consisted of a pork tenderloin sandwich the size of his head and a slice of strawberry rhubarb pie. The tiny Country Cabin was packed with overweight diners feasting on oversized meals. In the corner, a man who looked older than dirt jabbed away at a slot machine. Now that Illinois had opened the door to video gambling, the damn things were everywhere. The electronic burbling of the thing floated atop the murmur of dinner chatter.

Looking about the room, he counted three lamps—one on each nightstand and one on the desk—and the overhead light. He turned on the desk lamp, unplugged the two flanking the bed and unscrewed the three in the fan. A little trick he'd learned from trial and error.

Stepping into the bathroom, he stuck a nightlight into the outlet. Oscar the Grouch—it was all the ShopMor had.

Having successfully set a low light environment, he proceeded to set himself up at the desk. He pulled a deck of cards from his case and fanned them out. Each of the cards had a hole punched in it dead center. Casinos drilled holes in their cards once they'd been in play to cancel them out, to make sure cheats didn't try to slip a few extra aces back into the game. This particular deck was from the Big Muddy Casino, the riverboat where he had pulled in six hundred dollars last night after splitting a pair of eights. Free drinks, free cards and an extra six hundred bucks in his pocket. Not bad.

After cracking open a Red Bull, Wood turned back to the bed. The duffel lay there like a body bag. He glanced at his phone. 7:34. It was a shame he couldn't take advantage of the free HBO, but turning on the TV was a no-no. TV was a distraction just as sure as the bright lights were.

With the storm complaining outside, he steeled himself and walked over to the side of the bed. He leaned over the duffel and slowly unzipped it. A puff of dust rose as he spread the bag open. Staring down inside, a lump formed in his throat. He tried to swallow it down, but it remained.

Nerves. Happens every time, buddy.

The charred bones inside the bag were a mix of grey and amber and black. They sat in a pile of dust and ash. Ribs, thigh bones, part of a skull, some more blackened than others. Their proportions were off, and there were not enough, it seemed, to account for a single body. Let alone three.

Wood turned quickly to the desk and sat, his back to the bed and the bones. He instinctively pulled his vape and took a drag. The empty e-cig sizzled as it released one last unsatisfying spritz. His stomach cramped, clenching with the first of the pangs.

Not to worry. The night was young.

* * *

As Michael searched the ViddyBox, he heard the click of the keycard mechanism. A moment later, his father stepped into the room, pizza box in hand.

Michael grinned. "Mushrooms?"

"You bet."

The pizza proved underwhelming. Dad told him that he'd have to get used to it. "Midwesterners don't know squat about pizza. New York will always be number one in pie."

"New Jersey," Mom countered.

"New York."

"New Jersey!"

When his mother suggested he pass on a second slice in favor of another Ensure, Michael decided he'd had enough.

"Please stop treating me like I'm sick. I'm not sick."

Peter looked to Hannah. "What do you say we give the Ensure a rest?"

"Peter..."

"At least, tonight. The boy's doing great." He turned to Michael. "Aren't you?"

Michael nodded vigorously.

"See? He's got his appetite back, right? He's swimming."

"I know, but—"

"If we're even going to *think* about moving here, we're going to have to—"

Hannah rubbed her face until it reddened. "I don't want to take any chances."

"I understand."

"And I *don't* want to be the bad cop."

"No one would *ever* mistake you for a cop."

Hannah swatted Peter on the shoulder, but his playful retort had broken the mood. "Okay. No Ensure."

"All right," Peter said, clapping his hands. "Let's find something funny on TV."

* * *

Wood set the vape aside and shuffled the cards, eager to turn his attention to perfecting his blackjack strategy. Eager to lose himself in the cards.

Around 11:30, having shifted from blackjack to solitaire, Wood felt a tingle at the back of his neck. The temperature suddenly dropped. The desk lamp flickered. The room pulsed as it pressurized and depressurized like the cabin of a plane dropping from the sky.

It was the *thrum*—the vibration that announced their arrival. That made the shadows tangible.

Wood clapped his hands over his ears as the pressure mounted.

Ladies and gentlemen, this is your Captain speaking. Looks like we've got a little turbulence up ahead, so if you would fasten those seat belts, I'd be most appreciative.

It had begun.

* * *

Michael's folks were asleep, his mother already practicing her night chat, his father curled up next to her in a question mark.

It was time for the game.

"Say-mo-mo foor!" Michael whispered into the remote.

St. Elmo's Fire, the ViddyBox suggested.

"Chippy-shoo playdoh bleb-bling!"

Children Shouldn't Play with Dead Things.

"Jibby-jib cloo-cloo norf-norf!"

Michael.

Michael paused.

"Jiffy-jib..."

P.S. I Love You.

Electricity ran up and down Michael's arms. A thrill came over him like when he was playing the game Chompmaster II and was just about to unlock a secret level.

"Who are you?"

The room suddenly dropped ten stories. Or at least that's what it felt like to Michael. The only other time he'd felt such a rapid sinking feeling in his stomach was when he and his folks had visited the Empire State Building. On the elevator ride down, his ears had popped. Like now.

Ghost Dad.

Hands trembling, Michael pressed the info button.

Ghost Dad (1990) starring Bill Cosby, directed by Sidney Poitier.

The pressure pulsed in his ears and the air above him turned dark and thick. Swirling and angry, it beckoned the boy to reach up and touch it.

Michael dropped the remote and raised his hand.

* * *

Deep within the black womb, Peter felt the world go heavy as reality clicked into focus. Michael—*Michael!*—was below him, alive and so *tangible*. Whisper chittered and wailed at the *newness* of the experience, and while he had not intended they appear to the boy, appear they did.

Peter could only imagine what Michael was seeing. The boy stared up at him, spinning out of control.

"No," Peter thought. *"We're* the ones spinning."

Circling above the rollaway bed like a twister ready to drop its greedy funnel, Peter heard Whisper screech in fear.

No! Not doing! Not!

Someone or something else had released the floodgates, pulled out the stopper. He knew he should probably be as frightened as his clawing companion, but another thought rose to the surface instead and demanded he take action.

If I reach down, I can touch him.

The thought propelled him downward, and he stretched, finally accepting the fact that he was nowhere close to being human anymore. He strained downward, distorting himself as the dark one howled behind him.

Noooo!

Michael reached upward, curiosity and fear in his eyes, lower lip clenched tight between his teeth.

Almost there…

NOOOO!

With a cry, Whisper gave up resisting and the two tumbled downward, spinning headlong toward the boy, circling his outstretched fingers, his hand. Digging in to the savory *aliveness* of the boy's flesh. Grabbing hold until they orbited his wrist like twin moons of insanity. Held close by the gravity of his pulse.

* * *

"You okay, Buddy?"

Michael fell back in the bed, his arm dropping to his side.

"Yeah, Dad. Just a bad dream."

"Can I get you some water?"

"No, I'm fine."

"You sure?"

"I'm fine."

His father yawned and rolled over, already sliding back into his own dreams. "See you in the morning."

Michael wriggled in the covers until he found a comfortable position. But he wouldn't sleep for another two or three hours. Instead, he trained his eyes on the air above him, willing the swirl to return. And when it didn't, he grudgingly gave in to the night.

* * *

Jessie closed the door to the back room, stripped off her clothes and donned her oversized Elton John concert t-shirt. Her hip complained, but she steered her mind away from the fresh batch of pain pills Mr. Ecklund had given her. Nope. Best to leave the T-Rex alone.

Instead, she crawled into bed and indulged in five minutes of deep breathing. It didn't ease the pain, but it did help her separate from it, compartmentalize it. And once she'd accomplished that trick, the yawns commenced.

Jessie barely noticed when her eardrums constricted and the room went cool. And when an arm reached around her middle, pulling her close, she barely stirred.

"G'night," she mumbled.

The dead desk clerk of the Crossroads Motel held Jessie tight, the cold, wet O of his gut-shot belly kissing her lower back. Drawing warmth as they spooned.

* * *

The shower in the bathroom turned itself on, the gentle cascade of water echoing the falling rain outside.

Wood heard a pop like the crackle of a fire. The snap of a branch, the groan of straining timbers. But it wasn't firewood he was hearing twisting and bending—it was the bones. They were moving.

He concentrated on his game as he heard the bedsprings suddenly compress under a great weight. A familiar, bittersweet scent wafted his way, making his stomach do flips.

They were coming.

Once, he had made the mistake of looking back, but never again. What he had seen had threatened his sanity. Black and shiny and wild. And growing out of nothing.

No. Out of the duffel.

The thing he'd seen had locked eyes with him, and if he hadn't turned away, he was certain he wouldn't be sitting here right now looking for a place to play the nine of hearts.

THE HUNGRY ONES

The first one tumbled from the bed and onto the floor with a sickening crack, causing it to hiss. As it rose, the sound of bone splintering, knitting together and splintering again set Wood's teeth on edge.

His half-empty Red Bull began to shudder, and before he could catch it, liquid spilled across the desk, drenching his deck of cards.

The desk lamp sputtered, its light pulsing bright and dark, bright and dark. Fearing the bulb would burst, Wood quickly moved to dowse the light, but he was too late. In a puff of smoke and a final flash, the lamp went dead.

The room fell into darkness.

He heard a second drop to the floor followed by a third. Soon the room was filled with the sound of creaking, snapping bone. And under it all, a lone, dry voice hummed a quiet tune. The song sparked a childhood memory, and he was surprised to find that he knew the words.

Bringing in the sheaves, bringing in the sheaves. We shall come rejoicing, bringing in the sheaves.

CHAPTER 13

*B*ree *turned on the shower, stripped naked and faced the bathroom mirror.*

How long would it be before Rusty found out that she had altered the check he'd given her for his half of the bills? How long before he noticed that three thousand dollars—not three hundred—had slipped out of his account?

Hopefully long enough for her to get the hell outta Dodge.

And here I am at the Crossroads Motel. What a mess.

The bruise on her sternum had faded but it was still there. Bree let her fingers play across the discolored skin, remembering the argument. Remembering the blow.

Never again.

It wasn't enough that Rusty demeaned her in public, called her a whore in front of her friends—the few she still had left in this town. Now he had added beating to the menu. And unless she meant to kill the sonofabitch, she had to put Maple City in her rearview mirror.

The first time he hit her was last New Year's Eve. Apparently for Rusty Timmons, touching another man's arm was forbidden.

"You and Wesley were sure chummy," he said, picking up the rolled-up Penny Saver. Before she could answer, he'd struck her across the cheek with it. "Is that what you do out there at the river?"

What she did over at Quicksilver's, the strip club in Gulf Port half a mile from the Mississippi, was a hell of a lot more than arm touching. Rusty knew that, of course, but she had always suspected that he kept a clear picture of her job at bay. Her stinging face confirmed that.

Bree turned her gaze from the mirror to her bag. She unsnapped it, wrapped her fingers around the wad of hundreds and squeezed. She'd ditch the car in Carbondale with her friend Gareth, swapping it for another. Gareth was a car thief and had rather extreme views where race was concerned, but he had always been kind to her when he came north on 'business'.

She was heading south. Rusty would assume she was heading north—that's where all her people were. But since they'd made it abundantly clear that they didn't want anything to do with her, she was going to disappear into the Deep South.

I've always wanted to see Biloxi.

She snapped the bag closed and stepped into the shower. The water came as more of a gurgle than a stream, and the no-skid strips on the shower floor were curling up, but what did you expect for fifty dollars a night? She reached for the complimentary soap. Ladybug brand. It smelled like dish soap and disinfectant.

As she was lathering up her nooks and crannies, she heard a sharp sound that made her pause. She quickly turned off the water and listened.

That was a scream.

Bree reached for the towel and wrapped it about herself. She stepped out of the shower and stuck her head out of the bathroom. The moment she did so, a tremendous clap echoed from outside followed by another cry.

Something heavy hit the other side of the wall to her room. Someone was done for. This was quickly followed by pounding on her door. The horror had reached her room.

Bree dashed across the room, stuck her eye to the peephole and got a distorted view of a woman in a neon-yellow t-shirt and long black hair. There was terror in the woman's face, as well as blood.

"¡Abre la puerta!" the woman howled.

The thought of remaining in her room, of hiding and waiting for the nightmare to pass came and went instantly, and Bree unlatched the safety chain.

As she swung open the door, she came face to face with the woman.

"¡Gracias!" the woman cried.

Time slowed.

Relief on the woman's face. A flash. A concussive bang. The woman disappearing, replaced by a blast of red.

Bree went numb. Neutral. Unfeeling. And when time resumed its normal pace, what filled the void was not fear. It was anger. No...not anger. Rage.

Her face speckled with the t-shirt woman's blood, Bree screamed. At the violence inflicted before her eyes. At the gunman. At Rusty, at the grabbing, grasping patrons of Quicksilver's and at the whole fucking world of men.

Before she knew it, she'd grabbed up the desk lamp and charged out of the room.

The man with the shotgun was standing not five feet in front of her, reloading his weapon. He looked up at her with dull eyes.

Bree threw the desk lamp as hard as she could and caught the man square in the nose. The blood that poured from the fat man's nostrils had a dual effect. It snapped Bree out of her adrenaline-fueled fury, and it woke the man from his trance. He snarled in pain and finished reloading while Bree raced back into her room.

She was about to slide the safety chain back in place when she heard the man pump the shotgun on the other side of the door.

Bree dropped to the floor, and the door splintered inward over her head. She scrambled backward, losing her towel, beating a retreat to the bathroom. There was no window to be had back there, no escape. It was just...away. Away from the man reaching through the hole in the door.

The money. Perhaps she could distract him. She'd once heard a story of a man being chased by a bear. The man had disrobed as he ran, dropping another article of clothing each time the animal grew nearer. The bear would stop to sniff each piece of clothing. The man made it out of the woods safe. Naked but safe.

She grabbed the money from her bag, ready to toss it in the man's face. But before she could turn back toward him, she felt a slap to her back and saw the mirror go crimson.

What a mess.

Bree reached out and tried to wipe the red away, her blood-wet hands squeaking against the mirror's surface.

What a mess. What a...

* * *

Bree turned on the shower, stripped naked and faced the bathroom mirror.

How long would it be before Rusty found out that she had altered the check he'd given her for his half of the bills? How long before he noticed that three-thousand dollars—not three-hundred—had slipped out of his account?

Hopefully long enough for her to get the hell outta Dodge.

And here I am at the Crossroads Motel. What a...

Bree went suddenly cold.

I've done this before...

The mirror was red. *No it wasn't.* Her back was on fire. *No it wasn't.*

She leaned in toward the mirror, examining her reflection and found that she could see the door behind her. *Through* her.

And the door was opening.

* * *

Sister entered the bathroom first. The scent of the ghost was strong in her nose. Strong and ripe. Two years ripe. What a feast this would be.

She moved to one side, her body cracking and snapping as she did so. The larger of her brothers staggered into the room, a painful mass of blackened, cracking skin held together enough—just enough. The smaller remained behind. Waiting.

Sister hummed as her brother got down to it. As he pounced upon the spirit, ripping and shredding. She hummed to calm her hunger and drown out the cries. And in the end, she hummed to give thanks for this most welcome meal.

By and by the harvest, and the labor ended. We shall come rejoicing, bringing in the sheaves.

CHAPTER 14

Wood frantically worked his phone in order to illuminate the room. When he finally stabbed the flashlight option, the unnatural blue-white light hit him square in the face, blinding him. He quickly directed the beam at the wall before him.

Footfalls. One by one, the things that shared this room with him moved from bathroom to bed. He heard one crumple into dust, then the next.

Where was the third? Where was the—

A clawed hand grasped his shoulder.

Eyes straight, McKay.

Hot, sweet breath tickled the back of his head. The voice that followed was wet, as if the speaker had eaten an overly ripe fruit.

"Good," the voice cooed.

It wasn't fruit that the one who called herself Sister had been eating. Oh, no. Her meal was more *wet* than that.

"Take." The single word was followed by the proffer of a blackened hand with long blackened fingers. It reached out in front of his face, and it almost made him mad to look at it.

Bean pods!

As a child, he had collected dark brown bean pods that fell from a neighborhood tree. He and the other children used to swap the dried things as a sort of kid currency. Two bean pods for a ride on your bicycle. Five bean pods for a kiss from your sister.

Sister.

The hand floating before him was dry and dark. Any movement in the fingers caused them to crack—as if they were meant to be stationary, but the wearer of the shell was forcing them to move. Forcing them to *crack*.

"Take," the voice insisted.

And so, he took. He grasped the clawed index finger tightly and twisted.

Teeth gnashed in his ear, grinding at the pain, but they didn't bite. Not him, at least.

He twisted and pulled until the finger came free. A small spurt of black liquid accompanied the severing, but that was it.

At that, Sister withdrew, humming as she went. And soon, like the rest of her triumvirate, she fell into ash and bone on the bed.

When he was certain that she was gone, Wood thrust the raw end of the finger into his mouth and sucked.

CHAPTER 15

Jessie woke up gagging. Jesus, what was that smell?

Upon rising, she discovered a black, putrid stain on the sheet upon which she'd slept. Reaching back, her fingers found that the same damp foulness had soiled her shirt.

"Disgusting," she complained to the empty room.

She pulled the t-shirt up over her head and examined it. A greasy oval of black mucus obliterated Elton's tour dates, mimicking the dark stain on the bed. It smelled like roadkill. Like death. She dropped the ruined garment into a garbage bag, tied it tight, placed that bag into a second bag and tied it tight as well. Goodbye Yellow Brick Road.

Stripping the bed did little to solve the mystery of the offending goo. Jessie's first deduction was that a mouse or worse yet, a rat had curled up in her favorite t-shirt and died, leaving wet evidence of its demise. But search as she might, she couldn't locate a carcass.

She sprinted across the parking lot to room 109, showered, and dressed and sprinted back. Feeling a hell of a lot cleaner, she set about making the morning's coffee. Two pots regular, one decaf. By the time she was finishing up, Lin appeared at the door with two big plastic bags in hand.

"Apple turnovers," the young woman said.

"Great idea, Lin. Make sure you give me the receipt."

"No receipt," Lin said with a shy grin. "I made them."

Jessie bit into a warm turnover and the tart/sweet taste of the apple filling washed away all residual disgust at the morning's previous nastiness.

"These are heaven."

"Are they okay?"

"They're *heaven*."

"Good."

The office door opened and Steph barreled into the room. "You ready for this soft open?"

"Not even close," Jessie said.

"Cool." Steph attacked the coffee, ignoring the creamer but going heavy on the sugar.

The front desk phone rang, and Lin slipped past Jessie to answer it. "Have a turnover."

Steph's ears perked up. "There are turnovers?"

"Save some for the family. And for Mr. McKay," Jessie said.

"Are these going to be a regular thing?" Steph asked, gesturing with her half-eaten turnover.

"Just special for today."

"Because little niceties like these can add up."

"I know."

"But...damn, they are good."

Lin held out the phone. "Jessie? It's for you, but I don't...I can't quite catch what they're saying."

Jessie gestured for the phone. "This is Jessie Voss, how can I help you?"

Static crackled in her ear.

"Hello? Are you there?"

A woman's voice broke through the white noise.

"...needs to...home and...going...was just..."

"I'm sorry, I didn't catch that."

"...said that if...check on...because he's...today..."

"We have a lousy connection. Would you mind if I asked you to—"

"...very important...you...being stupid."

Jessie rolled her eyes. "And you have a wonderful day as well."

There was silence on the other end. Jessie was about to hand the phone back to Lin when the woman on the other end sighed heavily.

"Are you being sarcastic? I don't understand sarcasm."

The line went dead.

A white car with one brown door pulled into the parking lot. The driver, an elderly man with a stony expression waited as a middle-aged woman in a housekeeping outfit got out of the car and walked tentatively toward the office.

"C'mon," said Steph, stuffing the last of the turnover into her mouth. "I want you to meet my cousin Esther. She's starting today."

* * *

"Michael? You about done in there?"

"Five more minutes, Dad?"

"Three. We've gotta get moving."

Dad was in a state. As was Mom. The phone call from the nursing home had come early that morning, and ever since his parents had been riding on adrenaline. Something had happened, but no one was telling him what. Adults. Didn't they know he was already imagining the worst?

Michael turned on the faucet to add credence to his request. He opened his toiletry kit—a gift from his Aunt Gina—and rooted around until he found the yellow silicon band he'd hidden away. Until now. He fingered the lettering etched across its surface.

Michael Strong.

The band was his mom's idea. She'd sent away for a bunch. For support, she'd said. He could pass them out to friends, give them to family members as gifts.

"They're so you'll know you've got a team behind you fighting this thing."

But to Michael, the bands were an embarrassment. As if his bald head and sunken eyes hadn't been big enough clues of his illness, now he had to wear a taxicab-yellow confirmation of that fact? One night, he'd gathered up the lot and stuffed them deep in the wastebasket his mother reserved for medical waste.

All save for the one in his hands. Perhaps he could finally put it to good use.

He examined his left wrist. It was encircled with a beet-red rash. No, not a rash. Bite marks.

He knew what he'd seen hadn't been a dream. And his raw skin proved it. He knew he should be terrified, horrified at the realization that there was tangible, toothy proof of last night's nightmare ripped into his skin, but he couldn't get over the fact that, on the whole, he felt something quite different. Something far from fear. What was it?

Could it possibly be…joy?

Michael slipped the band about his wrist and found that it lined up well enough with the marks. Good. If it couldn't hide the bites, at least it could explain them. Some kids were allergic to silicone, right? His buddy Hervé at chemo had been allergic to latex.

"One time, a doctor screwed up and examined me wearing latex gloves instead of rubber," his friend told him as they sat in the waiting room awaiting their turn at bat. "I went into anaphylactic shock."

Three weeks later, Hervé was dead. It wasn't the latex that got him but a nasty bout of pneumonia. He was the second chemo friend Michael lost in six months.

"Time's up," his father said as he jiggled the door handle.

"Okay, okay."

"Five, four, three…"

Michael turned off the faucet and watched the water circle the drain.

"Two…"

Like the roiling air that circled his bed last night.

"One. Time's up."

Michael opened the door to find his father red-eyed and disheveled. He'd been crying. Dad crying made him nervous.

"Thanks, buddy."

His father slipped past him and closed the bathroom door. Michael turned to his mother, who was busy searching for her other shoe.

"Is Dad okay?"

"He's fine, Michael."

"But…"

Hannah retrieved her second shoe, sat on the bed and patted the spot next to her, telling him to join her. As Michael hopped up by her side, she noticed the band around his wrist. "I see you didn't get rid of all of them."

Busted.

"No."

"Is that irritating your skin—?"

"No."

His mother dropped the subject and draped an arm around him. "I know you want me to give you your space. Let you breathe. I know you think I've been acting like a mother hen."

"Mom…"

"And I probably have, but you're going to have to be patient with me. Mothers and sons—it's a tough game. The more you want to pull away, the closer I want to hold you." Hannah proved her point by squeezing her son tighter. "But I heard what you said last night. No more babying."

"You promise?"

Hannah smiled wanly. "No. But I'll do the best I can."

The shower turned on in the bathroom.

"What's wrong with Dad?"

"Oh, he's just—"

"Don't baby me."

Hannah sighed. "Grandma didn't recognize him."

"Did she have a stroke? Is that why?"

Hannah regarded her son. Too many hospital visits had made him an accidental expert in all things medical.

"They don't know but they're going to find out. And in keeping with my promise, I'm going to find you a sitter while I take your dad to see his mom. Give you some room. What do you think?"

"Yes!"

Hannah sighed. "Some day I'll get this mom thing down, kiddo."

Michael put his hand on her shoulder and nodded in mock sympathy. "Mothers and sons."

Hannah kissed the top of his head. "You got that right."

* * *

Jessie had wrapped up interviewing Steph's cousin when Hannah Larson stepped into the office with her son. The boy's eyes quickly fixed on the pastries.

"Mom. Can I?"

"Just one."

The boy raced to the coffee station, grabbed the biggest turnover he could find and went to town. "Mmm! Apple."

"I'm glad this is going to work out, Esther," Jessie said, shaking the woman's hand.

"Me too. Let me tell my husband and I'll get started." Esther practically bounced out the door.

"Poor thing had to quit Handel's Bed & Breakfast." Steph shook her head. "The folks who run that place are bastards, plain and simple."

Hannah cleared her throat. "Excuse me, but I was wondering if you might have any recommendations for babysitters." She caught Michael giving her the stink eye and amended her request. "For childcare. I'd like to hire someone to sit with my son today."

Jessie shook her head. "I'm sorry. I don't know of anyone offhand. Lin?"

Lin looked up from the computer. "You want me to do a search?"

"I'll do it," Steph said.

Jessie balked. "You?"

"Don't look so surprised. I'm childcare certified. Just one of my many skills. I'm also a notary and a fully accredited reflexologist."

"Really?"

"A gal's gotta do what a gal's gotta do. Besides, kids like me." The stone-faced woman turned to the boy. "What do you get when you cross a snowman with a vampire?"

Michael looked to his mom, who nodded for him to play along.

"Uh...frostbite?"

"He's a smart one." Steph gave Michael a wink and turned to Hannah. "Twelve bucks an hour."

The woman nodded her head a bit too enthusiastically. "That's great."

"Here's my number," Steph said, scribbling on the back of one of the new Intermission business cards. "You can text me every fifteen minutes, if you like—I don't mind. Office number is on the front."

"Let me give you my number," Hannah said.

"Already got it in the computer," Jessie said, amazed that Steph seemed to be pulling it off.

"Ah, right." Hannah knelt in front of Michael. "You okay with this, hon?"

"Yes." The boy looked thrilled. He didn't even seem to mind when his mom kissed him on the cheek and straightened his hair. One look back, and she was out the door.

Jessie turned to Steph. "So, what's the plan?"

"He'll help me and Esther do the rounds. Won't you, kid?"

Michael nodded vigorously.

Steph smiled. "See? That's settled."

The desk phone rang, and Jessie beat Lin to it. "Intermission Motor Lodge."

Ssszzz-zzzss!

The static was back.

"*...only listen...on, and if you...make everything...what to...*"

"Listen, if you're trying to book a room, I suggest you go to our website. The address is www.intermiss—"

"*...not you...think that every call...need...to Stephanie Hoyle...time, okay? Steph...if you...mind, sheesh!*"

Jessie held out the phone to Steph as if it were a rotting fish. "It's for you."

Steph frowned and took the phone. "Yeah, who is this?" She plugged her free ear with a finger. "Say again?"

Jessie was about to offer the boy a second turnover when she noticed that Steph's face had gone paler than normal, if that was even possible. No doubt about it—Steph was rattled.

"We'll see about that." And at that, Steph abruptly ended the call, tossing the receiver back to Lin who fumbled to catch it.

"Everything all right?" Jessie asked, even though it was quite obvious that everything was *not* all right.

Without a word, Steph headed for the door.

"Wait a minute, wait a minute!" Jessie cried, blocking the door with her foot. "What about the kid?"

"You'll be fine. I'll be back." Steph plowed past her, forced open the door and was gone.

"Boss?" Lin was nodding toward the kid.

Jessie turned back to Michael. The boy was staring past her, flecks of pastry stuck to his face.

"Michael?"

* * *

The man behind the counter was dead. Michael knew that instantly. He was dead, and yet he was standing there between the two women. Ratty t-shirt, mouth open as if wailing, the stink of rot filling the room. Black eyes stared from his white, doughy face, and his stomach...

Michael took a step back.

The man's stomach was missing. Scooped out like ice cream. Like blood-red ice cream.

Jessie caught him by the shoulder. "What's wrong?"

Michael doubled over and spewed apple pastry all over the floor.

CHAPTER 16

Wood's head pounded, but his stomach had settled. He'd caught the hunger just in time. Held it at bay. Now to make sure he could contain it for the duration of his stay.

Standing in the bathroom in his boxer shorts, he went about his practiced routine. The finger had already begun to harden. Last night, he'd sucked it dry of every drop of liquid, allowing the blackness to fill him up and quell his craving. The dry husk was all that remained.

In the beginning, he'd simply tossed the gnarled bits and pieces out the window en route to his next call, but a food network TV show had provided inspiration. It was a special on Indian cuisine, and the host had revealed his passion for his coffee grinder. It was the perfect thing for grinding cumin seeds.

The next day, Wood had purchased his own coffee grinder and set about testing out recipes. After a few mishaps—snorting the pulverized fingers brought on instant vomiting—he had settled on his current method: a course grind in a regular coffee filter with one cup of water. Chop up the dry flesh with his handy pocketknife, toss the bits into the grinder, pour the powder into the filter and brew. The resultant liquid was potent when vaped, and it kept the hunger at bay.

As the small coffee maker did its job, Wood glanced back at the bed. The duffel was open. Ash and bits of bone lay strewn about on the comforter. He'd finish making his brew, stash the liquid in a water bottle and get to cleaning up the bed. The clock on the nightstand read 9:22. He still had a good hour and a half before he'd check out of this room and into the next.

There was a knock at the door.

"Housekeeping."

Damn. He'd neglected to put the *Do Not Disturb* sign out.

"Just a minute!"

He heard the door open despite his protestation.

"Housekeeping?"

"Just a minute, I said!"

Wood dashed to the door. Thank God for the security latch. It kept the obviously deaf help from barging in on the scene of the crime.

He thrust his face out the door and glared at the stout woman in white.

"Do. Not. Disturb," he growled.

"I'm sorry. I—"

"Come back at eleven." He slammed the door shut and turned the lock. He thought twice, grabbed the *Do Not Disturb* sign and opened the door. The housekeeper smiled—perhaps she could be of assistance? Wood slipped the sign on the knob, flashed a toothy grimace and slammed the door a second time.

Damn. He'd let his guard slip. Both with the sign and with his demeanor. His charming mask had dropped for a moment, and he'd revealed his predatory nature.

He'd pull it together before he left the room. By then, he'd be all smiles.

As the coffee maker gurgled the last of the water, Wood turned back and approached the bed.

Fine, powdery ash blanketed the comforter. At the center of the bed lay the duffel containing the grey, charred bones. Silent and still once more.

Wood allowed himself a moment of regret at the role he played—serving up the ghostly lambs to the slaughter. He found himself wondering what happened to the souls that were feasted upon. Were they lost forever? Did they feel pain?

Yes. And yes.

I could run, he thought. Leave the bones for the nosy housekeeper to find. But what good would that do? He had tried once before and *only* once. The result had been torture, had driven him back to the bones. To Sister.

She would feed well here, she and her brothers. The rooms were filled with tasty morsels, ripening and growing more sustaining with each passing day.

And now there were a dozen of them, lined up like eggs in a carton.

No...now eleven.

And when they're gone? Swallowed up? Then what, Wood, old boy?

One thing at a time.

Wood retrieved the largest of the bones and stuffed it into the duffel. As he did so, he felt a sharp pain in his right palm and quickly withdrew his hand.

A shard of bone sat imbedded in his hand; a grey splinter piercing the ball of his thumb.

A rush of wind filled his ears as the room disappeared. The taste of cheap whiskey flooded his mouth, fiery and sweet, and he spat.

Cold! He was cold!

He tried to pluck the splinter from his palm but it wouldn't budge. The shard grew hot beneath his skin, singeing his nerves. He clawed at it, making a mess of his skin, ripping the flesh, drawing blood.

At last, he dislodged the splinter and tossed it aside. He stumbled backward, his breath coming in halting bursts.

"To hell with this."

He stalked to the bathroom and grabbed a bath towel. Using the thing as a barrier between him and the bones, he scooped the grey remains into the bag and zipped it tight.

Wood scurried about the room, gathering his things. He poured the fresh finger brew into a plastic bottle, pocketed his deck of cards and slipped on his shoes.

He tossed the ash-soiled towel into the shower, blasted the water and knelt. Working like a washerwoman at a river, he kneaded the soaked towel as a swirl of grey circled the drain.

The water got into his wound and stung like hell. He examined his palm. A slight, dark dash lay beneath the surface of his skin next to the ragged, pink hole. A piece of the splinter still in hiding.

I'm gonna need a needle to get that out.

Leaving the towel balled up in the shower, Wood made a beeline for the duffel, swiped it from the bed and left his room. The bright daylight hit his eyes like a bad joke.

"Whiskey."

But first things first. Time to secure the next room on the list. The next egg in the carton. Room 105. He knew because *she* had told him.

CHAPTER 17

L in wiped the floor with paper towels as Jessie cleaned up the boy's face.

"I'm sorry," Michael moaned.

"I think we should call his mom," Lin said.

"No!" The boy balled his fists. "I just ate it too fast. Don't call. I'm fine."

Lin dropped the paper towels into the trash bag meant for coffee cups and tied it tight, her nose wrinkling. "What do you think, boss?"

Jessie dropped to Michael's level and looked him square in the eye. "I think she's right, Michael." She pulled her phone from her pocket.

The boy put his hand over her phone, pushing it down. "Don't. Please. Dad's got to see Grandma. If you call, they'll come back. He's *got* to see her. I ate too fast. I *swear*."

"How's your tummy now?"

"Empty. But good."

Jessie looked to Lin. The young woman gave her a tilt of the head that Jessie could only interpret as *your call*.

She raised a finger. "You feel a *twinge* of discomfort and we're calling Mom, okay?"

"Okay."

"I mean it."

Michael nodded. He turned to Lin. "Sorry about making a mess."

Lin waved him off as she spritzed the floor with Febreze. "I have a cat that's lactose intolerant. I'm used to throw-up."

Jessie caught the boy staring past her at the front desk. "Whatcha looking at?"

"Nothing."

"Pretty intense stare for nothing."

The boy turned to her and seemed ready to blurt something out when the door to the office swung open and Wood entered, suit coat on and keycard in hand. The man caught the vibe of the room and stopped inside the door. "What'd I miss?"

Jessie rose. "Can I help you, Mr. McKay?"

Wood waved his keycard. "Swapping rooms, if it's okay with you. Your gal there told me it'd be okay. Just wanna get to know your motel as much as possible for my review. Mmm! Are those turnovers?"

Michael's stomach did a somersault but he swallowed it into submission.

"Help yourself," Lin said. "There's coffee too."

"Mighty kind of you."

"You want to get some fresh air?" Jessie asked the boy.

Michael nodded fiercely. "Fresh air. Yeah. Yeah, can we go?"

"Mind the fort," Jessie said to Lin. "And keep a sharp lookout for any last-minute emails from folks RSVP'ing for tonight."

"You got it."

Jessie rose and pointed the way down the hall. "Help me track down some folding tables? Pretty sure I remember seeing a couple next door."

Michael, whose attention had strayed to the front desk, to the spot where the man with the hollowed-out stomach had stood, roused himself. "Sure. Tables?"

"C'mon."

Jessie led the way down the hall toward the old restaurant, Michael at her heels.

Wood turned to Lin, his mouth full of turnover. "Dynamite pastry."

"You said you wanted to swap rooms?"

"I did at that." He flashed her a smile and scratched at his hand. "You wouldn't happen to have a sewing needle, would you?"

* * *

Michael took careful inventory of the space. The previous time he'd been in the great room was late at night. Now, in the daytime he was able to see what a mess the place was.

"You should call the American Pickers," he said, sidestepping a box labeled *Plates/Bowls.* "I bet they'd buy a bunch of this junk." Then, realizing his misstep, he added, "They love old stuff. Antiques, you know?"

"You had it right the first time, kid. It's all junk as far as the eye can see."

"Except the cow," Michael said, spying the plexiglass steer.

"Except the cow."

Jessie kicked a cardboard box and a cloud of Styrofoam peanuts jumped in the air. "You wanna tell me why you got sick in the office?"

"I…"

"It's no use lying. I've got a major lie detector sitting right here." Jessie tapped her forehead. "Works on everyone and everything. Except fiancés. It's useless where they're concerned."

Michael felt trapped. He wanted to spill the beans about the dead man in the office, the incident at the pool, the swirl of darkness in his room. But once he spoke, once he actually said the words, that would be that. It would be out there for her to judge. For her to pass on to Mom and Dad. And why should he trust her? Because she'd caught a glimpse beneath his mask? No way Jose. Better to stay silent and…

He felt his shoulders start to shake, his eyes begin to water. The skin on his arms raised up into gooseflesh, like when Dad scratched his back extra hard. The combo of reactions confused him, and he sat on a stack of old Penny Savers and sobbed.

"Hey," the woman said, drawing nearer. "Hey, now."

"This is so stupid!" he spluttered. "I'm not sad."

"I know."

"I'm *not* sad!"

"I believe you."

After a moment, Michael looked up. The woman was standing over him, a quizzical look on her face.

"You want to tell me about it?"

Michael shook his head.

Jessie glanced over at the plexiglass cow, who watched them with its painted, bovine eyes. "I've got an idea. Why don't you tell Elmer over there all about it while I root around for these tables."

"Okay."

Jessie led Michael over to the cow. She grabbed an old dining room chair and set it in front of the steer. "Michael, this is Elmer; Elmer, this is Michael. I'll leave you two to it."

The woman picked her way through the clutter.

Michael stared at the cow. Its dull, plastic face stared back.

"This is dumb," he said under his breath.

Still, the cow stared.

Michael shot a glance across the room. Jessie was occupied with a stack of boxes that nearly reached to the ceiling. No way she was going to hear a word.

He reached out and rapped the cow's snout with his knuckles, producing a hollow thunk.

Michael leaned in. "I saw a dead man in the office. He was dead and his stomach was gone and it looked like someone ate it."

The cow looked on with plastic interest.

"And something stole my breath in the pool and there was a tornado over my bed that whirled and whirled and see? It bit me!"

Michael raised his arm and pulled the bright yellow band down, revealing his reddened wrist.

A long silence followed, and in it, a dreadful thought began to sink in. And as it grew and took root in his mind, Michael gave voice to his fear.

"The cancer is back, isn't it? Only this time it's in my head. A brain tumor like Hervé. It's making me see things. Making me *feel* things. Making me—"

Noo-oo, the plexiglass cow mooed. Not out loud but deep inside his mind, doing a frightening job of proving the fear he'd just uttered. He scrunched his eyes tight. This was too much. He wanted Mom. For all his complaining, he wanted Mom.

Listen.

No, he refused.

Listen.

Get out of my head!

Listen to mmm-mee.

Out of his depth—and now apparently out of his mind—Michael finally gave in and listened.

* * *

The tables were not where Jessie thought they'd be. She could have sworn that they were lying out in the open, but instead they were tucked away behind a stack of menu boards. Funny how in the end memory was a totally unreliable thing.

She yanked on the first table and her hip screamed. Damn metal!

As she dragged the tables from their hiding place, she shot a look toward the kid. He sat entranced by the cow, every inch of his little body concentrated on the thing.

"How you two getting along?"

The boy flashed her a thumbs up but kept his eyes on the cow.

I should call his mom.

She should, but she wasn't going to. Not yet. She wanted to give the kid a chance to breathe. God knows he could use it. She could tell that the moment she saw him. He'd been through the wringer, that much was obvious. Her bet was cancer—the peach fuzz that masqueraded as his hair was her main clue—but there were new autoimmune diseases popping up every day, so she couldn't be sure.

Jessie knew a little something about taking a break from people, God knew she did. Donovan had hovered over her during her rehab, playing the role of dutiful boyfriend while all she wanted to do was to tune him out and get down to the fucking business of learning how to walk again.

The ferocity of the memory startled her but it didn't surprise her. Ever since her accident she'd experienced sudden flares of anger. PTSD, no doubt, although she was loath to call it that. In her book, PTSD was reserved for soldiers injured in the line of duty. Folks who watched their best buddy step on a land mine. Not for her. Not for Jessie Voss.

And so, when the opportunity for counseling came along, she'd casually declined. Forget therapy and counselors and yacking on and on about *feelings*. She'd muddle through like the rest of the Vosses. Her people were hearty folk, farmers and ranchers from way back. Had any of them been knocked on their ass? You bet they had. Had any of them lain on a couch and spilled their guts to a shrink? Not a chance.

And still the fits of anger and depression and anxiety remained. Perhaps she wasn't as smart as she thought she was.

The boy stood up, seemingly done with his chat. He petted the cow's snout like it was the most natural thing in the world and then headed her way.

"You found the tables."

"Yeah, I did," Jessie said, presenting the tables as if they were trophy kills. "These should do."

"How's your hip?" the kid asked.

Jessie cocked her head at this. "How do you know about my hip?"

"The cow told me."

"Oh, yeah?" Jessie shook her head in mock annoyance. "I just can't tell him any secrets. What else did he tell you?"

"That if we climb the ladder we can see the whole motel."

What the hell? The kid was full of surprises.

Jessie was about to respond, but the boy was already searching the room.

"Can we go up there?"

"Absolutely not," Jessie said. "How'd you know about the ladder?"

"I told you. That's it, isn't it?" He was pointing at a wall-mounted ladder in the corner next to what used to be the checkout counter. It led up to a small trapdoor in the ceiling. "Please, can't we go up? Please?"

Despite her better judgment, Jessie found herself walking toward the ladder. She'd been up it only once before when she went up to the roof to figure out how to get Elmer down. Getting him down the trapdoor hadn't been an option. Instead, Steph had called in a favor with her cousin at Public Works, and he and his crew had retrieved the cow in exchange for a round of beers at Sullivan's Tap.

She laid her hands on the rungs. "Promise you won't tell your mom?"

"Are you kidding me?"

"Okay, okay. Just wanted to make sure." She stepped back. "You first so I can back you up. But go *slow*. You got that?"

"Got it." Instantly proving the truism that kids don't listen to a thing adults say, Michael leapt onto the ladder and started climbing like a monkey.

"Slow it down! Sheesh!" Jessie forced herself to climb faster than she normally would and paid the price in jolts of pain. "When you get to the top, stop and don't move an inch, you hear me?"

"Should I push this door open?" Michael was already at the top and already doing just that.

"No! Wait for me."

"Come on, slowpoke."

Jessie reached the top and hovered over Michael. She gripped the rung firmly. "Okay, give it one quick push. It should—"

The boy didn't need any further instruction. He shoved the trapdoor open so hard that he nearly broke it free from its hinges. A square of bright, blue sky appeared overhead.

"Careful!"

Michael was up and out of sight in a shot. Jessie swore under her breath and double-timed it up the final rungs until she broke through to the outside. With a bit of straining, she clambered onto the roof's tarry surface.

The boy stood two feet away, waiting patiently. Good. At least she didn't have to explain to his mother why he'd fallen over the edge and broken every bone in his body.

She grabbed the back of his shirt for good measure, and when the boy frowned at her, she said, "Scowl all you want, kid. My rules."

"You can see the whole town from up here," Michael said.

That wasn't exactly true, but Jessie agreed that the roof afforded them a pretty killer view. And something about the perspective made her feel bold enough to ask, "So, what's your story? It's cancer, isn't it?"

The kid didn't bat an eye. "Yup."

"You doing chemo?"

"No, I'm all done."

Her curiosity sated, Jessie fell silent.

"How'd you hurt your hip?" The boy's eyes were still on the view.

"I tried to tangle with a semi."

"A truck?"

"Yup."

Again, the silence.

"So we're both hospital people," Michael said, finally glancing up at her.

Jessie nodded her head and grimaced. "Jell-O."

"Ensure."

"Hospital gowns."

"IVs."

"Bedpans."

"Bedpans are the *worst!*"

They sighed in tandem, their new fellowship firmly intact.

"I died in the hospital," Jessie said, surprising them both with her revelation.

"Really?"

"I sure did. For three full minutes I was outta here."

"That must have been scary. Was it scary?"

"I don't know. Like I said, I was gone. I made it through surgery easy peasy, but afterwards when I was recovering…"

She let her words trail away when she noticed Michael shifting nervously, eyes on the ground.

"I'm sorry. I'm not sure why I told you that."

"Because friends tell each other stuff."

"We are friends?"

"I thought so. The cow said we were."

The boy looked up at her, and Jessie nodded. "I guess the cow's right."

Below, a delivery truck ran a red light, earning the honking disapproval of his fellow motorists.

"She's not a boy, you know. She's a girl," Michael said.

"Oh," Jessie said, going along with it. Anything to break the mood. "That would explain a lot."

"And her name's not Elmer. It's close, but that's not her name."

A strange look came over his face. It was as if, standing here at the top of the world, the boy saw a different view than she did.

"Why did you buy this motel?"

The boy's words hung in the air like a bird riding an updraft, and Jessie's heart skipped a beat. She started to give her stock response—*because I always thought motels were romantic*—but it didn't quite cut it. The question unsettled her because at that moment she didn't know how to answer.

As she fumbled for something to say, she saw Steph's car pull off Main Street and into the parking lot below.

"You want to spend the morning with Steph?"

The boy said nothing.

"Or do you want me to call your mom?"

The boy nodded.

Suddenly eager to get down off the roof, Jessie dialed the front desk and asked Lin for Hannah Larson's number.

CHAPTER 18

*T*he telephone rang. Patrick finished perusing the sports page
before picking up.

"Crossroads Motel, how may I help—"

"Stupid...stupid...stupid," said the voice on the other end.
"Too soon!"

The caller hung up.

"Screw you too," Patrick spat as he set the phone in its
cradle.

This was his last week at the Crossroads. In fact, it was
everyone's last week. The owner, a guy by the name of Fitz who
lived out in Vegas, had decided keeping the motel open wasn't
worth the effort. It was all the same to Patrick. He'd been trapped
in this spider's web for far too long. Time to move on. Maybe
take a drive down to the Keys where the water was always warm.
A green sea for Patrick C. Greene.

He'd have to break the news to the residents sooner rather
than later. Some were paid up until the end of the month—not
many but some. The owner was probably required to give at least
a month's notice to those people, but he knew Fitz didn't give a
rat's ass. Upon further reflection, Patrick decided he'd avoid the
unpleasant task of notifying the guests altogether. His last
paycheck had bounced, so he'd taken some of the motel's
furniture to the Second Hand Rose and paid himself out of the
proceeds. If he wasn't getting paid, why should he go through the

hassle of telling folks they had to find someplace else to live? No. He'd simply slip out some morning, leaving nothing but questions and a fresh turd in the toilet.

I wonder how much I could get for the cow on the roof...

He glanced out over the grounds. That damn stray kid was back at the pool smoking it up, but the gawky motherfucker wasn't hurting anybody. Again, Patrick wasn't being paid to police the place—he wasn't being paid at all.

There were lights on in a few of the rooms, and Patrick was surprised to find himself suddenly nostalgic. His pop used to make it a habit to take him and his little brother Rod on road trips in the summer, and the highlight of those trips was a stay at a roadside motel. Those were good times—black-and-white TV, a foldable luggage rack and, if they were lucky, Magic Fingers. For twenty-five cents the bed would vibrate the fillings right out of your teeth. It was better than the mechanical horse outside the grocery store.

But Pop was ten years dead, and he hadn't spoken to his brother since the old man's funeral. There was no bad blood between them. Rod worked some government job in DC, and Patrick was lucky if his latest gig paid him anywhere close to minimum wage. Seeing each other made them both feel bad. And so they'd let their hug at the cemetery be their last.

The office window lit up white as a pickup truck pulled into the lot. Cool. He'd insist on cash and pocket it. In fact, for the next week, the Crossroads Motel was a cash-only business.

Patrick put the newspaper away and slapped a smile on his face for the new guest. Having worked the front desk on and off for the past five years, he had a pretty good sense of what sort of person would walk through the door based on how long it took between the time they parked and the time they opened the door. The longer the wait, the more tentative the person, and tentative meant either low on cash looking for a bargain or first to arrive for a tryst. Women were quicker than men to enter, possibly eager to assert the fact that they were comfortable staying in a dive like this.

He couldn't read the person in the pickup. That's because they were taking their own sweet time. They were probably on their phone looking up alternative lodgings.

Hell, that's what I'd do.

Patrick reached below the desk for the beer he'd been nursing for the past twenty minutes when the owner of the pickup kicked in the door and fired.

Kicked in the door and fired.

Kicked in the door and fired.

Kicked.

And fired.

Kicked.

And fired.

Each time, the blast ripped through Patrick's middle, exploding his belly.

Each time, Patrick dropped his beer. Each time, he let out a low woof as his breath escaped in a rush.

Each and every time.

He hit the back wall and slouched. The fat man with the shotgun turned and exited the office.

Each and every time.

He slid down the wall, leaving a smear of red, his heart racing and then stumbling like a drunk man falling down the stairs.

Like a dead *man.*

I'm hit.

The realization came to him over and over again. Even as the room shifted around him. The light strobed—day-night-day-night-day-night. People came and went. EMS workers, police, a dozen others he couldn't recognize. Paint peeled on the walls as the artwork went missing. Invisible hands ransacked the place, stripping it bare and leaving it a mess.

All the while whispering to himself...

I'm hit.

Time jolted and he lurched with it. Two women stood on the opposite side of the desk taking stock of the place. The younger of the two looked so warm and inviting, and Patrick found himself drawn to her. He was freezing. Had been *freezing for what seemed like forever.*

Warm me.

As he reached out for the woman, she flitted away. In her place stood a young boy who stared at him with open-mouthed fear and wonder. Then, the kid doubled over, losing his lunch.

Patrick laughed as if it were the funniest thing in the world. Were all ghosts mad? They must *be. They* must *be! For that's what he was, wasn't he? The Ghost of the Crossroads Motel? Killed over and over again, doomed to haunt this shitty office for the rest of his life? Ha! For the rest of eternity!*

Ha ha!

Ha! Ha!

HA HA HA HA HA!!!

CHAPTER 19

As soon as Jessie entered the office, she covered her nose and mouth. "God, what a stink!"

Lin was spritzing the room with perfume. "I checked everywhere—the trash, the storage closet. I can't find what's causing it."

Steph stepped through the front door. "I know what you're going to say, Jess, and I'm...holy hell, what died in here?"

The boy wrinkled up his nose, and for a moment Jessie was afraid he was going to hurl again. "Febreze!" she shouted. The last thing she needed during her soft open was an office that smelled like a charnel house.

Steph disappeared out the door and returned shortly with a carton of spray bottles. "Take two and get busy." Even Michael joined in.

After filling the small room with a sickly sweet mist to mask the putrid smell, the three stepped back to assess their work.

"That's better," Steph said. "But I think you might have a rat problem."

"We had a rat at school named Wolverine and he didn't smell," Michael said.

"Woulda smelled if he died."

"Enough rat talk, okay?" Jessie said. "Let's get some fresh air in here."

Jessie cracked the window in the back room, Lin wedged the front door open with a rock and Steph set up a standing fan. Soon the smell had dissipated to a tolerable level.

"Set up an appointment with the exterminator," Jessie said.

"Way ahead of you, boss," Steph replied.

"Where'd you go that was so important?"

Steph looked down, a hangdog look on her face. "Something came up. Family business."

"Anything serious?"

"Yes and no. Love to keep it to myself, if you don't mind."

"Of course." Jessie knew the woman well enough that if she didn't want to talk about something, she wouldn't. She nodded toward Michael. "But you owe me."

"Sorry. But I did pick up the grub for your shindig."

"Did you get the donuts?" Lin asked.

"I got the donuts."

Jessie turned to the boy. He looked a bit pale, as if he expected someone to jump out of the woodwork.

"Hey kid, you want a pop?"

* * *

A few minutes later, Hannah Larson returned sans her husband. "Dad's going to grab a cab back so he can stay with his mom. How's the tummy, buddy?"

Michael gave a root beer burp. "It's a lot better."

"You want to put on your swimsuit?"

"Sure," he said, doing his best to smile. He had no interest in getting back in the water with whatever was down there in the deep end. But if he balked at the chance to swim, the questions would come fast and furious.

And so Michael soon found himself at the pool's edge, tentatively dangling his legs in the water.

"Aren't you going in?"

"In a minute. I think it's going to rain."

Looking across the pool, he watched as Jessie and the other women set food out on twin tables. *Soft open* they called it. That meant that the motel was opening tonight...but not really. It didn't make much sense to him, but then again adults did a lot of things that didn't make much sense. Like keeping secrets from kids, like smiling when they were actually sad. None of it worked, but they did it all the same.

* * *

Jessie's hip warned her of the approaching storm well before her weather app did. Up until half an hour ago, the app showed smooth sailing. It wasn't until the first car pulled up containing Glenda Wickes that the sky had begun to sour.

"So sorry to hear about you and Donovan," Glenda said as she gazed sadly at the spread of buffalo wings, stuffed potato skins and donuts. Glenda was the head of the snack bar and a favorite of the students. Jessie placated her with a jumbo plastic cup of wine.

Glenda and two couples had taken her up on offers to stay for the night at the Intermission Motor Lodge in exchange for filling out a brief survey. There were Glenda, the ever-charming Dr. Evans from the English Department and his wife Helen, and Diane and Lisa. The latter two both worked in admin and had always gone out of their way to see how she was doing after the accident.

"Quality turnout," Dr. Evans said as he munched on a stalk of celery. "The place looks great, Jessie. Really it does."

"So do you," Mrs. Evans added. "Such a lovely dress."

"Thank you." She'd ordered the dress online, and the fit left something to be desired. A couple of safety pins remedied that. She'd never been a dress kind of person. To her, it always felt like putting on a costume. But the compliment helped.

She had emailed out invitations to two dozen or more friends but had only received a few replies. She'd forgotten that when a relationship goes belly up, half of those friendships do as well.

Dr. Evans took up the task of leading the conversation and was soon regaling the group with tales of his latest trip to Scotland. "The food is terrible but the people are lovely."

But the chat and the wine and the niceties were soon interrupted by a gust of rain so fierce that it threatened to upend the snack tables.

"Just like the weather in Scotland!" Dr. Evans cried.

Steph tugged on Jessie's arm. "What's the backup plan?"

Backup plan? There was no backup plan. A flash flood wasn't on her radar.

"The office," Jessie said, hoping against hope that the air freshener was keeping the stench at bay.

As Steph and Lin herded the group toward the office, aluminum trays of hot wings in hand, Jessie looked out over the parking lot toward the pool.

Thank God. Apparently the Larsons had the good sense to come in out of the rain. Mother and son were making a mad dash for their room.

A particularly wild wind ripped the plastic tablecloth off of the nearest table at the same time it knocked over the lemonade. Jessie made a grab for the tablecloth and succeeded only in twisting her hip, bringing a stab of sharp pain. Wincing, she retrieved the boxed wines and limped to the office, a drumroll of thunder urging her on.

* * *

Wood was waiting at the front desk when the group descended upon the office. "What's this? A moveable feast?"

"Ah!" said Dr. Evans, toasting Wood. "A fellow Hemingway fan?"

"Only Hemingway I know anything about is that Mariel. Almost sixty and still a knockout." Wood turned to Steph who was cradling two aluminum trays. "Lighten your load?"

"Thanks," Steph said as she handed over the tray of wings.

Jessie stumbled into the room toting the red and white wine boxes. Her hair was wet and flat, her blowout having blown away with the wind.

She surveyed the clutch of people huddled together in her office.

"Thank you all for coming. It really means a lot—"

Lightning flashed, followed closely by a tremendous crack of thunder which shook the windows and made Glenda Wickes screech. The power dipped but it held.

"Especially in the middle of a monsoon," Jessie finished.

Dr. Evans raised his cup. "I've yammered on enough for one evening, so I'll keep this brief. In the words of Mary Shelley, 'The beginning is always today.' And so, Jessie Voss, may this new beginning of yours truly prove to be—"

"Brief, dear," Mrs. Evans nudged.

"Yes, of course. To Jessie!"

The room erupted in applause, and it was enough to make Jessie laugh and cry at the same time.

She nodded to Lin. "Let's get these folks checked in, shall we?"

* * *

As it turned out, Glenda opted out of the free night. She explained that she had a skittish Whippet at home that was probably demolishing the house.

"He *hates* thunder," she said as she slipped out the door.

Two comped rooms, two surveys. Well, it was a start.

"I think I drank a box of that damn wine all by my lonesome," Steph said. "Mind if I crash in one of the rooms?"

"Give her 108," Jessie snickered.

"108?"

"That's where we found the cat skeleton."

Steph gave an exaggerated shudder. "You're *so* kind."

Jessie noticed a small vase filled with miniature white roses sitting on the front desk.

"Who's this from?"

"Oh," Lin said. "That Mr. McKay. There's a card."

Jessie retrieved the card and read.

Best of luck from the Midwest Independent Lodging Association!

"I already checked him into his other room," Lin said.

Jessie turned. "His other room?"

Lin glanced back at the computer. "He said he wanted to try a different room each night. Don't we do that? He said it was for his review."

Multiple rooms meant multiple full cleanings, but a review was a review.

"It's fine," Jessie said, more for herself than Lin. "All the rooms are ready to go. It's fine."

Steph surprised her by placing a hand on her shoulder. "You did good here, boss."

Jessie smiled, and the tears came.

Yeah. You bet your ass I did.

CHAPTER 20

Framed local ads from newspapers past adorned the walls of Wood's new room. The one nearest him read, *Best Prices in Town and that's No Fib! Fibber's Liquors.* A black and white photo accompanied the text—a young woman popping the cork from a champagne bottle. Maple City didn't really seem like a champagne sort of town. If anything, it was a Schlitz town, an Old Style town. What the heck was that old brew with the Shakespearean name?

"Falstaff," he said, snapping his fingers. That professor at the party with the verbal diarrhea would love that one. Wood had played dumb when the man asked him about Hemingway. Being on the road more often than not, he listened to a lot of audiobooks, and *The Old Man and the Sea* was one of his favorites. He knew that Papa was an Illinois boy, born outside of Chicago. He also knew the old boozehound blew his head off with a 12-gauge. Funny how things circled back around.

The storm had made a surprise entrance, but that was all well and good with Wood. No reason to hang around and chitchat with strangers when there was a barstool with his name on it.

His palm itched like hell. The girl at the front desk had found him a needle, but it hadn't done him much good. As soon as he was ensconced in his new digs, duffel tucked away under the bed, he'd gone to town on the splinter. He'd heated the needle with his lighter until its point turned black. Then, he dug in with all the gusto of a prospector.

As much as he poked and prodded his flesh, he couldn't seem to extract the last bit of bone from his palm. And each time he made contact with the splinter with the tip of the needle, it seemed to dig itself deeper, eager to burrow its way into his veins.

Keen for distraction, Wood slipped out of his room, into his car and was soon tooling down the town's main strip. Downtown Maple City had seen better days. The majority of the large storefronts were empty, and those that weren't were home to insurance agents and dollar stores.

Wood had his pick of taverns—oh God, did he ever. In the space of five square blocks he'd spotted Sullivan's Tap, Dede's Bar, The Village Pump, Pappy's and El Lobo Gris. Flags touting *SLOTS!* waved outside each and every one. None of the places seemed inviting, although he thought he could get a decent meal at the Mexican joint. He decided to circle the downtown area one more time before venturing to the outskirts where he undoubtedly would find sketchier watering holes.

He rounded the corner next to the Maple City Diner and spotted a sign he hadn't seen during his first pass. *Blind Rock Tavern.* And of course there were the obligatory waving flags announcing that *SLOTS!* could be found within.

He pulled over to the curb and parked behind an old Jeep. Why this place—which looked from the outside like every other joint in this burg—caught his interest was beyond him. He just had a feeling about it. And Woodrow McKay made a habit of following his gut.

The itch in his palm flared, and he jumped out of the car, determined to drown the irritation with a shot of Jack.

The one thing Wood required of a bar was that it was dark as hell, day or night, and the Blind Rock had that in spades. The sound system pumped out contemporary country, while football was the main event on the flat screens. Aside from two old boys playing pool in the back and a woman feeding bills into a slot machine, he was the only customer.

Instead of bellying up to the bar, he opted for the comfort of one of the booths. Sliding in, he couldn't help wondering how many of these dives he'd visited in his lifetime. Probably best not to linger on that thought.

"What can I getcha?" The disembodied voice came from behind the bar.

"Shot of Jack and keep 'em coming."

"Man after my own heart. Gimme a sec, I gotta change this damn music."

The country song cut out, replaced by the musical stylings of Mr. Jimmy Buffett.

A man popped up from behind the bar, his Hawaiian shirt confirming his love of everything Margaritaville. "If I gotta be here during the doldrums, I'm gonna play what I wanna play."

"You serving food?"

"Kitchen's on a temporary hiatus until I can find a new cook. But if you're starving, I can throw a frozen pizza in the toaster oven. I was gonna make one myself. You're welcome to half."

"Sounds good."

"You like pineapple?"

"I do not."

"Pineapple on my half then." The man reached for the Jack Daniels and paused. "Those lushes drank all my Jack last night. Gonna have to run downstairs and grab you a fresh bottle."

Wood nodded, and the burly fellow disappeared through a doorway. Pulling the needle and lighter from his coat pocket, he baptized the needle with fire before digging once more into his palm. He couldn't see what he was doing, but he could feel that he was getting close. Making progress. He gave the needle a sharp twist and felt the splinter shift beneath his skin, making contact with a nerve.

Blood...

and bone...

mixed.

Wood swerved back into his own lane, barely missing the oncoming truck.

"Sorry. My fault," he called back to the semi as it vanished into the night. "I dropped my smokes is all. I...sorry again."

He fumbled with the pack of cigarettes and slipped his finger inside, hoping to pull out one last smoke. Like pulling a rabbit from a hat. Abracadabra alakazam! But no such luck. The pack was empty. He held it over his mouth and shook the last, loose bits of tobacco onto his tongue.

"Just a pinch between your cheek and gum," he snorted as he tried to maneuver the mess with his tongue. When that didn't work, he spit it onto the pile of hamburger wrappers and ATM receipts that littered the passenger seat.

Another 18-wheeler whooshed past, kicking up snow and causing his car to slip on the ice. The sign on the bank in the last town had read -10 degrees; -35 degrees with wind chill, the radio said.

"But I'm as warm as a bug in a rug!" he hooted as he blasted the heater and threw back another swig of Dickel Rye. *"Warm as a goddamn lightning bug! No...a firefly. Warm as a goddamn firefly!"*

"Don't mind if I join you, do you?" the bartender asked as he set twin shot glasses on the table.

Wood flinched and nearly drove the needle through his hand. Where the hell was he?

"Easy, buddy." Then, noticing the needle in Wood's hand, "That's not...drug related, is it?"

"No," Wood said, holding up the needle. "Trying to fish out a splinter."

"Ah! Splinters suck ass." He poured two shots. "What's your handle, partner?"

"Wood."

"Well, that's fuckin' ironic. Good to meet you, Wood. The name's Riggs." The man raised his shot glass high. "As you slide down the banister of life, may the splinters never point in the wrong direction."

Wood took hold of the shot glass and downed the whiskey. It burned but not enough to tame the pain in his palm.

"Men's room?" Wood asked, sweat rising on his brow.

"Shitter's thataway." Riggs gestured toward the back of the room, near to where the old men were cheating at pool.

Wood rose and quickstepped it past the row of beckoning slot machines and slipped into the bathroom. The scent of urinal cakes was heavy in the air. He gripped the edge of the sink and stared into the decal-encrusted mirror.

The man who stared back at him looked frightened as hell.

I was on the road.

He spat into the sink, half expecting to see flecks of tobacco, so strong was the taste in his mouth.

What the ever-loving fuck?

As he stared, he felt his innards shift as if great, writhing worms moved within his belly. He pulled his newly-filled vape from his pocket, put it to his lips and inhaled deeply, begging the mist to calm his stomach and his head.

As the vapor settled in his lungs, his eyes widened and his pupils shrank to points. Good.

It's going to be okay, you hear me? It's going to be okay.

The man in the mirror didn't believe him one bit.

Wood took another hit off the vape. And another. And another.

CHAPTER 21

A peal of thunder woke Sister, and although she sensed it was not yet the dead of night, she rose nonetheless. Cracking and snapping into being, she slit the canvas fabric with a newly-formed claw, dragging herself from the bag. Crawling from under the bed.

"Shall we rise as well?" her brothers asked, puzzled by her early awakening.

"No. Sleep."

"You won't leave us?"

"Never."

And so they slept on, comforted by her false promise.

The lights were low, and grand flashes of lightning snuck through the gap in the curtains and the peephole in the door.

Sister paused in the middle of the room, finding her balance, waiting until there was more of her. *Becoming* was painful, almost as painful as the hunger. Almost.

The man was not here. The man. Her pet. The dog who brought her meals and settled for scraps. Her Wood.

She caught her reflection in the mirror above the desk and paused. Her brothers wouldn't dare look, but she did. Staring back was a maddening horror—a charred mosaic of blackened skin and broken teeth. Her shattered face, framed in rotting hair, fought to hold its structure. And peeking through the

130

cracks in her shell-like skin, raw flesh. Red and angry in its encasement.

She smiled at herself and an incisor fell free. She didn't care. Anything was better than nothingness. Even this nightmare she'd become.

She looked back to the bed beneath which lay the bones of her brothers. Not brothers by blood but by choice. Without her, where would they be? *Lost.* It served her to continue the charade. But should their triumvirate no longer prove beneficial, well...she'd been alone before.

She sniffed the air. There were three spirits here, all of them ripe, each with their own sweet scent. A man, a woman and a child. A little one. *Niñita.*

She couldn't see them yet. They needed to be drawn forth. And for that to happen, she needed to...

Thrum.

Her neck quivered and a deep rumble rose from her throat. The vibration split the skin across her neck, drawing blood, and yet she continued...

Thrum.

The first of the figures appeared. It was the man. The Papa. Growing luscious and beefy. Perhaps she would eat him herself—make a private meal of the man. Devouring a ghost wasn't like feeding on flesh. Oh, no. It was so much more. You tasted *everything.* Dreams, love, fear, hate—every minute of their lives. And yes, their deaths—their deaths were the most delicious morsels of all. They filled her up, gave her the strength to *become.*

Yes, she'd feed on him alone.

Thrum!

Fattening him up. Bringing him into focus.

The ghost was aware of her now and turned. In his face she saw delicious terror.

Sister raised her clawed hand—claws growing longer by the second—ready to rip him to shreds…

A soft cry came from behind her and she paused. Whirling about, her spine splintering, she came face to face with a wisp of a child hovering in the corner.

The little one.

Looming large above the ether-like child, a memory sparked deep within Sister's ruined skull.

There was another girl once. Older than this and wearing a homespun dress.

Something was perched on her shoulder.

A bird…

Before Sister could capture the memory in whole, the little girl slipped through the wall and into the rain.

* * *

Michael stood at the window and stared at the glowing neon sign across the parking lot. Even though their room was protected by an overhang, the wind had kicked up and errant drops of rain beaded and trickled down the glass. Michael pressed his eye to the window and looked through a cluster of raindrops. The neon sign bulged, the two faces twisting and distorting.

Dad had returned about an hour ago and crawled into bed. There was whispered talk between his parents from which he could only glean snippets: a house, a visit, a new beginning.

Whenever his parents colluded like this, it usually meant he wouldn't like the outcome. Like the hushed conversation they'd had when he came home fired up after visiting the adoption dogs at Union Square. He had pled his case vehemently, but after conferring, his folks had tried to sell him on a goldfish instead.

He'd said no to the fish, more out of disappointment than anything else. And so, the Larson family had gone petless.

Until now.

Not that the cow was a pet. Not that the cow was even *real*. But one of the hushed secrets she had told him was that she was *his* cow. Not Jessie's. *His*.

She also told him to keep his eyes open.

Michael breathed on the glass, fogging it. He wrote *MOO* in the moisture and watched it evaporate.

His stomach dropped.

Oh, no…

A piercing cry broke his concentration and he tripped himself up stepping back from the window. The cry came again, distant and close at the same time. Was the person outside? Were they in his head?

Thunder rolled and Michael looked back to his parents. They were entwined on the bed, oblivious to the storm. How was that possible? Dad didn't like storms. One crack of lightning and he was up and pacing. He lied and said that he found storms exciting, but in reality they jangled his nerves. Michael could tell.

But now? Both of his parents were dead to the world.

A razor-sharp shriek nearly split his head in two, and this time he could tell who was calling out but *not* what they were saying.

It was a girl. And she was crying.

¡Ayúdame!

That's it. Time to wake his folks.

No, said the cow who was Elmer but not Elmer. *Go. Now.*

With competing voices in his head, Michael ran to the door, released the deadbolt and dashed into the windswept night.

* * *

With the last of her guests off to their rooms and Steph and Lin gone as well, Jessie could finally reflect upon the evening, despite the rumblings of storm. She felt good, like she'd snapped a piece of the puzzle that was her life into place. Plenty of pieces to go, but tonight...

Why did you buy this motel?

The kid's words came back to her, throwing a monkey wrench into her reverie. It was an important question, but he'd put her on the spot. Still, it was a loose thread she wanted to pick up.

"Because I saw its potential," she told the coffee maker with confidence.

Nope.

"Because it called out to me."

Warmer.

Annoyed at herself, Jessie stepped behind the front desk and skirted into the back room. Off came the dress and on came her t-shirt—this time a pink Aledo Rhubarb Festival tee.

"Because…"

Colder.

"Because…"

Colder.

Resigned to the fact that she wasn't going to crack it tonight, she crawled into bed and pulled up the covers.

A deep *thrum* roused her from her sleep. And when she heard a distant scream, she shot out of bed.

Thunder boomed. The lights in the office flicked out. Jessie scurried to the front desk. The neon sign was out, as were the golden arches across the street.

She reached for her phone and tapped on the flashlight icon. A harsh LED light pierced the darkness.

Something swatted the phone from her hand and it went flying. It hit the far wall and landed on its flashlight side with a thud. Darkness returned.

Jessie stepped back and as she did so, her right heel landed on something cold and familiar. It was a bare foot—she could feel the toes quite clearly.

A pair of arms slipped around her middle, and a hollow voice whispered into her ear, the words riding on fetid breath.

Warm me.

CHAPTER 22

The pizza burned the top of Wood's mouth, but he barely felt it. Not even the fifth or sixth shot of whiskey could awaken the exposed nerves. He ran his tongue over the roughened skin.

Like eating Cap'n Crunch with Crunchberries.

The childhood memory made him giggle and he took another toke off the vape. He was running low on liquid, but there would be more. Much more. In fact, Woodrow McKay was set for a good long time.

"You mind taking that outside, buddy?" Riggs asked, approaching the booth. "It's getting a little whiffy in here."

"You got a ban on vaping?"

"Naw, but...c'mon." The bartender wrinkled his nose.

Wood grinned and took another hit, exaggerating his enjoyment. "Then, what are we talking about?" His lungs were burning but—*ah!*—the mist filled a need that he couldn't quite put his finger on.

Finger. Ha!

Riggs frowned. "Geez, I give you half my pizza and this is the thanks I get?"

One of the older fellows at the pool table cupped his hands and shouted, "Did you tell him to cut it out?"

"I did, T-bone, but..."

"But what?"

"Gimme a sec."

"It's giving me a headache!"

Riggs leaned into Wood. "Man, you're pissing off my regulars."

Wood clumsily rose and leaned in toward the bartender. "And you're pissing *me* off." The words were out before he knew what he was saying. Too much. He'd taken in too much of the liquid. And now it was in the driver's seat and steering him toward the edge.

"Don't you get up in my grill," Riggs warned as Wood moved even closer.

Wood's lungs seized and his lips curled back. Yup, he was definitely just along for the ride.

"I'll do whatever the fuck I want."

He took a swing at the bartender, who, though sporting a beer belly, knew his way around a belligerent patron. Riggs dodged the blow before delivering one of his own, sending Wood tumbling to the floor.

Wood's forehead slammed against the steering wheel as the car plowed into the ditch, the airbag remaining stubbornly encased. A bright pulse of white light accompanied the pain that shot across his brow.

I'm dead.

But no such luck. The engine clattered for a moment, trying to remember its job and then gave up.

Wood felt a warmth and realized that he'd pissed himself in the crash. Another highlight of a banner day for McKay. Easing himself off the wheel, he felt a pop in his neck and felt a tingling rush spread down his shoulders and spine.

That can't be good.

He fumbled for the seat belt release and tumbled out of the car and onto the edge of the shoulder. There were no flashing blinkers, no steam rising from underneath the hood like in the movies. Instead, there was the dark silence and the bone-chilling cold.

He rose on shaky legs. Aside from his throbbing head, he seemed to be intact.

Intact? Yeah, right.

As he saw it, he had two options. Stand here next to a wrecked, uninsured vehicle and flag down the next trucker, or...

He stepped around the car and took off across the field. Without gloves, his hands began to numb. The tilled, frozen earth made for uneven travel, and he stumbled as often as not. Undeterred, he continued on.

Freezing to death had a nice ring to it. Better than wasting away in prison. For that's what was awaiting him, wasn't it? Eight withdrawals he'd made on company checks—each one for a greater amount. His brother would never forgive him for that. The clerk's position he'd offered Wood came only at the behest of their sister. And he'd screwed it up. Willingly and with gusto.

Where had the money gone? Better yet, where hadn't *it gone. Fifty-seven thousand dollars didn't go far when you were intent on spending it. Liquor—yes. Women—sure. The horses— of course, of course. With each action, he divorced himself from the old Woodrow McKay until he didn't recognize the person in his mirror.*

And so, with the final thousand retrieved from ATMs, he'd lit out in search of one last hurrah. The night was a montage of greatest hits—all sins indulged. The final chaser was to be a dive into the Mississippi River, but as he slowed on the bridge between Iowa and Illinois, he'd balked.

Instead, he drove on, perhaps hoping to outdistance death and debt and his brother and, well, the whole damn mess of his life. Curbing the occasional urge to steer toward the headlights of an oncoming semi.

But then his escape had come to a screeching halt. And now he was walking across a frozen landscape, stripping off his coat and kicking off his shoes. Marching toward his death.

He had gone far enough that there were only two elements to the world: the black earth and the purple sky.

But no...there was something else. Jutting below the horizon. A faint halogen light illuminating a tangled tree. Or was it a sculpture?

Wood gulped cold air as ice formed on his lips.

Was it a cross?

He began to shiver, as much from the realization as from the subzero temperature, and in a rush of blind emotion, he ran toward the light.

His foot caught on an embedded stone and he went down hard, his forehead receiving its second blow. He struggled to his knees and realized that his muscles were growing stiff, and he imagined rows of chickens in the frozen food aisle.

Which came first? The chicken or the...

He sat back down, his legs splayed—one sock off, one on.

Damn stone. If it hadn't tripped him up, he would have...what? Get real. If it hadn't tripped him up, he would have frozen a bit farther off, that's all.

He stared at the offending stone. It was blackish-red, the color of blood in moonlight. He realized it had a grey companion on either side. And those companions had companions of their own. Turning his stiffening neck, he saw that he had stumbled into the center of a circle.

What the hell was this?

A tickle of warmth raised the hairs on his arms and neck. Is that what freezing to death felt like? The opposite *of freezing to death?*

"Take," a voice said.

"Who's there?"

"Take."

This must be it. The moment when his brain froze solid. He was hearing things.

"What do I take?" Each word was an effort.

The warmth traveled down to his fingertips and melted the soil beneath.

"Dig."

He dug. And when he unearthed the collection of dark bones, he blindly followed the voice's command.

"Eat."

Wood McKay sat in the middle of the field, growing warmer as he gnawed on the cold, charred bone.

"Shit, man, you made me do it!"

Wood opened his eyes and found he was staring at the bartender's feet. His nose was painful and wet.

"Let's get you up." Riggs hauled Wood to his feet and set him back in the booth. "Sheesh, that's a busted nose if I ever saw one."

Wood put his hand to his face and it came away bloody. He deserved it. That and more.

"I can snap it back in place if you want. Or you can tell me to go to hell. Take your pick."

"Do it," Wood mumbled.

Riggs slid Wood's final shot of Jack toward him. "Down it when I'm done." He set both thumbs on either side of the crooked nose. "One...two..."

Crunch.

Wood's eyes went wide and he howled. Not because of the pain in his nose, which was something fierce, but because of the pain in his palm. The snapping back in place had reignited the throbbing sting of the buried splinter.

He grabbed his latest shot of whiskey and dowsed the wound. He'd expected the red hole to roar, but there was no change in the agony. It spread up his arm, across his chest and to his heart—a gripping, screaming pain the likes of which he'd never known.

Not true.

Wood's heart sank as the realization kicked in.

A thunderclap echoed from outside and the power dipped. The woman sitting at a slot machine cursed as her game rebooted.

"What time is it?"

"Going on ten-thirty."

Ten-thirty? So early and yet there was no doubt. He'd felt this driving, stabbing sensation before. Only once.

When I tried to leave her.

Wood jumped up, startling Riggs. "Whoa, buddy. You want me to call you a cab? Lemme call you a cab."

With the bartender calling after him, Wood raced for the door, knocking over chairs as he went.

Ten-thirty. She was coming.
And he wasn't there.

CHAPTER 23

"Wake up!"

Peter hovered above the bed where Hannah and the other Peter slept. *Slept!* While their son was moving ever closer to danger, things were waking in this place. Bad things. How could they sleep?

He felt a rush of wind as the boy slipped out the door.

Peter strained against the grip that Whisper had over him. The demon dug deep, ripping at his mind with tooth and nail, bleeding him of memories. High school friends, books he'd read, tender moments with Hannah gushed from the wound and dissipated into the massive black shroud in which he was imprisoned.

So be it. Let them go. Nothing mattered but Michael.

"You want more? Here!" He tore at his own injury, flinging snippets of his life left and right. This sudden turnabout startled the demon and it cried out.

Back. Bad!

"I've got to follow him."

No.

"I've got to warn him."

No!

Peter turned on Whisper. "If you try to stop me, I'll split myself in two and drown you in life, every single second of it.

And then you'll be alone—half of what you were. Wounded and *alone*."

The thing shuddered at this. Threatening and posturing, it flapped about, hating him and hating this prison. But it did not strike.

"Let's go."

* * *

The moment Michael stepped outside, the world went dark. First the streetlights, then the motel itself. The last thing to dim was the neon Intermission Motor Lodge sign.

Emergency lights came on, doing their best to replace all the illumination that had vanished and doing a poor job.

Another scream pierced the night, seeming to ignite the sky with streaks of fire. There was no question about it—it was a little girl and she was one floor below.

Michael headed for the staircase, his bare feet pat-pat-patting on the cement. As he bounded down the stairs, leaving the protection of the overhang, sharp rain stung his face and drenched his pajamas.

He reached the bottom row of rooms and paused. What would he do if he found her? The girl? She was crying out for help but from what? How was he equipped to do anything? Even the short dash down the steps had him winded. He should go back upstairs and get Dad. This was stupid. This was...

No-oo.

The damn cow—her crazy, lowing voice in his head.

"Shut up!"

Cold and wet and feeling suddenly stupid, Michael was about to turn around when a girl stepped through the wall not ten feet ahead of him.

The child was younger than Michael and was as insubstantial as the rain. Just a sketch of a girl—details but no substance. He could make out only a few features: dark hair, dark skin, wide eyes. And when she turned and screamed in his direction, he spied the gap where one of her baby teeth had been.

The sketched girl ran straight toward him. *Past* him.

The door to the room from which she had fled swung inwards, and a terrible hand wrapped its blackened claws about the doorframe.

Michael turned and raced after the girl.

* * *

Jessie ducked, letting the twin arms of her assailant close above her. She tried to make a graceful move from ducking into standing and succeeded only in tripping herself up. She landed on her ass, striking the back of her head on the wall with a loud *thock*. The blow momentarily rattled her, allowing the man to step forward.

Warm me!

If there were ever any doubts about where the stench in the office had come from, those doubts were suddenly exploded. The man who lurched toward her reeked. The sour look on his face made it appear that he was all too aware of this fact. His stomach was open and leaking, and the wound reached all the way to his back and out. She could see the doorway through the hole.

No. It wasn't that deep. She could see through him. Not just his stomach. Through *all* of him.

Jessie scurried backward into the corner and raised a foot.

"Get back or I'll kick your balls across this room!"

Her words only seemed to make the man more anguished. He stepped forward again and Jessie kicked. Her heel hit home and slowed as it passed through the man's groin.

Unfazed, the man dropped to his knees, arms outstretched like a baby reaching for his mama.

Warm.

As the man tumbled onto her, Jessie scrambled to her feet. Scrambled *through* him. It was like fighting through pelting rain. The lights sparked and died in counterpoint with another monster thunderclap.

Now behind the intruder, Jessie made for the door. As she opened it, the ghostly man let out a wail. It was heartbreaking and horrible, and all she wanted to do was to drown it out with the sound of the storm.

Please!

* * *

Although smaller than Michael, the girl quickly outpaced him. She stuck to the light cast by the emergency lamps. Each pool of light she passed through had the effect of diffusing her form, solidifying the fact that he was, indeed, pursuing a ghost.

Whatever possessed the clawed hand gave chase as well. He could hear it skittering behind him, cracking like a tree branch with every step it took.

The girl disappeared momentarily, and Michael was afraid that she had given up what little there was of her in the world. But as he passed the last room in the row and came to the corner of the building, he caught a glimpse of the girl slipping in through a side door. *Through* the door.

Michael's heart was racing, and he had to force himself to bridge the distance between himself and the door as the sound of gnashing teeth and scuttling claws drove him on.

As he passed through a stretch unilluminated by the halogen lamps, he recognized the door that was fast approaching. The laundry room. He also recognized a frightening possibility: that the laundry room might be locked.

Emerging from the darkness into the harsh light, he slammed into the door and gave the doorknob a twist.

Locked.

He tried again, straining with wet hands, willing the door to open, but it was no use.

He heard footfalls behind him and a dry, guttural cough. The thing was close enough for him to smell—it gave off a sickly-sweet aroma, like a pumpkin gone bad.

I'm not looking back. I'm not looking back.

Two more steps and the thing was directly behind him. Inches. It cracked as it breathed. In. *Crack.* Out. *Crack.*

As he stood there, frozen in place, his hands welded to the doorknob, a nightmarish hand reached around him and gently pried his fingers away. Trembling, he complied. Then, with as much effort as it would take him to break an egg, the dark hand turned the knob, ripped it free and pushed the door open.

The creak of the door snapped Michael back into action. He elbowed his way through the doorway, positioned himself on the other side of the door and shoved it closed.

Or at least *mostly* closed.

The hand that had made quick work of the locked door hung limply between door and frame. It twitched once and then lost its connection to the creature at large, dropping to the floor like a hand of spoiled bananas.

The door closed. The lock clicked.

Michael stood panting, the scent of bleach stinging his nostrils, determined to hold the door closed with sheer will, if necessary.

He flicked on the light switch but no luck.

Across the room in the glow of a lone emergency light stood the girl. Through her he saw the stack of industrial dryers, their mouths as slack as his own.

The hand twitched and twitched again. Like the spider he'd rescued.

And then, it began to grow.

* * *

Jessie opened the door, and the rain hit her with such force that for a second she thought the man had somehow gotten ahead of her and she was once more plowing her way through him.

Her first thought was for her phone. She'd left it in the office. No way she was going back in there.

Steph. She was staying in Room 108.

Jessie lit off in the direction of Steph's room when the power popped on again, disorienting her. She whirled about, rain flying from her hair, taking stock of the newly enlightened landscape and promptly twisted her hip. The resulting pain was fierce and threatened to bring her to her knees.

She glanced back at the office. No movement. No sign of the man.

As she turned back, she caught sight of the neon sign. Whereas a regular flow of power had returned to the rest of the block, the Intermission Motor Lodge sign had suddenly turned vampire, sucking up electricity at a monstrous rate. It blazed madly against the night sky.

Pop! A tube burst. *Pop-pop-pop!* A second, third and fourth. Sparks rained down, and she could hear the hiss of electricity and rain intermingling. When the sign finally calmed and resumed its regular order of business, it was shy a couple of characters.

INT RMI ION OTOR LODGE

The comedy mask indicating a vacancy blinked *ES* instead of *YES*.

Her designer's brain kicked in. She did her trick, making a quick tally of the missing letters before swapping them about in her head.

M-E-S-S-Y.

A swirl of movement in the distance caught her eye, but she couldn't bring it into focus through the pounding rain. Whatever it was was outside the laundry room.

* * *

The spirit girl darted into one of the dryers.

Michael stepped back from the creature as it sputtered and cracked, growing an arm, twisting out ribs. Eyes grew in the hollow sockets of the shifting skull; one trained itself on him, and he felt cold pierce his heart.

As soon as it had grown two hands, it lurched forward, dragging itself with new arms. It moved past him, making its way toward the girl in the dryer.

"Leave her alone!" he cried. It didn't matter the girl was mostly air. She was terrified.

The creature kept moving. He had to do something. Michael looked about, his eyes lighting upon a laundry cart loaded down with miniature shampoos and other toiletries. He grabbed it, aimed it directly at the thing and charged.

The cart's squeaky wheels alerted the thing of Michael's approach. It whirled about, catching the brunt force of the cart square in the mouth. Its face shattered like obsidian glass, revealing raw meat beneath.

"Come on!" Michael shouted as he dashed for the door. "Come on!"

He didn't look back to see if it was following him—looking at it *hurt*. Plus, he could hear the thing shoving the cart aside. Moving his way.

Michael yanked open the door, ready to race to Dad—*yes! Dad*—and came face to face with a wall of smoke. The entire doorframe was filled with it, swirling hypnotically. It was as though one of the storm clouds had come down from the sky and was now blocking his path.

The smoke billowed into the room. It engulfed him before flowing past. But in that moment when it blotted out the world, he had heard someone whisper.

Stand back, buddy.

Dad's voice.

He stood back as he'd been told, and the smoke condensed, forming itself into the crude figure of a man. It stood between Michael and the snarling, black demon.

* * *

Sister stopped in her tracks, watching in wonder as the smoky man approached. She twisted her head, trying to get both eyes to focus on the figure.

How could it be? He was changed but...it was still he.

"Whisper..."

A thrill went up her still-knitting spine.

"Family!"

At that, the dark figure lost all coherence. It collapsed into a swirling mass.

She stepped forward, arms outstretched, and the whirling cloud retreated, howling in fear and spitting off wisps of itself. Frantic to escape, it rushed the boy, jetting through the air and down his throat.

* * *

Michael recoiled as the gush of blackness poured into his mouth. It was like breathing thick smoke and swallowing broken glass at the same time. He trembled and choked, his

151

lungs fighting to be rid of the invasion. And when his spasms subsided and he reopened his eyes, he found the creature inches from his face.

Its eyes bore into his, shifting from red to black to white. Its mouth twitched, splitting its lips, multiple tongues darting in and out.

The nightmare reached out with one careful finger, sliding the nail between his teeth. Pressing gently, it lowered his jaw, opening his mouth and peered inside.

Michael's stomach clenched as the nail in his mouth turned claw, grew and snaked toward his gullet.

The power kicked in and rows of fluorescent lights flooded the room. The thing rose up in the sudden light, one face splitting into two, two arms into twenty, fanning itself out, brushing the very ceiling in joy and anger. Reaching its full height, it dashed itself to the floor where it shattered. Pieces scattered everywhere. Its jaw hit Michael's foot. It turned pale grey before collapsing into dust. Soon, there was nothing left but dust and bits of ashen bone.

Michael stood in the aftermath of the creature's self-destruction, swaying and fearing he'd topple over. He shot a look at the girl in the dryer. Her eyes met his and then...she faded away like breath on glass.

All was silent in the laundry room save for the sound of rain coming through the door.

And his father's voice.

I've missed you.

* * *

Jessie found the laundry room door open. Inside was the boy, standing wet and barefooted on a floor strewn with ash.

"Michael? My god, are you okay?"

The boy smiled. His PJs were soaked through and hung loosely on his thin frame. And still he smiled.

"I'm fine."

"What are you doing in here?"

Michael looked around the room. "I don't know."

"Let's get you back to your room."

"Okay."

Jessie grabbed two towels, one to place around the child's shoulders, the other to cover his head and she led the boy back out into the rain. When they reached the Larsons' room, she knocked, and the boy's mother answered.

"Oh my gosh, you're soaking wet. What were you thinking?" Hannah said.

"I must have been sleepwalking. Sorry, Mom."

The pass off complete, Jessie beat a path to Steph's room. Her friend greeted her at the door in her underwear, her hair smashed to one side.

Jessie slipped past her and into the room.

"What the hell, Jess?"

Jessie steeled herself before saying, "I'm shutting this place down."

CHAPTER 24

Wood pulled into the parking lot, the car hitting the curb with one tire and scraping bottom.

The door to his room was open.

Fighting through the whiskey and the rain, he stumbled to his room.

The duffel was sticking half out from under the bed. A trail of ash led to the door.

Gone.

Frantic, he stepped back out of the room. She could be anywhere. *They* could be anywhere.

A sharp pang ignited in his palm and he almost cried out. He bit at the flesh, trying to gnaw the pain into submission. He held out his hand and it curled in on itself, cramping horribly.

All save for the index finger—it was pointing. Still reeling from the Jack and the vape, Wood followed his finger.

In his drunken state, he stumbled sideways and thumped against a motel room door. A man with a dour look poked his head out of the room. It was the professor—Dr. Verbal Diarrhea.

"Some of us are trying to sleep!"

Wood plowed on, and when his finger twitched right, he went right until he found himself standing in front of a second open door. The laundry room.

Stepping inside, he found what he was after.

He could hear her voice whispering low but couldn't make out her words. Grabbing a dustbin, he gathered up her bits and pieces, filling a laundry bag and cinching it tight.

Wood made his way back to his room and set the deadbolt. He placed the bag on the bed and instantly, her voice rang out cutting and clear.

"You left us."

"I know."

"You left *me*."

"I'm sorry!"

The laundry bag shifted, as if threatening to open.

"New bargain."

"What?"

"Come close."

Wood obeyed.

"Open."

He fumbled at the drawstring and opened the bag. Inside, the bone and ash undulated as if breathing.

"Come closer."

Wood dipped his head into the bag.

"Do as I say and you are free."

"Free?"

"Free."

The pain in Wood's palm vanished and he felt something he hadn't felt in a good while.

Hope.

He dared to grin. "Anything."

CHAPTER 25

Michael lay tucked in between his parents. His mother was kicking herself for taking a Xanax before bed and for feeding his father one as well.

"I would have heard him get up. But you needed to sleep. We *both* needed to sleep."

"Breathe, honey. He's okay. Aren't you, sport?"

Michael smiled and nodded.

But he wasn't okay. Not by a long shot.

Can you hear me? His father/not father's voice.

Michael nodded again.

"What was that thing in the laundry?" Michael mouthed, whispering without making a sound.

I don't want you to worry about that...

In the space of two breaths, the memory of the dark creature that he had stared in the face slipped from his mind and twirled down a drain behind his eyes.

Is it gone?

"Is what gone?"

That's better. Don't worry. Everything's going to be okay.

An angry howl rose from deep inside his mind, blotting out the calming voice.

Michael curled in on himself and begged for sleep to come soon.

CHAPTER 26

A fter hearing Jessie out, Steph grabbed her clothes.

"What are you doing?" Jessie asked.

"Well, I'm not going to go check out your office half-naked, now am I?"

The rain had slowed to a drizzle, the storm having moved off east to bother Peoria. Jessie led the way, with Steph on her heels.

"You are *not* shutting down. We're getting to the bottom of this, okay?"

"Okay. Careful, he's in the office."

The man wasn't in the office, but once again he had left his stench.

"Jesus..." Steph gagged.

A thorough search turned up nothing but the disarray caused by Jessie's struggle. Steph picked up the prescription bag and raised an eyebrow.

"Oh, please." Jessie shook her head. "I'm not popping pills. Besides, that stuff doesn't give you hallucinations."

"I don't know. Once in the hospital you told me there was a dog under your bed."

"I know."

"And that the balloons I brought started looking like heads."

"I was on morphine, Steph. Mor-phine."

Steph yawned.

"Sorry if I'm keeping you up."

"Come on. You're staying in my room."

"What if one of the guests needs something?"

Her friend grabbed a Post-it, scrawled a message and slapped it up on the door. *In Room 108.*

"Satisfied?"

Back in Steph's room, Jessie found that her friend had pilfered one of the wine boxes.

"So sue me."

Steph poured them both plastic glasses of red and sat on the bed opposite Jessie.

"Okay," Steph said, taking a deep gulp of wine. "I believe you."

"Fantastic."

"Don't give me that tone. I'm trying to help."

"Fine," Jessie said, taking a sip.

The other woman leaned in. "I've seen a ghost too."

"Really."

"Cross my heart. My mom."

"Okay. But—"

"Shut up and listen, will you? It was a week after she passed. There was always bad blood between us, so I was surprised when she popped in on me out of the blue. It was in our kitchen. I was baking bread—not her recipe, her *sister's* recipe—when she just...well, when she was just *there*, okay?"

"You saw her?"

"No, but I knew that she was snooping around. I could feel it. There was bad blood with her sister, too, so I figured she was pissed that I was baking *her* recipe—"

158

"Wait. So you didn't actually see anything?"

"No, but I—"

"Nothing grabbed you?"

"It grabbed you?"

Jessie set her wine on the floor. "Steph. I *saw* something. It...hell, do you want to smell my shirt?"

"Okay, okay."

The two sat for a moment without saying a word, Jessie debating knocking on her guests' doors and telling them that the night was off.

Steph broke the silence. "I need to come clean about something, boss."

Jessie frowned. "Yeah?"

"Yeah. Can I steal you tomorrow?"

"For...?"

"Can I steal you?"

"Fine...yes."

Steph downed the last of her wine and shuddered. "You able to get any sleep?"

"Probably not."

"Mind if I...?"

"Go ahead."

One final crack of distant thunder put a period on the storm. The phone between the beds warbled in reply and was then silent.

Jessie flipped on the TV and tuned into an old Katharine Hepburn and Cary Grant flick while Steph climbed into bed and promptly started snoring.

"I want to know how I stand, where I fit into the picture, what it's all going to mean to me," Cary Grant exclaimed.

That makes two of us, Cary.

* * *

Morning brought fog and the reviews from Jessie's soft opening guests.

"Once I was able to get to sleep, everything was fine, just fine," Dr. Evans said. "There were children making noise until all hours. And that fellow from the party—I believe he was stumbling drunk. And that storm…well, you can't be faulted for that, now can you?"

Jessie nodded them all to death, hurried them on their collective ways and tossed their comment cards in the trash.

Lin arrived with a fresh batch of turnovers. Jessie couldn't eat if her life were on the line.

"After Esther does her rounds, make sure she sees to the laundry room. We had an…accident."

"What do you mean?"

"I'll show you."

But when Jessie led Lin to the laundry room, she found nothing but a few piles of dust. No big mess—just dust.

Steph was waiting for her in her Impala.

"Where are we going?" Jessie asked.

"To see if we can't get some answers."

"That's not very specific."

Steph looked pale. "I know. I'm giving myself wiggle room in case I want to back out."

"What are you talking about? Where the hell are you taking me?"

THE HUNGRY ONES

Her friend didn't answer. Instead, she threw the car into gear and pulled out onto Main Street heading south.

CHAPTER 27

Michael dreamed of flying.

He was high above Maple City, catching the breeze, dipping and gliding, diving with such speed he thought his heart would explode.

I've missed you.

He woke up drenched in sweat.

The shower was on in the bathroom. He could hear his father's trademark singing. Dad couldn't hold a tune, not even in the shower, and the result was a bellowing glissando that sounded like the whales he'd seen on the Nature Channel. Any other day, the sound would be comforting; today it creeped him out.

Mom came in from outside with two plastic bags in tow. "Hey, sleepy head. I bought yogurt and bananas and you are going to eat them."

Dad popped out of the bathroom wrapped in a towel, steam pouring out from behind him. "Is that my bride?"

Hannah set down her bags and gave Peter a quick kiss. His hand went around her waist, insisting she give him another.

"Someone's feeling better this morning," Hannah laughed. She turned to Michael. "What about you, hon?"

"You gave us a scare, Michael. You want to tell us what happened?" Really, if Dad wanted to be taken seriously, he needed to put clothes on.

"I told you."

"Tell us again."

Michael scooched up in bed, kicking the covers aside. "I was sleepwalking."

His mom sat on the end of the bed. "You haven't done that since you had that spate of high fevers. Come here."

Reluctantly, Michael crawled to his mother and offered up his forehead. "I'm fine, see?"

"Cool as a cucumber," Hannah said. She raised a finger. "Symptom countdown."

"C'mon!"

"Michael."

It was a 'game' they'd played when he was sick, a way for him to share what was ailing him—joint pain, itchiness, bad stomach—while not dwelling on it. In the past, he would shout out his symptoms like Captain America, announcing to the world that he had *A SORE THROAT!* and *BLURRY VISION!* and *GAS!*

No more.

"I said I was fine. Stop badgering me, Hannah." His words caught the entire Larson family off guard, including himself.

"Hey, now," Dad said. "We don't talk like that in this family. You tell your *mother* that you're sorry."

"Sorry!" Michael blurted out. *What the heck?*

Dad retreated into the bathroom. Mom looked at him quizzically but didn't pursue his outburst. Instead, she handed him a blueberry yogurt and a plastic spoon.

We need to talk.

No, we don't.

I need to explain.

163

Go away.

His head was becoming Grand Central Station. First the cow—*a cow!*—and now these new people—one who sounded just like Dad and another. The other hadn't spoken, at least not yet. But it made its presence known. Even now, it was screaming.

"Mom?"

"Yes, honey?"

"Can I have an aspirin?"

"Do you have a headache?"

"Yes," he said, lying. He was hoping the pill would quiet the cacophony, still the horde.

"How about an ibuprofen? The doctor says you'll tolerate that better."

Mom. He knew his sickness had changed her. Weighed upon her. She was always the free spirit, dragging his father and him to neighborhood fairs, flea markets and anything that had a Groupon discount. She drank a bit too much wine at Christmas and forced her two city boys to go camping in Maine. But ever since his cancer? She was diminished. And it made him sad.

"Maybe we can go to the Fall Festival?" he asked, trying to throw an enticing lilt into his voice. Dad had mentioned the festival a couple of times to no avail. Michael gave it another shot. "Play Skee-ball?"

His mother picked up on his tempting offer. "Ride the Ferris wheel?"

"Eat fried food?"

"Finish your yogurt."

The two smiled at each other, for a moment seeing an earlier Michael and an earlier Hannah sitting before them.

"I'll talk to your father. In the meantime, you need to get dressed, mister. We've got an appointment to go see a house."

Michael shuddered. Or had the one inside him shuddered? "What house?"

Hannah took her son's emptied yogurt container and spoon. "The house that Big Bear bought."

As soon as his mother's back was turned, Michael felt an incredible urge to remain rooted to the bed. When his father came out of the bathroom and called for him to bathe next, he reluctantly complied.

The water from the shower brought back the previous night's rain as well as his encounter in the laundry room.

Don't worry.

The voice rose up inside, speaking to him from a place within where the darkness from the laundry room had gone into hiding. Michael had often wondered what his cancer might sound like if it could speak. He imagined it might sound quite similar to the hollow voice that spoke to him now.

I'm here.

Michael scrubbed his face hard with the harsh motel soap, wishing his new companion down the drain.

CHAPTER 28

The hangover awaiting Wood when he awoke was big and boisterous, and he promptly threw up for the first time since college.

Steadying himself at the sink, he felt a sense of renewal despite the rope of drool hanging from the side of his mouth. He wiped it away and treated himself to a handful of cold tap water.

Freedom.

It was a ways off and would take some hefty effort on his part, but...she had said it was there for the taking.

Wood moved quickly about the room, gathering up his things. Imagine—getting a reset. Having the chance to erase the past five years. Moving on. Putting this all behind.

He had waited up in case a late night feeding was on the docket, but apparently those who dwelt in the ashes had taken the night off. Did it mean that he should swap rooms or no? The room was still ripe with spirits. He had felt them as he sat at the desk, willing himself awake. It was one of the vape's small gifts—the ability to sense the presence of cold, dead things.

He opted to request the room directly next to the Larsons'. Earlier examination had informed him that a number of the rooms had twin sets of communicating doors to accommodate guests intent on spreading out. The Larsons' was one such room.

166

"You're really taking a tour of the whole motel, aren't you?" the young woman at the front desk said.

He smiled and poured himself a coffee. The scent of air freshener was heavy in the air, curdling his stomach, and so he opted out of a complimentary turnover.

Upon entering his new room, he set the duffel on the bed and pressed his ear to the wall. The muffled sounds of conversation confirmed that the Larsons had yet to venture out.

No worries. He could wait. Over the years, he had become nothing if not patient.

He decided to get a jump on the first of his tasks and unzipped the duffel. Rooting through the ash, he selected a small bone and zipped the bag closed. Even looking at the bones made his stomach lurch.

Wood extracted his coffee grinder from his luggage, plugged it in and set it atop the desk. Same view but a mirror image of the morning before.

The first time he fed on the bone he was desperate. Half-frozen in the middle of a field and willing to sacrifice his pearly whites if it meant saving himself. But now he'd have to grind the bone to dust if he wanted to ingest it—swallowing it whole was not an option. Not for him. Just the thought of it made Wood gag.

But swallow it one way or another, he must. After Sister had the boy—and Whisper—in her clutches. He would partake of their unholy communion one last time to sever their tie and wipe away his hunger for good.

They lie. His father's voice.

"I'm not listening," Wood said, dropping the bone into the coffee grinder. He pushed the button, and the blades clattered the shard about like a crazed roulette ball.

They're playing you for a chump.

He turned the grinder off and removed the lid—the bone remained untouched.

How could that be? He pulled the vape from his pocket and took one short hit. The vapor calmed his stomach.

You gotta stand up to those types or they'll get the best of you over and over again. His father's advice on how to deal with the neighborhood kids when they stole his book bag and rode off with his bike.

"That's great, coming from you!"

They had gotten the best of his father, that was for sure. The company worked him for the better part of his life only to fold up shop a year before his retirement.

Reluctantly, Wood placed the bone in his mouth and tentatively bit down. It crumbled as easily as a Smarties candy. It *wanted* to be chewed.

He spat into a plastic cup. Nothing but powdery ash. Not even a hint of moisture from his mouth. Dry as a bone. He wanted to swallow it down and be done with it, but he had been told to wait. *Ordered* to wait.

"Until Sister has the child…"

They'll leave you with nothing if you let 'em.

"Shut up!"

He heard a door slam next door, and when he ran to peek out the curtains, he caught the Larson kid's eye as he passed.

When he was certain that the family was in their car and gone, Wood opened the door on his side and tried the communicating door.

He was pleasantly surprised to find it unlocked.

CHAPTER 29

The Loving Pet Food silo towered next to the railroad tracks, shrouded in mist. A stretch of freight cars stood ready, awaiting their cargo, the far end disappearing into the fog.

The houses were older in this part of town, some well maintained with potted plants and Cubs flags, others on the verge of total collapse. The first of the *No Trespassing* signs appeared, then the first dog on a chain. Stacks of firewood took up space where cars once stood, and every other block or so, the skeletal remains of a once proud house now reduced to a pile of burnt lumber.

"I grew up two blocks from here," Steph said with what Jessie deemed misplaced pride. "I was a home birth. Didn't cost my family a dime."

"And you're worth every penny."

"Har-dee-har-har."

"Seriously, Steph. What are we—"

"We're here."

They pulled up before a small white house with an awkward addition. After examining the place with her designer's eye, Jessie figured out that the addition was once a carport that had been boarded over in a haphazard way to form an extra bedroom. The result was a house that any realtor would run from as quickly as possible. The one tree on the property bent at a strange angle, like a broken leg that no one had bothered to set.

"This is Hilde's place."

"Okay…"

Steph turned the car off and took Jessie's hand. The uncharacteristic gesture made Jessie worried as hell.

"There are three families that run through the heart of Maple City. All of us have mixed and mingled at some point or other. That's one of the reasons I'm half convinced to take JR's ring—to change my damn last name."

Jessie waited for an explanation that never came.

"Remember that call I got? When I bugged out and left you with the kid?"

"How can I ever forget?"

Steph got out of the car, and Jessie followed suit.

"*This* is why."

An old pit bull next door barked incessantly. Although unchained, it didn't venture near. As the two women drew closer to the house, Jessie noticed blankets in the windows where blinds should have been. The porch was a porch in name only. Gaping holes offered the perfect nesting place for vermin. Beds of leaves and ample droppings proved that. An American flag reduced to ribbons hung next to the front door.

Steph winced and knocked. When there was no answer, she knocked again, harder this time.

"Hilde! Open up."

"I don't see a car," Jessie offered.

"That's cuz there ain't none," said Steph, slipping into a dialect Jessie hadn't heard her friend use before.

Steph gestured for her to wait and then circled the house. When she returned, she seemed pissed.

"She's in there but she's hiding."

"Who? Who's in there?"

Pulling a bit of wire and a miniature screwdriver, the type they sold at Ecklund's Pharmacy for adjusting eyeglasses, Steph went to work on the lock. A second later, there was a click and her friend swung the door open.

Heat wafted out of the house, and with it the scent of...what was that? Vapor rub? Disinfectant? Whatever it was, Jessie was instantly reminded of the hospital with all its various odors. Yes, there was excrement as well, hiding beneath the more medicinal smells.

The two stepped inside, leaving the comparatively bright day behind as they entered the cloaked darkness of the small house.

A lone parakeet eyeballed them from the corner in its newspaper-lined cage. Jessie hated birds—always had. Her elderly Aunt Bix had owned an enormous parrot by the name of Tee-Tee whose main source of joy was biting little children's fingers. But Aunt Bix insisted upon her niece petting Tee-Tee if she wanted a silver dollar.

"What's wrong with you, Jess? Show Tee-Tee some love."

Over the course of her childhood, Jessie had amassed a treasure trove of silver dollars and endured her share of bites.

This bird simply stared.

Jessie had half expected the place to be a hoarder's paradise, but instead it was sparsely furnished: a framed print of Jesus on the wall, a small dining table with two matching chairs and the birdcage.

"Hilde!" Steph shouted.

A startled cough sounded from the back of the house, followed by the slamming of a door. Floorboards creaked as an elderly woman in a *Bingo Queen* sweatshirt maneuvered herself down the hall, aided by a rolling walker. Her face was flushed and angry.

"Get out!"

"It's me, Hilde. It's Steph."

"What?"

"Turn your hearing aids on."

"Is that you, Steph?"

"Turn your hearing aids on!"

The woman stopped in her tracks, bracing herself with one hand while the other fumbled at her ear. The hearing aid squealed, causing the bird to chirp in reply.

"Only got the one. God knows where the other is." She stood defiantly before them. "How'd you get in, girl?"

"I picked your lock."

"What?"

Growing impatient, Steph made a move for the hallway. The old woman shoved the walker to block the way.

"I told you yesterday I don't want you nosing around."

Steph turned back to Jessie and said under her breath, "Play along."

The old woman made a grab for the phone on the wall. "That's it, I'm calling—"

"Who? The police?" Steph shook her head. "That's funny, cuz guess who I've got here?" She stuck her thumb at Jessie, who stood stock still, wondering where her friend was going with this.

"Who's that you say?"

"Hilde, this is Detective Voss. She's doing a home inspection to make sure everything is A-OK."

"Detective? Don't look like no detective."

"She's undercover. That's how she likes to roll. Detective Voss, this is Hilde, my second cousin once removed. Or as most folks call her, Grammy Long."

"Long?" Something clicked in Jessie's mind.

Steph took a step toward Hilde. "She wants to make sure that you're getting enough assistance from the State. She'll be in and out before you know it."

"What?"

"She's here to get you a bigger check!"

Grammy Long's eyes lit up. "Oh! Why didn't you say so, you silly girl?" After a few grunting pivots, the woman cleared the way. "Be quick. It's almost lunchtime."

Steph gestured for Jessie to follow. The old woman sized Jessie up as she passed, breathing heavily through her nose.

The hallway walls were lined with framed photos, all of them black and white. The odors present in the front of the house were stronger here and growing stronger with every step.

They passed a couple of rooms with closed doors until they reached the one at the far end of the hall.

"I'm sorry I didn't tell you." Steph rapped once on the door before opening it.

Butch Long was awake and ready to receive visitors.

CHAPTER 30

Once inside the Larsons' room, Wood quickly set the *Do Not Disturb* sign on the door. No need for a repeat with the cleaning woman.

He took stock of the room. Queen-sized bed, a rollaway, dressers, mini fridge. The bed it was.

In his experience, most hotel beds sat on platforms that didn't allow for guests to leave items beneath. Or corpses. He recalled a story he'd heard about a hotel guest in New Jersey finding a dead body underneath his bed. From the guest's description, the body must have been there for some time. But the Intermission Motor Lodge was old fashioned in that respect, allowing him to stick both the duffle and his head underneath the bed.

At first he was simply going to leave the bag close to the wall, out of sight of anyone trying to retrieve a stray shoe. But there was the kid to think about, and who knew what toys might go sailing under the bed.

Wood wriggled under the bed. His face was practically touching the thin fabric that lined the bottom of the box spring. Pulling his pocketknife, he cut at the fabric until a flap of material hung down making a hole big enough for him to slip the duffle through and wedge it into the empty space between wooden slats.

The bag weighed down the lining, bulging downward, making the box spring appear pregnant. Working the duffle up toward the head of the bed, his fingers coaxing it through the fabric, he found a sweet spot where the bulge was not so noticeable. The hanging flap, though, was a problem. Oh, for some duct tape.

He extracted himself and scoured the room for something, *anything* that would do. His search ended in the bathroom where he found a box of superhero-themed Band-aids. Snagging six or so, he returned to the bed.

Once again underneath, he peeled and pressed, peeled and pressed until he had accomplished a crude repair.

He was about to work his way out from under the bed when it sagged abruptly.

Someone's up there.

The bedsprings twanged and now the fabric *was* touching him. In fact, it was covering his face like a shroud.

Sweet breath wafted over him and he saw movement on the other side of the thin material.

"Are we set?"

"Yes."

"Are you certain?"

"Yes! Yes."

"Not going to betray us..."

"No. Why would you think that?"

"We were *listening.*"

"I didn't say a word."

"Not your mouth. *Here...*"

A black fingernail pressed against the lining, piercing the fabric. The sharp tip tapped his temple.

His father's voice returned. *You gotta stand up to those types...*

Wood's stomach dropped. "I was just daydreaming. Don't you know what daydreaming is?"

The nail pressed insistently, and Wood feared it would draw blood. Pain erupted once more in his palm as the embedded splinter came to life, twisting itself even deeper into his flesh.

"Be good."

"I will. I *am*."

"Promise?"

"I promise!"

The nail withdrew and the bed lifted. He was once more alone in the room.

Wood quickly retrieved his knife, dragged himself out from under the bed and slipped through the communicating doors. Safely back in his room, he cradled his throbbing hand and let out a trembling cry.

Enough. Enough.

He flicked open the largest blade in his pocketknife and sunk its sharp point into the screaming meat of his bloody palm.

CHAPTER 31

Butch's appearance caught Jessie off guard and she quickly averted her gaze.

The man had no face.

"Lunch in ten minutes, Butchie!" called Grammy Long from down the hall, setting a timer on the visit.

When Jessie looked back up, she realized that she'd been mistaken in her initial impression. Butch *did* have a face, technically speaking. But it was the stuff of nightmares.

Butch Long lay propped up in bed—a regular twin bed, not some fancy hospital bed, although he sure seemed to be a candidate for one. A mound of pillows cradled his misshapen head, which was cocked to one side as if he were intent on hearing whatever his guests might have to say.

Steph spoke up. "Got someone here I want you to meet." She gestured for Jessie to move forward, which she did, reluctantly.

Butch stared at her with his one eye. The idea that he might say hello was negated by the fact that he clearly had nothing close to a working mouth. Instead, a gaping maw stretched from his chin to his rebuilt upper lip. There was no nose in the mix—just two indents that sucked air. Loudly. The rest was a patchwork of surgeries on top of surgeries, the tenderest sections moistened with some sort of jelly.

Jessie pulled Steph roughly aside. "What is this?"

"I thought we could get you some answers."

"He was dead. Jesus, I *thought* he was dead!"

"He's spent the last two years shuttling between hospitals and the Pontiac Correctional Center."

"Why's he here?"

Jessie looked back at the man in the bed. The eye watched them with keen interest.

"They call it compassionate release. The man's had three strokes, every infection in the book and now...he's dying, Jess. They give him a week, tops."

"Aren't they afraid he might—"

"Try to escape? To where? Look at him."

Jessie looked. There was no rise in the blanket where a right leg should be.

"Five minutes!" Grammy Long cried. She was speeding this visit along.

"You got questions? Ask them."

Jessie stepped forward. As she did, Butch pulled a quaking hand out from under his covers. He reached for a phone charging on the side table alongside prescription bottles and a humidifier. The eye dropped to the phone and a swooshing sound came from the device signaling the opening of an app.

The eye found her again.

Jessie swallowed. "You...you're the one who shot up the Crossroads Motel."

Tap-tap-tap...

A woman's voice spoke his message.

Yes.

Stupid question and a waste of time.

"*Why* did you do it?"

Tap-tap-tap...

I was hungry.

Jessie was about to ask a follow-up question when Butch waved her off.

Tap-tap-tap...

I was hooked.

"On what? On drugs?"

Worse.

"Can...can you explain that?"

No.

Jessie found that she was leaning farther over the bed with each answer. She corrected that by standing up straight.

She frowned at Steph. "I'm not sure this is helping."

Steph approached the bed. "Is there anything you can tell us that might explain why something attacked my friend? In her own goddamned motel?"

Butch let out a long, low moan but his thumb remained still on the phone's screen.

"Can we get out of here?" Jessie begged.

"Yeah. Sorry."

The two women turned to go.

Tap-tap-tap...

Goats.

A frustrated groan.

Tap-tap-tap...

Ghosts.

Jessie stopped cold.

He said—

"Who said? Said what?" Jessie insisted, gripping the foot of the bed.

—that I give him ghosts I get feed.
"Who?"
Fed.

A jolt of adrenaline shot through Jessie's veins and she shook the bed. Butch's head wobbled and threatened to topple over.

"That's it! You gotta go! Lunchtime, lunchtime!" Jessie could hear the clatter of the approaching walker.

"Who!"
Woo...
"Spit it out."
Word...
Grammy Long breached the doorway. "Time to go!"
Wood.

The eye went wide. Butch's chest heaved. His hand seized and he dropped the phone. His lone leg kicked off the covers, revealing streaks of black veins running underneath waxen skin.

"His pills," Grammy Long cried as she tried to get past Jessie and Steph. "He needs his pills."

A deep gurgle rose out of the man's gullet and a concussive cough released a spray of spittle. His tongue lolled from his maw, extending to a disturbing length. On its surface sat a sharp, stone-like object. Butch rolled his tongue and the mess dropped off, his breathing returning to normal, his single eye at last closing.

Jessie looked. Lying on the sheet, slathered in glistening bile was a pale, white bone.

CHAPTER 32

Michael stared out the car window at the foggy landscape whipping past. Fields stripped of their corn, clusters of trees starting to show their autumn colors, farm houses invariably flanked by enormous pickup trucks. And that was it. Aside from the occasional billboard touting legal services or far-off attractions, rural Illinois kept it simple.

His mother and father were silent, opting instead to fill the air with an oldies station.

The discussion during the first part of the ride had been brief but memorable.

"What's this woman's name again?" Hannah asked.

"Lillian Dann," Peter replied.

"I thought Dan was a first name," Michael said.

"She spells it D-A-N-N."

"Oh."

"Did she happen to mention when your dad bought the place?" Hannah asked.

"Nope, but I get the sense he's had it a long time," Peter said, flipping through radio stations.

"A bit odd, isn't it?"

"Dad was always buying one thing or another. If it wasn't a house it was a car wash, an old truck. He couldn't pass up an auction."

Michael's mother peeked back at him. "What about you? Are you looking forward to checking out an old house?"

"No." Michael's hands began to shake. He wasn't the one speaking.

"Really? You're not even a bit curious?"

"I think we should stay the fuck away from there."

"Michael!" his parents said in tandem.

His father slowed the car. "Do you need to get out for a bit and think about what you said?"

"No. I'm sorry."

Tell him to turn around.

"No."

Fine, I'll do it...

"No!"

His father pulled onto the shoulder and stopped the car. He leaned back. "Are you going to behave yourself?"

"Yes."

Peter checked in with Hannah, who nodded. He turned on the radio, and for the next few miles, no one spoke a word.

Well, almost no one.

Look at me.

Michael kept his eyes on the passing landscape.

Don't be stubborn.

He counted the houses. One...two...three...

Michael, look at me!

The voice startled him with its volume and he whipped around. Sitting next to him in the backseat was his father. Or at least a *version* of his father. The man was gaunt and grey. His clothes hung loosely on his frame. And that grin...

Michael had watched a program on TV once about a group of mountain climbers who went missing. When they were found, they said that they were so hungry they had eaten their boots.

The man beside him had that same starved man's grin.

"I don't know what to say," the man said, tears rimming his eyes. "Look at you. You're the most beautiful thing in the world."

The man reached out to touch his face and Michael shied away.

"Mom!" Michael cried only to realize that there was no one in the front seat. His parents had vanished. And yet, the car still barreled down the road at sixty miles an hour. "What happened? Where are they?"

"I'm tuning them out so we can have a chance to talk."

"Who are you?"

The pale man looked pained. "Take a good look."

Michael looked. Every feature was the same as his father's—the upturned side of the mouth, the earnest eyes. But in this man, they were diminished.

"Are you sick?"

"Yes. Sick from missing you."

The man gripped his hand and his touch was as cold as death. Michael wanted to pull his hand away, but something in the car had shifted. The sky outside darkened and the car increased its speed.

"Michael, he makes me watch. *Everything.* Every minute, every day. He takes me back and makes me watch."

At first, Michael didn't understand, but then...

A stream of images flowed past him like he was falling into a movie screen. There he was, laughing with his father in the subway, his father trying to put on his child-sized Yankees cap. The scene shifted and now he saw himself curled up in bed as his mother sang "Sweet Child O' Mine" while tousling his hair. Another shift. He was pale and gasping, grabbing at the oxygen mask pressed to his face as the ambulance hit a pothole. Shift. Dad was filling a hypodermic needle, his face grim and...

"That never happened," Michael said, squirming in his seat.

Mom again, this time sitting on the floor of his now empty room with an old IV needle in her hand, her arm peppered with self-inflicted wounds.

"Stop it!"

His parents holding each other in a bar restroom weeping over his death, Mom barely holding it together.

Tears flowed down the face of the man gripping Michael's hand. "You see? Who am I if I'm not your dad?"

The car swerved, and Michael could swear he heard something laugh.

"Shut up!" the man who looked like Peter Larson shouted. He looked back to Michael. "My *friend* can be cruel."

Michael squeezed his eyes shut, willing the scene away.

"I just want to protect you."

Michael's fear mounted as the car seemed to speed up. "Really? Because no one's driving the car!"

"Don't be scared. The last thing I'd want to do is scare you."

"Then *go away!*"

"Open your eyes."

"Go away!"

"Michael?

It was his mother's voice.

"We're here."

Michael opened his eyes. Through the glass, he saw an imposing farmhouse with a solemn demeanor, his father standing with a well-dressed woman in high heels, holding a clipboard.

A wretched wail rose up within him which was soon joined by another. He listened inward, trying in vain to separate the two voices, but one thing he was sure of was that one of the anguished cries belonged to the man in the back seat.

* * *

"Run."

Peering through Michael's eyes, Peter screamed with all his might. Whisper screamed alongside him, the demon lending him its voice, robbing him of his own.

He didn't have to enter the place to know what awaited him because the memories were tumbling all around him. Every moment he'd spent beneath that roof with Hannah, from their first visit—a carbon copy of the scene being played out before him—to the nasty end where he had forced himself upon his screaming companion.

Whisper went suddenly rigid. He snarled and spat like a cornered dog, and Peter knew what was coming next. Feared what was coming next. All he could do was steel himself to the fact that Whisper was about to…

"Run."

Peter had thought the word was his own, him begging the boy to jump from the car and head off across the cornfield, but instead he now recognized that it was his companion's voice. And it was not a command but an exclamation of purpose.

"Run!"

The world lurched and Peter lurched with it. Whisper was off like a shot, not forward in motion but backwards in time, retreating down a path of yesterdays. Fallen trees rose, broken shutters mended themselves and the walkway to the house, once nothing but dirt, populated itself with stones.

A truck appeared out of thin air, and standing next to it was a man dressed in coveralls—a working man. *The Old Man,* Peter thought, recognizing the person he had called Father for the first few years of his life. The man opened the passenger door and a young woman stepped out.

She was younger than the man by decades and wore the plain, homespun dress of a character in a Steinbeck novel. Her skin was dark but her hair was darker—a wild raven mane.

A yearning the likes of which Peter had never felt gripped him tight, suffocating him. The woman across the yard turned and looked his way, and he longed to go to her.

He turned to the demon and came face to face with himself. They had intermingled to such a degree that he didn't know where he ended and it began. All he knew was that he wanted to fly to the woman—*Willa! Willa wait!*—and sink his teeth into her heart and be loved and cherished and...

"Who's that lady?"

Peter turned, and because Peter turned, Whisper turned. Michael crouched behind them, peering intently at the young woman.

Whisper bolted for Willa, but Peter held him back. Terrified, Michael gripped his hand. The incredible strain between the two threatened to rip him in half.

Suddenly, the small hand gripping his disappeared.

"Michael!"

* * *

"Come on. Let's take a look."

Michael sat frozen, reeling from the encounter. His mother cocked her head in puzzlement and continued speaking, but Michael didn't hear a word she said.

Run.

But how could you run from something that was inside you? This was too much for him. He was just a kid. He shouldn't be asked to figure this out. He should be doing kid's stuff—swimming and playing catch, but there was something in the pool and the Dad more intent on his company cried to him from inside his head.

Michael!

Must run!

Be quiet...

Run!

The cow. Crazy as it sounded, he wanted to see the cow. To touch her head and hear her voice. She was his touchstone in all this madness.

"I want to go back to the motel."

"Listen, young man..."

"I want to go. *Now.*"

CHAPTER 33

A determined Jessie drove back to the motel as fast as possible. Wood, that bastard—he was wrapped up in this. She'd get answers out of him, oh yes. Even if she had to beat them out of him.

Steph, who hadn't said a word as Jessie demanded her keys, sat shotgun. Finally, she could stay silent no longer.

"Go ahead. Yell at me. C'mon, say something!"

"How could you let me buy the place?

"Look—"

Jessie ran a stop sign.

"You should have talked me out of it."

"Okay, first off you already knew the place's history. Second, how was I to know that ghosts came as part of the package?"

"Why didn't you tell me that you were related to that monster? I thought you were my friend."

"I am your friend. I just wanted…"

"Wanted what? Spit it out."

Steph grimaced. "Fine. I wanted you to buy it and fix it up so folks could forget about all that bad business. You know what it's like being related to him? What it's like for my family? It's a nightmare. And then I get a call telling me they're releasing him?"

"So you decided to sell me out—"

"I *didn't* sell you out."

"You decided to leave me holding the bag and there's nasty stuff in that bag."

"I'm sorry."

"You're going to help me fix this."

"How?"

"I don't know, but you're going to help me fix this, Steph!"

"Okay!"

Jessie whipped the car right, lurched into the Intermission Motor Lodge's parking lot and pulled up to the office.

Lin poked her head outside. "Hey, the exterminator called and—"

"Give me your master, please," Jessie said.

Lin complied. "Is everything okay?"

"What room is Mr. McKay in now?"

"208."

Jessie turned and headed toward the stairs. "Come on, Steph," she said. "Let's see what this guy has to say for himself."

* * *

Michael made a move for the ViddyBox control but Hannah grabbed it before he could.

"No way, mister. If you're in too much of a mood to check out our new digs, then you're *definitely* not up for TV."

Michael's jaw tightened. He needed something, *anything* to distract him. The dual voices in his brain were loud and throwing elbows. He sat on his rollaway bed and tried to drown them out.

Michael, listen...

No good. Can't stay. Must fly...

Please. I'm begging you...

Bad-bad-bad-bad-bad! FLY...

He thought his head would split in two—no, three—no, a *million* pieces, scattering him to all corners of the earth.

Dad knelt before him. "You want to tell me what that was all about back at the house?"

The voices returned, both clamoring for attention.

"I'm okay, Dad."

"That's not what I asked."

"I want to be alone, that's all."

"Your mother and I—"

"Give it a break!" Michael shouted. "The boy wants to be alone. Why can't you leave him alone?"

"Excuse me?"

"Fly!" Michael cried in a horrible, screeching voice. "Fly!"

His father stared at him, alarmed at his son's outbursts. He turned to his wife. "Honey? Do you think we need to take him to the—"

"Yes."

"Leave. Him. Alone," their son growled through gritted teeth.

"Let's get a bag together," Peter said.

A loud pounding came from next door. Michael clamped his hands over his ears and balled up on the bed.

Peter scowled. "Now what?"

* * *

Getting no reply, Jessie knocked on Wood's door again, harder this time. "Fair warning, Mr. McKay. We're coming in."

Steph grabbed her shoulder. "You do realize the guy could be armed…"

But it was too late to stop Jessie Voss. She slipped the master keycard into the slot, waited for the blinking green dot and threw open the door.

Wood stood swaying in the middle of the room. In one hand he held a bloody pocketknife; the other hand was the source of the blood. A large red divot of flesh had been cut away from the palm. The man stared not at the women who had forced their way into his room but at his angry hand.

"It's gotta be out, doesn't it? Doesn't it?"

The man winced in pain and proceeded once more to dig at his flesh with the blade.

"I'm calling the cops," Jessie said, barely above a whisper. *Jesus, he's almost cut straight through his hand.*

Steph, likewise shocked by the scene, raised her phone as if it were a weapon. "Yeah, buddy. We're calling."

Wood looked back up, this time finally focusing on the women. The knife tumbled from his hand and bounced on the carpeted floor, leaving a crimson stain.

"It's still in there," he croaked.

"That's too bad," Jessie said, doing her best *not* to look at the knife on the floor by the man's feet. "I think you need a towel."

"A what?"

"A towel. There are plenty in the bathroom."

The man looked dumbly down at his hand. "Yeah. I think you're right." Wood's shoulders started heaving, and at first

Jessie thought the man was about to break down. Instead, a mad giggle rose from his throat. "You caught me red-handed."

"Towel. The bathroom?"

"Right."

Still chuckling, Wood shuffled off to the bathroom. As soon as he was inside, Jessie stepped quickly across the room and pulled the bathroom door shut. She braced herself, leaning backward slightly, hearing the *click* of her hip.

Steph promptly kicked the knife under the bed. "No screwing around. We need to call 911."

Before Jessie could answer, the doorknob twisted in her hand. Wood cursed and yanked on the door. It opened an inch or two before Jessie managed to pull it shut again.

"Don't just stand there, Steph! He's going to bust out."

"What do you want me to do?"

"Where's his knife?"

"Under the bed."

"Hey! Let me out! Help! Let me out of here!" Wood's voice was a mix of anger and anguish, and Jessie feared what he might do should she let go of the doorknob.

"Why is the knife under the bed?

"Because I kicked it! It was covered in blood, and who knows what kind of diseases this guy might—"

"Get the damn knife!"

"Help!" Wood screamed. "Help!"

* * *

The murmured voices in the adjoining room had given way to frenzied shouts.

Michael was rocking now, hands plastered to his ears. He could feel black fissures streaking across his mind.

As Peter packed Michael's pajamas and underwear in his overnight bag, Hannah sat on the bed and put her arms around the boy. "Don't worry, honey. We're going to get you checked out. Okay?"

Another shout, this time clear enough to make out.

"*Help!*"

Peter set the bag aside.

"I'm going to see what's up."

* * *

The door shuddered as Wood yanked harder.

"Steph!"

Jessie's friend grabbed the coffee grinder sitting on the desk and raised it over her head like a bludgeon.

Jessie dug in her feet as Wood yanked on the door again, and this time her hip did much more than click—it *howled*. She'd have to let go or risk really fucking herself up.

A shadow fell across the wall.

"Is there a problem in here?"

The voice startled Jessie. It wasn't so much the suddenness of the words as the *voice* itself. It was so familiar that it set her brain in motion, searching frantically for a memory to attach it to.

She glanced back over her shoulder to find Peter Larson standing silhouetted in the doorway. Her momentary distraction was all Wood needed. With a powerful tug, he pulled the door open, and the doorknob slipped out of Jessie's sweaty hands.

Wood was clear-eyed once more and he quickly surveyed the situation. He bolted past Jessie and headed straight for the exit.

Sensing an imminent collision, Peter sidestepped as the man raced toward him. Wood hit the railing hard and kept on going. With a yelp, he toppled over the railing and disappeared over the edge.

Jessie and Steph joined Peter at the railing. Wood lay motionless on the hood of his car, the windshield buckled inward and safety glass scattered all about. A moan from the prone man signaled that he was still alive and kicking.

"Peter, what the hell's going on?" Hannah asked, joining the group.

"Our next door neighbor seems to have gone nuts."

"There's no *seems* about it," Steph said with a snort. "That man is a grade-A lunatic."

Unseen by those gathered at the railing, the door to the Larsons' room slowly swung closed and locked with a definitive click.

CHAPTER 34

Michael smelled smoke. The scent roused him and he glanced about the room.

"Mom?"

The overhead light flared and died, and the room went suddenly dark.

"Dad?"

No answer. Just the rumble of conversation beyond the door. Michael had no intention of remaining alone with the voices howling in his head and he *definitely* had no desire to remain in the dark. Though shaky, he got to his feet and took a step toward the door.

Something rattled underneath his parents' bed. It was a dry, threatening sound. His father had once brought him home the preserved head and tail of a rattlesnake, a souvenir all the way from Colorado. The twin trophies came with their own glass display case. Michael would stare at the thing from across his bedroom—the snake's fanged mouth open, its dried tail sitting alongside it. After too many sleepless nights, he chucked the head and tail into the trash and heard the tail *rattle* one last time.

Perhaps the snake had followed him, growing to monstrous proportions. Because he couldn't imagine anything else that could make such a sound.

He didn't have to imagine. A black hand reached out from under the bed, pulling itself forward with ever-lengthening nails.

Michael's throat went dry and his legs turned to stone. He tried to shout for his father, but panic robbed him of all breath. He was glued to the spot, his eyes trained on the awful hand. Then the arm. Then the body. A foul collection of blackened body parts piecing themselves together.

The laundry room. The memory slammed back into his head, nearly knocking him off his feet. *The laundry room!*

The thing rose up before him on creaking insect legs, its skin snapping and splitting as it grew. Something resembling a face formed itself at the center of the mass. It drew one thin nail across its skin, cutting it and two red, ulcerated eyes burst forth from the wound. It raked its chin and teeth sprouted, gnashing together to rip open a mouth.

With the ragged approximation of a grin on its face, the creature rose up over him.

"Wake, brothers. Time to go home."

The bed shuddered as two dark figures emerged from beneath. It was nightmare overkill. Michael was already petrified by the sight of the monstrous thing that swayed above him, cooing to him in its—*her?*—brittle voice. Now there were two more writhing, growing beasts to contend with.

Snarling and snapping, the two lumps of putrid, burnt flesh formed themselves into twin guards, rooks flanking their queen. A rancid-sweet scent like mulberry intermingled with the smoke, and soon the room was filled with the nasty stench of spoiled barbeque.

"Mom! Dad!" The words so quiet not even Michael could hear them.

The first creature—*she called them brothers, does that make her their sister?*—rested two arms on her companions' heads while she reached out a third, palm out. A strange sound emanated from her chest—a low, chittering sound. She slowly drew her hand into a fist, and as she did so, Michael felt his stomach churn. She closed her fist tighter, finger bones cracking, and Michael's gorge rose in response.

Just when he thought he couldn't stand the pressure any longer, something let loose inside him. A visceral untethering.

Michael!

BAD!

A frightening feeling of relief swept over the boy as he gave up control. Blackness poured from his mouth. And not just blackness, light as well. *Everything* that was not of his body gushed forth until it formed into a twisting pillar of smoke before the dark creatures.

* * *

Sister shot out her hand and gripped the blackness, forcing it to congeal. It was all leather and wings and teeth and cries—shifting and shifting again. She squeezed harder and brought the squirming, scratching mass to her face. Yes, *he* was in there but there were others as well. No matter—as long as he could hear her.

"Home, Whisper," she insisted. "Home, Mr. Tell."

The wriggling blackness in her grip bit once and then…

* * *

Michael toppled to the floor, his head bouncing on the carpet.

"Michael?" his mother called from the other side of the door.

"Open up," his father ordered.

There was a flurry of conversation, the click of a lock and the door opened, flooding the room with light. Jessie stepped aside, making way for two frantic parents.

Michael's mother cradled him in her lap while his father shook his arm and lifted his eyelids. It was no use. For although their boy's heart beat steadily and his lungs sucked air, Michael Larson was gone.

CHAPTER 35

Hannah Larson let out a wail that struck Jessie in the gut. Peter gathered up the boy in his arms and rushed toward the door.

"Hannah, get the bag."

Jessie and Steph stood out of the way as the Larsons went through their well-practiced maneuvers, placing a blanket around the boy, gathering up prescriptions and double-checking insurance cards and phone chargers. And then…out the door.

Jessie chased after them down the stairs. "Do you need directions to the hospital? It's only six blocks down—"

"We know where the hospital is." Peter passed Michael off to Hannah who was already in the backseat.

The boy is pale. God, he's so pale.

Before Jessie could offer to help further, the Larsons took off in their road-weary Prius, kicking up gravel in their haste.

As she watched the car disappear down Main Street, her mind flitted back to her conversation with the boy on the roof.

"We are friends?"

"I thought so. The cow said we were."

It hadn't made sense. *None* of this made sense. The only thing she knew for certain was that *she* was responsible for what was happening to Michael. It was her decision to raise this motel from the dead, to unearth what should have been left buried. Could she be certain that the child's stay at the Intermission was the reason his parents were now spiriting him away to the emergency room? Yes. As sure of that as she was that Wood was the one who...

Wood...damn. Where is he?

Jessie whirled about in time to see the man hopping into his Lincoln. The engine started up and her stomach dropped.

"Shit! Steph!" She pointed toward Wood's car which was now backing up at a rapid pace.

Steph made a dash for the vehicle. Wood spun the car around and hit the gas. Jessie could see his terrified face through the mosaic of the shattered windshield.

She'd screwed up. She should have called the cops.

The Lincoln's wheels squealed as it made a beeline for the street. Just as it looked as if Wood's escape was a fait accompli, a second car came into view. The vehicle was a small beater, an off-white Geo Metro, the last of its breed. The car pulled into the path of the Lincoln and...accelerated.

Steph was out in the open and in the danger zone of the two cars' imminent impact. "Get out of the way!" Jessie hollered. Her friend dove right—it was a fifty-fifty shot—and her choice proved lucky.

The Lincoln swerved left and the Geo Metro slammed into its passenger side door, checking it like a small but sturdy linebacker. Wood's car veered toward the dumpsters and came to a metal-crunching halt.

Jessie watched as the small off-white car sputtered slowly toward the office and came to a slow stop, bright green coolant spilling from its undercarriage.

Steph picked herself up and raced over to where Wood sat dazed behind the wheel. She yanked the door open and leaned over him, switching off the ignition and taking the keys.

Jessie heard a string of swear words coming from inside the Metro, and then the driver threw open the door and crawled out.

"My insurance is going to take a hit for that." The young woman to whom the voice belonged was short in stature and dressed head to toe in black. Even her lips and nails were black. "Didn't even want to learn to drive in the first place."

She pushed the driver's seat up and retrieved a similarly black portfolio from the back—a large one, the kind Jessie had sported about campus when she was going for her degree in design. White twine stood in for a broken zipper. A mass of scrawled pages poked out from the portfolio's interior like a hoarder's prized possessions.

Without another word, the woman marched toward the front office, forcing Jessie to catch up.

"Excuse me!"

The woman in black stopped and turned to Jessie, annoyance spreading across her wide face.

"Yes?"

"Who are you?"

The young woman harrumphed, stuck her free hand into her pocket and came out with a handful of business cards. She tossed them in Jessie's direction—they fluttered in the air and landed at her feet.

"There's no time for this," the woman said in a firm monotone. She promptly turned tail and headed into the office. "Where's the cow?"

THE HUNGRY ONES

Jessie retrieved one of the business cards. It read:

ELLEN MARX
author/medium/psychic

CHAPTER 36

Lin stood wide-eyed behind the counter, looking as if she
wanted to bolt.

"Is the Larson boy okay? What's going on? Who was that
woman?"

"Where'd she go?" Jessie asked. Lin pointed down the
hallway to the unfinished restaurant space.

Steph dragged Wood through the door. His wounded
hand hung limply at the wrist, his nose jutted to the side—
another break. Steph had his good hand trapped behind him.
He let Steph lead him, all his fight sapped away.

"Take the rest of the day," Jessie said to Lin. The young
woman seemed all too eager to comply. She grabbed her bag
and slipped out the door.

"What do you want me to do with this piece of shit?"
Steph asked.

"Bring him."

Jessie headed off down the hallway and Steph followed
with the captive Wood.

The young woman clad in black stood in the middle of the
collection of boxes, furniture and refuse. She'd set her portfolio
of pages on a round table and was staring at the plexiglass cow,
shaking her head.

"I thought it'd be on the roof."

"It was," Jessie said, walking up to her cautiously. "I had it brought down here until I can get the restaurant in order."

"Still say that's biting off too much—"

"Hush, Steph."

The woman turned to face Jessie. As she did, Jessie noticed something in her left hand. Doing her best not to stare, she recognized it as a child's toy—a small, black Angus. The woman's thumb worried its head.

"It's my touchstone," the woman said, gripping the toy cow. "It helps me key in. Communicate. Cow at the motel— cow in my hand. Don't know how it works but it does. Are we going to get on with this?"

The woman furiously stroked the toy with her thumb, and Jessie realized that this must be the woman's constant ritual. The toy cow's head was worn flat like a polished stone.

"First things first. I'm Jessie."

"Huh. Got that wrong."

"Excuse me?"

The woman smacked her lips. "Thought your name was Jersey. Like the cow. At least that's what I picked up."

Jessie was flustered. "And you are?"

"I gave you my card."

"Ellen…"

The woman let out a wearied breath. "Ellen Marx. Now, can we *please* get started?"

Ellen Marx. Jessie rolled the name around in her mind. *Ellen Marx…*

Michael's words popped into her head once more.

"She's not a boy, you know. She's a girl. And her name's not Elmer. It's close, but that's not her name."

205

The penny dropped. The boy had said the cow spoke to him, told him things. Secret things. But her name wasn't Elmer. Close, but not Elmer.

It was Ellen Marx.

"What exactly are we getting started—"

Ellen slipped the twine from the portfolio and threw it open, revealing a collection of writings on newsprint, yellow legal pad paper and the stray napkin. She proceeded to leaf through the pages, casting every other one aside.

"Not relevant. Not relevant," the woman in black muttered, leafing through the pages.

Jessie's patience was wearing as thin as the layer of paint on the toy cow's head.

"Explain yourself," she said, her voice booming in the open space. "God knows I can see you're connected to this whole…whatever this is, and I insist on knowing how."

Ellen kept her attention on her pages. "No time for that. I already told you. Now, will you just let me—"

Jessie pushed over a stray chair, making much more noise than she had planned on making. "Explain!"

Startled, the woman in black turned. "I don't like people slowing me down when I'm on task. But I need you so I'll explain. What do you want to know?"

"Who are you?"

"I'm Ellen—"

"No, *who* are you?"

Ellen cocked her head like a Spaniel. "Oh. Sometimes I miss the subtleties. You should be more precise when you talk."

"Yes?"

"I've been keeping an eye on you folks for a long time. Couldn't help it, actually. This place and everything that's happened here sort of crawled into my brain and won't get out. You ever hear of earworms? Tunes or phrases that stick in your head? This motel is my earworm. Annoying, actually. Lost a lot of sleep over it…"

Jessie looked to Steph, who was watching the woman the way one watched a circus act. "Watching us?"

"Keeping tabs. Not that I had any choice in the matter. One day about eight years ago I was at the library doing some research when I heard a gunshot. I thought some wacko was shooting up the place, so I ran down to the basement and hid in the periodicals section. I hope they got the smell out. The library had flooded two months prior to that and the basement still had the funky, mildew smell that only damp books give off."

Ellen paused, and Jessie wondered if the woman thought she had explained herself through sheer volume of verbiage. But then, she continued.

"There was no shooter. It was only in my head. I chalked it up to the new meds I was on and got back to my reading. But the gunshot came again each day at the same time. 12:07 pm. In my research, I've found midday is just as powerful a time spiritually speaking as the hours between midnight and—"

"The gunshot?" Jessie asked, guiding her back to the subject.

"Yes. I soon came to realize each gunshot was actually a blast of information. When they came, I was ready with a pen in hand to write down everything I could pick out. Okay, I see how you're looking at me. Do you want me to stop or am I misinterpreting?"

Jessie turned back to Steph. Her friend had settled Wood in a chair, where he sat slumped over to the side. His face was ashen and his hand looked nasty. She'd have to call an ambulance soon, she knew that. But not yet. She had to get to the bottom of this.

"Ellen?"

"Yes?"

"There's a lot going on inside your head."

"You're telling me."

Jessie spoke slowly, softly.

"You say this all started eight years ago?"

"Yes, because that's when I fired my shrink because he wouldn't tweak my meds so I could better tune in on this place."

"The shooting that took place here…it happened *two* years ago."

"Yeah, well it had a massive cold front. You know how the air chills before a big storm? That's what it's like before traumatic events. I can feel the chill before the kill, so to speak. People like me—not that there are many, you wouldn't *believe* the number of fakers out there—we're sensitive. We feel the cold before anyone else. In B. F. Chesteron's *Psychic Consciousness*, he writes—"

"Ellen? I need you to give me the mega-dumbed-down version of what the hell you're doing here and why I should care."

This seemed to hit the woman in black the right way. She took a step toward Jessie and put a tentative hand on her shoulder, as if comforting a child.

"I'm exactly what my card says. I see things others can't. I talk to them; they talk to me. Sometimes I can make a difference. Bad things happened here. I think we can fix them."

"What do we do?"

"First," Ellen said, nodding at Wood. "We need to get him to talk."

CHAPTER 37

Jessie turned to Wood.

Steph no longer had to restrain him—the man sat slumped and beaten. His injured hand hung down at his side like an afterthought, and if Jessie's eyes didn't deceive her, drool dripped from his slack-jawed mouth.

She and Ellen approached the man in tandem. Jessie gave his foot a gentle kick. His eyes fluttered open but did not seem to focus.

"What?" Wood moaned.

"We're going to get you to a doctor, but first you're going to answer some questions, do you hear me?" Jessie asked.

"Yeah, yeah, yeah…"

Jessie gave his foot a harder kick. "Do you hear me?"

"Yes."

"How do you know Butch?" Steph jumped in.

"Who?"

"Tubby guy, shot this place up. Used to have a face," Jessie said.

"Oh…yeah, he was one of mine."

"One of your *what*?"

Wood looked at his hand as if seeing it for the first time. "God, my hand."

"You were talking about Butch?"

"I got him hooked. Hooked good."

"On what?" Steph asked, leaning in. "It wasn't booze. He's been a drunk since high school."

"Meth?" Jessie offered.

Wood winced and glanced about. "Where's my vape?"

Jessie quickly patted the man down and located his vape pen. "What's in this?"

"You wouldn't believe me."

"Try me."

Wood finally seemed to rouse, taking in the trio of faces around him. "You all come in threes," he chuckled under his breath.

This caused Ellen to break her silence. "There's a gap in what I've been able to see. Three gaps, to be precise. They are at the center of a lot of pain. I've been able to make a rough sketch of them in my mind based on the outline of their absence. Like you can tell the size of a foot from a footprint, or the shape of a head from the..." She shook her head. "Back on point. What have you done and who did you do it for?"

"I'm just the middle man."

"Between?"

When Wood didn't answer, Steph reached down and gave his bad hand a squeeze. He squealed and grit his teeth. "Between Sister and guys like Butch."

Ellen's brow furrowed. "*Guys* like Butch? How many guys like Butch have there been?"

"Four or five. No...definitely five. Maybe six."

"I don't get it," Jessie said.

"How many people have these *guys* of yours killed? Tell us or I'm sure this woman would be happy to have another go at your hand," Ellen said, nodding to Steph, who feigned another twist of the hand in response.

"Not many before this. One-offs, mostly. Convenience store shootings, arson. The Charburger Castle fire, that was mine. I'd hook them—they'd do the dirty work. But it wasn't enough to satisfy her. And she needed them to marinate a bit. Make sure they were nice and ripe. One to two years, that's what she said. So I've been..."

A wave of sorrow passed over Wood's face, and for a second Jessie could almost imagine him as something other than the inhuman monster he was revealing himself to be.

"The motel. I thought maybe one big score and I could get out from under. I wanted to stop, but she wouldn't let me. I tried to run, but..." Tears rolled down Wood's face. "May I have my vape, please?"

Ellen took the vape from Jessie and held it out before the man's eyes. "What's in here?"

"Something to curb the hunger."

"Specifically?"

"Pieces. Pieces of her. Give it to me."

The three women looked at each other. Ellen was looking more alarmed than before. Wood broke into a shoulder-shaking sob that tugged at Jessie's conscience. Time to call 911.

Ellen had one last question. "Where is this Sister you talked about?"

Suddenly, the man was out of his seat. He handily shrugged Steph off and grabbed at the vape in Ellen's hand. The woman in black was fast but not fast enough. He swiped the pen from her grip and retreated to the far corner of the room.

Wood looked at his vape pen like a long lost friend. "She's gone. Along with the others." The man put the cylinder to his mouth and fired it up. He closed his eyes in expectation and then...

His eyes popped open and he spat dust. He looked down at the vape as if betrayed. "No..."

From where she stood, Jessie could see the liquid inside the vape's tank had gone jet black. Spoiled black.

Wood's mouth opened into a distorted O as his eyes clouded over grey. His stomach retreated into his body as if suction were pulling it inward. The same was happening to his muscles and fat—all moving to the center of his body.

He shook his head frantically as if trying to deny what was happening to him. His ribcage buckled in on itself and he toppled to his knees. It was if something were vaping *him*—sucking him dry.

The man collapsed altogether, grabbing desperately at the boxes around him, spilling old menus across the floor. His hands curled into useless husks and his eyes shrank in their sockets. His skin flaked and fell from his body, and with a final gasp, Wood collapsed, leaving behind a pile of ash, his salesman's clothing and his vape.

Jessie and Steph stared in disbelief. Ellen, by contrast, leapt into action, rushing over to her portfolio and leafing through the pages.

"Holy shit," Jessie said.

"Fuck me," Steph agreed.

Ellen continued digging through the pages, tossing some aside and setting others in a pile.

Jessie turned to the hyperactive Ellen. "What just happened?"

Ellen ignored her, all attention on her pages.

"What the *hell* just happened?" Jessie asked again, her mind threatening to unhinge.

"Yeah! What the *hell?*" Steph echoed.

"He's gone. Dried up. I don't know how or why and right now I don't care. We've got to get busy."

"Busy doing what?" Jessie asked.

Ellen whirled about, her dark eyes flashing. "Didn't you hear what he said?"

Jessie threw up her hands. "Which part?"

"I asked him where she went, this Sister of his. *Gone*, he said. Did you hear that? Gone!"

"So?"

"With. The. Others."

Jessie tried to piece it together but it was hard with Ellen staring at her with fire in her eyes. "Meaning…"

"The boy. They took the boy."

"Michael?" Jessie looked back to Steph for confirmation. "No. His parents took him to the hospital."

"They took his *body* to the hospital."

The gravity of the woman's words hit Jessie like a Mack truck. "So, wherever Michael is…"

"He's disembodied. And with things hungry for souls." Ellen turned back to her pages. "Now, snap out of it. We've got work to do."

CHAPTER 38

For a moment, Michael thought he was dead.

When the thing from under the bed drew the dark stuff out of him, the dark stuff grabbed hold, taking him along for the ride. He'd tried to hold on, but the pull was too great. Out of his body he slipped and into this nothingness.

Death was a constant fear when he lay awake at night during his months of chemo. When his brain was at its foggiest. And its trickiest. Often he'd respond to questions no one had asked. When it became a nightly occurrence, his father brought home a white noise machine to help him sleep, but his mind had found voices in its hiss.

His prankster brain also conjured up visions. One vision, in particular: a misty man. He would catch it moving across the room, and when he turned to look it would stop, imitating a shadow cast by the lamp. A misty man. No...a *messy* man. For that's what he was, wasn't he? He drew near when the bad stuff happened to Michael. The messy stuff. When his fever spiked and he spit up black tar. When the IV missed its mark and his arm swelled purple. When...

The Messy Man.

His cancer had brought along a menagerie of strange symptoms—numb feet, specks that floated and danced before his eyes, the taste of pennies in his mouth—and so he considered the arrival of the shadow man only part and parcel of the ordeal. But now that he thought about it...

How could I have forgotten about the Messy Man?

At that, other voices rushed in, blocking out his own, and Michael knew quite clearly he was *not* dead. But he *was* falling. They were all falling—he and the others who howled and shrieked around him. Only one of those voices was familiar to him, and it whispered instead of shouted.

"Stay close to me, Michael."

It was Dad.

Not *his* Dad but the Dad from the car.

The one with the drawn and pale face. He was pressing close, shielding him in this pitch blackness as they fell, as the others fought all around him, snarling and biting and screaming venom.

It was getting colder, and Michael sensed they were approaching the end of the road.

A sudden rush of wind billowed up and the voices scattered. Michael felt a sudden separation from the group, and he was falling solo. He tumbled to the ground amidst the receding cries of the others. He waited a moment before opening his eyes, unsure if he wanted to see the next chapter in this nightmare. He lay there, hands pressed against the ground.

I won't open my eyes. I won't.

Until at last, he did...

CHAPTER 39

It took Ellen Marx a scant five minutes to sort through her collection of writings and pull out the ones she wished to use. The rest lay scattered about the floor in heaps.

"This should do," the woman said as she propped a felt menu board up against the table. The pushpin letters still announced *BLT* as *Today's Lunch Special.* Ellen yanked out all the letters and used them to tack up her writings scribbled on yellow pages and stained cocktail napkins.

"Get my bag out of the car," Ellen told Jessie. "Back seat. The purple one, not the red one."

Jessie nodded and headed for the hall.

Ellen stopped her with a shrill whistle. "Hold on. I don't have a red bag this time. Never mind. Purple, it's purple."

Jessie shot Steph a look, but her friend was busy poking at Wood's empty clothing with a broom handle. She acquiesced and made quick work of making her way to the woman's crippled car. Digging through the mess of old magazines, clothing and fast food wrappers, Jessie finally found the bag. It wasn't purple—it was black, the same as the rest of the woman's attire.

As she pulled it free by the strap, the bag opened, spilling half its contents. Cursing, Jessie grabbed up Ellen's prescription bottles, tissues and a small bottle of Boo-Hot, the label on the glass touting it as America's finest ghost chili-pepper-flavored sauce.

Returning to where Ellen stood stooped over, pinning pages to the menu board, Jessie set the bag on the table.

"Sheesh. Black bag," Ellen spat. "Get it right, Marx."

"What did you mean when you said you didn't have a red bag this time?"

Eyes still on her work, Ellen raised the bag and shook it. Pills chattered in their bottles like teeth. "I don't. It's black."

"No," Jessie said, trying again, speaking slowly and deliberately. "What did you mean by *this time?*"

The woman in black pulled the bottle of hot sauce from her bag and downed a few drops. Jessie could smell the heat of the pepper from a few feet away. Ellen grimaced and when she opened her watering eyes, they were trained on Jessie with a new sense of focus.

"Sorry. I have little tricks to check myself. Darn that's hot." Ellen tucked the bottle away. "Lemme explain. In life, things happen or they don't. But for me, as of eight years ago, things happen *and* they don't. Do you understand?"

The look on Jessie's face said she didn't.

"Up until then, everything's going fine. High school's the worst but I'm managing. And then...*boom*, on goes the radio. Instead of picking up one signal—which is bad enough—I'm picking up every signal on the dial all at once. Take you for example, Jersey."

"Jessie."

"When I did my thing and set my thoughts out toward this place, sometimes you were married, sometimes you weren't. Sometimes you bought the motel, sometimes you didn't. *This*

time you're not married and *this* time you bought the motel."
Ellen dug into her bag and pulled a stray pill from the bottom
and popped it into her mouth. "After dealing with this for the
past eight years, I think I'm handling it quite well."

"And why have you been thinking about this place at all?"

Ellen snorted as if it were obvious. "The boy. I think I
helped him before or am helping him now or helping someone
else help him. It's all wrapped up in the kid. And if I can solve
this, maybe I can sleep without the horse tranquilizers. That's a
joke. I don't take horse tranquilizers—they'd kill me. I'm no
good at jokes."

"Michael must be around eight years old," Jessie said.

"Isn't that a coincidence?" Ellen said, raising an eyebrow.
"Show me where the boy got snatched."

"The Larsons' room is on the second floor." Jessie ushered
Ellen toward the hall.

Steph waved them down. "Hey!" She pointed at the pages
tacked up on the board. "Don't you need your notes?"

The woman in black rolled her eyes at Steph and gave the
board a quick glance, taking a mental snapshot. "Got it.
Where's this room again?"

* * *

The Larsons' room was as they'd left it. The mattress on the bed
was askew, chairs toppled over. And something Jessie hadn't
noticed before: a fine layer of grey dust on the carpet.

Ellen plopped down on the mattress and immediately
closed her eyes and held her hands out, feeling the room. An
hour ago, Jessie would have chalked up the small woman as a

charlatan, and a rather obvious one at that. Now, she stood silent beside Steph as the woman tuned her mental radio.

Ellen's eyes shot open. "I've got a bead on the kid, but...shit. If the guy with the vape hadn't vaporized, I could have used him. This is going to be tougher than I thought."

"How do you mean?" Jessie asked.

"Someone's going to have to take a dip in the pool."

"What does that even mean?" Steph asked, tapping her foot. Jessie nudged her and she stopped.

"Someone has to disconnect so they can lead the boy back."

"Disconnect?" Steph howled. "You mean die. She means *die*, Jess."

"I don't mean die, I mean...haven't you ever read *Riding the Silver Cord* by—"

"How would I lead him back?" Jessie asked, her mouth set.

Ellen stared at Jessie and clucked her tongue. "Physical contact is best...well, as physical as you can get on the spiritual plane."

"Jess, don't listen to this woman."

"So, I'd just wrap my arms around him or...what?"

"That should do the trick."

"Jess!" Steph stepped between Jessie and Ellen. "What the hell are you thinking of doing?"

Jessie gave her friend a reassuring nod. "I'll be right back."

* * *

Jessie found the white, paper Ecklund's Pharmacy bag next to the Aerobed, the bottle of Rexaphine still stapled inside.

220

She made a mental calculation, multiplying the number of pills by their strength. It should do the trick. She walked to the front desk and rummaged for the first aid kit.

The boy's words popped into her head.

"Why did you buy this motel?"

She hadn't had an answer for him then, but she did now, and it was as true as anything she'd ever known.

So I could save you, Michael.

* * *

Jessie returned to the room, the prescription bottle gripped firmly in one hand, a small white package in the other.

Steph stepped between her and Ellen. "I'm not going to let you do this."

Jessie tossed the empty bottle to her friend. "Too late."

"You've gone off the deep end, you know that?"

Jessie held out the two-pack of naloxone nasal spray. "Which is why I'm going to need someone to pull me back out."

CHAPTER 40

Sister hit the ground and was immediately on point, ears ripping from the side of her head to move forward, eyes splitting and staring in four directions, not two.

Home she had said. *Home* she had wanted. But this was not home. This was a barren field, an insult to the reunion she had in mind.

Sister screamed to the heavens and heard her brothers scream in kind. They were not far off. She'd collect them and sort this out. And then she'd sort Whisper out as well.

The smaller of her brothers limped into view, legs bending in all the wrong places. Without sustenance, he would wither and die. Best not to let that happen.

"Come, Brother. Take comfort beneath my wing." For she suddenly had a wing, formed from the shattered remains of her arm. A large, black, sweeping thing that mended itself into a protective flap.

Her brother hurried to take shelter at her side, and when she could feel his heat on her skin and smell the rot of his failing flesh, she fell on him and fed. Drinking, chewing, gnawing with one mouth, singing him to sleep with a warbling lullaby with another. Ignoring his squeals as she ate. Gaining strength in the betrayal.

The third of their now dissolved triumvirate crawled into view, sniffing the air, wary of the scent of death in the air.

"Fear not. Come and feed. You are my kin."

The creature came, bowing its cracked head low to the ground, careful not to look Sister in the eye. When it reached the fallen corpse of its companion, it buried its face deep in the obsidian gore.

It was good he fed. He could be counted on to provide food later. In a pinch.

No kill.

She felt the sting of guilt. Yes, others had killed for her, but up until now, she had refrained. Bound by the rule.

No more rules.

Sister stared off across the field at the motel a mere half mile off.

Whisper. I will make you pay for this.

CHAPTER 41

Jessie led the other two to Wood's room. It wouldn't do to have Mr. or Mrs. Larson return for some of their kid's clothes only to find their host lying on their bed, drugged to the point of death.

The Rexaphine was kicking in hard. She'd chewed the lot before swallowing. She didn't have much time.

"Your friend isn't going to let you stay out for long, so you're going to have to work quick," Ellen said.

"Give us a sec," Steph said sternly, guiding Jessie to the bathroom.

Jessie closed her eyes and stood swaying while she heard her friend turn on the faucet. Then, the feel of a cool, wet cloth on her face caused her eyes to pop open again. Steph was standing in front of her, dabbing at her brow with a damp washcloth.

"You were looking clammy," Steph said.

"I feel clammy."

"You should have let me do this for you, you idiot." Steph choked back a sob, and Jessie noticed tears rimming the woman's eyes.

"And risk losing my best friend? Not a chance."

"I'm your best friend?"

"Didn't you know that?"

"Yeah, well, I just never thought you'd fess up to it."

"Well, you are, you pain in the neck." Jessie gripped Steph's arm. "You'll bring me back?"

"If I have to kick the Devil's ass myself."

"Atta girl. Now get me to the bed, I think I'm going to—" At that, Jessie slumped, her leg muscles no longer willing to keep her vertical.

Grabbing her like she was a sack of flour, Steph hauled her up and transported her to the bed, where she flopped back.

Jessie's vision suddenly narrowed, and her mind flitted back to a childhood vacation she'd taken with her family to Florida. The beach was hot, but the breeze was cool, and she'd found a toy telescope half-buried in the sand. She had spent the better half of the morning spying on sunbathers. And when she'd turned it around and peered through the larger lens at the water, the green Atlantic receded into the distance. The motel room was withdrawing from her in much the same way.

No. I'm the one withdrawing.

"The boy's still here?" she said, begging Ellen to confirm this. "Here at the motel?"

The woman closed her eyes and raised her hands like a television psychic. The gesture might have looked comical if Jessie hadn't felt a tickle of static electricity crawl up her neck.

"Yes. He's confused. Scared and confused but definitely here."

The room was starting to dim. Jessie reached her hand out for Steph. "You've got the spray?"

"Wouldn't be much use to you if I didn't."

Ellen muscled in close and leaned into Jessie's ear.

"Jersey?"

"Jessie," Jessie mumbled, her jaw going slack.

"Find the boy, bring him back. I'll do my best to talk you through this from my end. So, I want you to listen to my voice. Concentrate on *nothing* else. Listen to me and everything is going to be okay."

"Promise?"

"I promise. I'll be with you every step of the way."

And with that, the world blinked out.

* * *

Ellen promptly left Jessie's side. She perched on the edge of the desk, pulled out the toy cow and proceeded to worry its plastic head.

Steph glared at her. "What the hell are you doing? You told her you were going to talk her through this."

The woman in black continued stroking the cow. "I already did."

CHAPTER 42

At first, Michael couldn't understand what he was seeing. The sky was dark purple and he could hear a cricket choir chirping in the distance. The last thing he remembered, it had been daytime. How was it suddenly night?

He rose from the gravel. He was in the parking lot—no question of that. And yet, something felt off. *He* felt off.

Trying to gain his bearings, he glanced up at the neon motel sign and was once again thrown for a loop. The sign should have read *Intermission Motor Lodge*. Jessie had designed it herself, and he had convinced her to put it up. It was a work of art with all its color and its cute little yes/no emoji faces.

But instead, another sign blazed garishly over his head, and it announced something quite, quite different.

The Crossroads Motel.

A quick look around told him all was not well. Gone was the renovated motel with its freshly painted walls and neatly kept parking lot. In its place sat this monstrosity, its walls the pale beige of dead flesh. There wasn't a car under twenty years old parked in the lot. In all, it was as if the Intermission had died and begun to decay.

This is the motel before the motel.

As soon as the thought came to him, he knew it to be true, and it frightened the hell out of him. How had he gotten here?

Where were his parents? And where were the others who had traveled with him to this godforsaken place?

Michael considered making a dash for the office, but if this truly *wasn't* the Intermission Motor Lodge, then he had no reason to believe he would find Jessie waiting for him behind the front desk.

There was movement to his right, and he whirled about. Standing across the lot next to a rusted-out car missing its two back wheels was a girl. Michael recognized her immediately.

It's the sketched girl. The girl from the laundry room.

The child cocked her head, her dark hair falling to one side in exaggerated puzzlement.

Michael instinctively raised his hand and the girl responded in kind. She took a tentative step forward, then another and another. Soon, she was standing an arm's length away from him, her brow furrowed, her fingers wiggling.

"¿Eres un fantasma?"

"Hi. I'm Michael."

"Michael…"

"What's your name?"

"Rosa."

Michael didn't know how to speak Spanish, but he had picked up a smattering during his time waiting with his chemo buddy, Hervé. The girl in front of him was Rosa, and Rosa was looking at him as if he were a…

The girl stepped forward, and for a second Michael thought she meant to give him a shove. Instead, she placed her hand on his chest and pressed. Wonder flooded both of their faces as her hand passed through him.

Warm! Her hand is so warm!

The thought was quickly replaced by another.

I'm a ghost.

In an odd counterpoint to this startling realization, the girl laughed. She proceeded to poke both of her hands in and out of his chest, reveling in the sensation. Her final move was to stick her face into his. When she drew back, she was laughing even harder than before.

"¡Rosa!" a voice called from one of the rooms. "Ven a la cama."

The girl rolled her eyes. "Okay, Mamá." She smiled at him and then suddenly her gaze shifted to over his head. Her smile widened even further and she clapped her hands together. "¡La vaca!"

Michael turned to see what had caught her attention. Spotlights were coming on atop the shuttered restaurant, and the plexiglass cow flickered into view, outlined by a glowing halo of light, its gaze directed down at Main Street.

Ellen...not Elmer. Her name is Ellen.

The flash of headlights erased the magical scene as a beat-up pickup truck bounced over the curb and came to a lurching stop in front of the office. Thick exhaust curled from the pickup's tailpipe. The driver—it was a man, and a big one at that—did not get out of the truck. He sat behind the wheel as if listening to something. The radio? His phone?

The girl Rosa drew to his side, and Michael saw she too was staring at the scene ahead—the cow, the driver, the pickup and its smoking tailpipe.

He felt the air ripple about him, a tingling sensation that rushed straight through him.

"Run."

It was Ellen. It was the voice of the cow. Had the girl heard it too? Had she—

"*RUN.*"

Michael took a frightened step back. He half expected the cow to turn her plexiglass head and call to him a third time, but instead the driver of the pickup chose that moment to exit his vehicle. He stepped forward, and in the glare of the pickup's headlights, Michael could see the big man held something in his hands that looked to him like a bat or a stick.

The girl's startled cry alerted him to the truth.

It was a shotgun.

CHAPTER 43

"*Oh, wow.*"

Blissful darkness surrounded Jessie, and all thoughts of anything previous to this moment melted away. In fact, she herself seemed to be melting—becoming one with the cool calm of the void. Her part in the great game of life was over now, and she breathed a sigh of relief, prepared to shed herself of every last remnant of Jessie Voss.

The next thing she knew, she was flying through the air.

Screaming brakes heralded her flight, and the squeal of rubber drowned out her landing. Jessie felt the whoosh of massive tires as they passed inches from her head. Gone was the warm numbness of the dark; in its place was a bright, sunlit world of pain.

"Jesus! I didn't even see you. Lady? Lady!"

Jessie rolled her head to the side and looked down at her prone body. Her running shoes were missing and one of her legs looked…wrong. Not only was it flashing *agony-agony-agony* but it was…wrong.

"Don't move her," said another voice.

"Put your coat under her head."

A flock of strangers circled round, staring down at her.

"Did you call 911?"

"Oh God, look at her leg."

"I think I know her."

"My boss is going to kill me!"

Go away. Let me finish my run.

"She's going into shock."

Jessie felt herself drop as the scene playing itself out above her receded. As she withdrew.

Bleep.

"I'm supposed to be doing something," she whispered to the void. "But what?"

Bleep.

A high grinding sound and the smell of burning bone jolted her awake. Two men in white flanked her leg and they were drilling—*drilling!*—a hole through her knee. Her pain hit the roof and shot into the heavens.

Bleep.

Once again, a black wave swept over her, and she begged for it to take her with it—out to sea where she could sink below the surface, to the quiet ocean floor. *In an octopus's garden in the shade...*

Bleep.

"C'mon, Hank," a woman's brusk voice boomed. "You can daydream about your golf game later."

"Holy cow! She's awake."

"You think?"

Jessie gagged on the tube snaked down her throat. Her eyes fluttered open and a rush of images poured in: a surgeon in blood-spattered green scrubs holding a devilish tool in her hand, a flock of interns staring intently, a giant red mouth where her hip should be.

"Pushing the Propofol."

232

"Thank you, Hank. Can someone please turn up my music?"

A rolling Mozart concerto filled the room as Jessie slipped back into the darkness.

Bleep.

"That's enough," Jessie thought, willing the night to return. "That's enough."

Bleep.

Reluctantly, she opened her eyes. Donovan was fast asleep in the chair next to her bed, a People magazine draped across his chest.

A woman was leaning over her. A nurse, no doubt. Though why would a nurse be wearing black?

Ellen?

She placed a pair of headphones over Jessie's ears. Jessie tried to speak, but she was finding it harder to breath. It felt as if someone had placed a stone on her chest. No longer able to focus her eyes on the woman in black, she closed them.

A man's voice whispered in her ears.

"*Q&D Audio Presents…*Messages from Beyond, *by Ellen Marx. Read by Peter Lar—*"

"Come on, Ellen. Get to Track 21."

The audio jumped forward.

"*Afterword.*"

She knew that voice.

"*If you have read this far, perhaps you will journey a bit farther.*"

It was Michael's father narrating Ellen's words.

"*Imagine if you would that you yourself were one of the dead.*"

The weight on her chest increased, and Jessie began to panic. She tried to open her eyes—she could not. She tried to grab for the call button—she could not. All strength was abandoning her at a rapid pace.

And still, the calm voice went on.

"Imagine yourself at the moment of your passing. Feel the darkness creeping in, see the world dim."

Jessie didn't have to imagine anything. She was experiencing it all and it was terrifying.

"When people ask me, 'Ellen, what's it like when you die?' I give them one of two answers. If they come to the question with a flip attitude, I reply, 'It's like you're dead. Next question.'"

Unlike the times before when she had played with the thought of giving herself over to the blackness, now Jessie fought back. She didn't want to go, didn't want to be numb. Pain? Screw it. Fear? Screw it twice. She wasn't ready. Not yet. There was something she still had to do. Something she…

Michael.

She wasn't at the motel. She was supposed to be at the motel. And the moment she was living—*reliving*—had already come and gone. The boy was drifting two years of tomorrows in the future. Her overdose was in vain!

Jessie's heart seized…

"But if I sense they truly want to know, I tell them, 'It's like stepping from one side of the room to another. Nothing to be afraid about. Just as simple as that.'"

…and her breath caught in her throat.

Blee-ee-ee-ee…

With that, Jessie rose, crossed the room and stood at the foot of her bed. She watched as the zigzag of her heartbeat flattened out. The monitor adopted a single, warning tone. Soon after, a red light flashed on the wall and a new, more alarming tone sounded, alerting the staff, bringing a nurse into the room and rousing Donovan from his nap.

"Jess?"

She watched as all manner of people made a fuss over her lifeless body.

"I died in the hospital," she'd told the boy. And now here she was, spectator to the actual event. What would happen when they revived her? Would she be back at Donovan's side? Back to rehab? The long, slow struggle to learn how to walk again, to drive past a semi without flinching, to re-wage her war against the goddamn Rexaphine?

No.

If she stayed here, woke here, the boy was lost.

That means staying is not an option.

She headed for the door, past the crash team and down the hall.

"If you've got *anything* to tell me, Ellen Marx, you best get talking!"

Peter Larson's voice was back in her ear.

"If you can handle life, you can handle death. So, as I lay out these, my final thoughts on the matter, just know I'll be with you every step of the way."

CHAPTER 44

Butch Long made his move. It was time to get this party started. And then he could claim his reward.

He reached for the office door and paused. Something was niggling at the back of his brain and he had learned not to ignore such whispers.

Looking about the landscape, he saw he had two, no…three witnesses. One was a stringy-haired stoner peering at him from the pool. The other two were children.

What were children doing out at this hour? Didn't their parents know what targets they made, standing in the middle of the parking lot?

Abandoning the office, he moved toward them. The children cowered at his approach but did not run, which surprised Butch. And it gave rise to a single question.

Are you seriously *thinking about killing children?*

Like the first cracks in a frozen river, the question sent fractures through his brain, breaking his concentration and unsteadying his course.

Hell, no. I wouldn't hurt a fly. I wouldn't—

A lightning strike of pain shot through his head and his stomach turned on itself. The hunger planted there by that devil Wood—*oh, the promises the man made*—was beginning to open. It was a ravenous thing, this need, and it swallowed up any sympathy the sight of the two children had brought to the fore. It gobbled up his will, ordering him to level the shotgun at the boy.

No!

The child stepped in front of his companion and Butch's mind glitched. He could see the girl *through* the boy, her face frozen in terror. *Through* him.

Grammy Long was a God-fearing woman, and many were the nights she had tried to steer him toward the path of righteousness. One of her prime weapons in this regard was her firm belief in life in the hereafter.

"You don't want to end up a banished spirit, do you Butchie? Wandering the earth bereft of the company of our Lord?"

That's what the boy was, wasn't he? One of Grammy's banished spirits.

But the girl? She was a different story. The same was true for the man gawking at him now from the office, the young guy crawling from the pool. He'd make them all spirits. At least that's what the hunger told him, for it had begun to rise again, whispering to him to get it over with and find relief.

The urge to raise the gun was strong, but he resisted. The weapon trembled in his grip, and yet he refused.

Butcher, they'll call me in the papers. The Butcher of Maple City.

"No."

The gun begged him to let it do its job.

"No!"

* * *

Michael saw the man's hesitation and chose to take advantage of it.

He leaned into the girl's ear and said in a low voice, "Run across the street to the McDonald's. Look both ways but *don't* look back."

The girl glanced at him, giving away their secrecy.

"¿Qué?"

"McDonald's!" Michael urged, pointing at the golden arches.

"What are you whispering about?" the man with the gun snarled.

"Go!" Michael shouted. At the same time, he made a dash toward the man's left, away from the girl. The girl obeyed, dodging right and past the man.

Michael ensured he, not the girl, remained the man's primary focus. He raised his arms, giving his best impression of a ghost. "Ooooo!" He felt silly doing it, but it seemed to work. The fat man was taken aback, and for a moment Michael thought he might drop the shotgun and turn tail. But an ill-timed cry from the pool area made certain that was not to be.

"Get outta here, asshat!" the wiry guy in the swim trunks shouted.

The man whirled about and fired in the direction of the voice. The shot went wide, taking out the pool rules sign instead. Startled, the lanky teen dove back into the pool.

The night clerk stepped from the office just in time to notice the shooter noticing him. Michael couldn't hear what the man said, but it must have been a curse word with the vehemence with which the man shouted it. Instead of ducking back into the office, the man simply took off, running toward the highway as fast as he could, disappearing into the night.

Now, lights along the rows of rooms started to flicker on. A woman in a neon-yellow t-shirt exited her room. "¡Rosa!"

No!

Michael shot a glance at the street and his heart sank as he saw the young girl pause midway across, pivoting on the center line.

"Run!" he shouted, hoping the fear in his voice could trump her mother's command.

No such luck. The girl let a motorcycle pass and then retraced her steps back across the street toward the motel's parking lot, her path leading right toward the man with the gun.

"¡Mamá!"

There was only one thing to do. Take the man on himself.

Michael rushed the hulking figure and took a flying leap. Remembering how the girl's hands had slid right through him, it was his hope this move would disorient the man, at least long enough for the girl to run to the safety of her mother's arms.

Instead, when he jumped the fat man, he stuck—not *to* the man, but *in* him. Michael felt a pull like the draw of a magnet and he slipped fully inside the man's body.

At first, all was silent. Then, he heard the beating of the man's heart and the rasp of his rapid breaths. All he could see was dark muscle and sinew floating before his eyes and so he screamed at himself, "Open your eyes!"

That did the trick. He found himself staring straight at the approaching girl, saw he was raising the shotgun...no, the man was raising it with his beefy, hairy arms.

"Drop it!" Michael commanded, and the man's hands obeyed. The shotgun fell to the ground with a thunk. Just in time—the girl dashed past him, not even bothering to look up as she made a beeline for her mom.

"Kneel!" he ordered, and the man struggled to his knees. Michael felt the bite of the gravel through the thin fabric of the man's pants, but he didn't mind. He was in control.

This is better than a videogame.

But then he felt it. He wasn't the only one in here besides the panicking man. There was something else. Something dark and squirming. Something *hungry*. And its hunger was infectious, because it was now *his* hunger as well. The urge to lean forward and grab the gun was powerful; the rotten nastiness of the blackness was almost too much to bear.

"Michael."

At first he thought it was the hunger saying his name, appointing him as its next meal. But then the voice spoke again.

"Michael."

Hope rose inside him and he let go of the fat man, running from the darkness, clinging to a solitary word.

"Dad!"

He burst forth from the fat man's chest and landed before a pair of feet. Slowly, he looked up.

Before him, bathed in the neon glow of the motel's sign, stood the man who looked like his father—and he seemed to be having a terrible time keeping it that way. His face molded and unmolded the likeness of Peter Larson, holding and breaking. Half the time, rather than a face, there was nothing above his shoulders but a swirl of black smoke and gnashing teeth. But then, his father's image would return and it was this face that spoke.

"Get behind me."

As odd as the scene was, Michael had kept a grasp on the rules of this scene. Rules were what made it possible for a kid like him to play *Chompmaster II,* and he was pretty darned sure the rules said fatso here couldn't hurt him. Guns and ghosts didn't mix.

Still, he obeyed his Dad/Not-Dad and slipped behind him. As he did so, the fat man took hold of the shotgun. He planted the butt in the gravel and used it to hoist himself up. His eyes blazed at the newcomer, the intruder.

"I won't let you touch him," the man with the shifting face said.

The man with the shotgun trained it on the other man's head. "Oh, no? We'll see about that."

"I wasn't talking to you."

Two blackened hands gripped the shooter's shoulders from behind. Then a third and a fourth. The sound of tight, charred skin cracking rose behind him as Sister grew larger, shifting black sheets of hardened skin to make room for more muscle, more meat. Ripping herself apart only to mend into a larger, more twisted version of herself.

Coming around to her side slunk another of her kind, and he had fashioned himself multiple mouths. Claws sprouted from every limb—some curved, some hooked, some barbed, some needle-straight.

Sister held the man with the gun close against her belly, nails biting into flesh, as she spoke directly to the man protecting Michael.

"Speak, Whisper. Did you really think you could hide from me?"

CHAPTER 45

Glancing at the clock on the wall as she passed the nurses station, Jessie saw it was just after midnight. The hospital was busy for this time of night.

As she rounded the corner, taking a shortcut through the emergency room, she saw why. Doctors and nurses busied themselves over half a dozen patients, some in neck braces, some moaning in pain. A policeman speaking to a young woman gave Jessie her answer.

"Did your husband mention seeing the driver leave the scene?"

A multiple car pileup. All these people now related in pain. *This* is why she hated hospitals. It was the sheer sorrow of the place. No one in a hospital was there for a good time—every day at the ER was someone's worst. Hers certainly had been.

As she headed for the exit, an elderly man waved her down. "Excuse me."

Knowing she moved unseen through this crowd of suffering people, she kept on moving. But as she passed, the old man reached out and grabbed her.

"Miss, please, excuse me."

Startled, Jessie stopped.

The man looked down and Jessie followed his gaze to a gurney. Wrapped in blood-soaked sheets was the man himself, wide-eyed and still.

"I don't understand," the man said.

Jessie's fought back the urge to tell him *that makes two of us* and instead put her hand on the man's arm. "I'm sure everything is going to be fine."

A doctor who looked no older than a high school senior stepped up to the gurney with a nurse, a clipboard in hand.

"I'm calling it. 12:05 am."

"12:05 am," the nurse repeated with a yawn. "June 4th…"

"5th," the doctor corrected. "It's after midnight, Sue. Sheesh, when was the last time you slept?"

"I honestly can't remember."

"Calling it? What does that mean?" the old man asked Jessie.

Peter Larson's voice piped up again, seeming to suggest an answer with Ellen Marx's words.

"You're screwed."

Jessie smiled at the old man and kept moving.

"That's what you may think at the moment of your death. But nothing could be further from the truth."

She sidestepped another gurney, this one carrying a man she recognized as Bert Endicott, her old mail carrier. From the look of his mangled lower half, Bert had delivered his last letter.

Jessie slipped out the door and into the warm night air. She shivered, suddenly realizing how cold she was. Her eyes lit upon the barely visible Big Dipper, and that slight bit of normality gave her strength.

Jessie's mind snapped alert.

June 5th.

The day of the shooting at the Crossroads Motel.

"*But it's no coincidence you are where you find yourself. Einstein said, 'Coincidence is God's way of remaining anonymous.' Well, actually he didn't, and no amount of stupid internet memes can make it so. But the sentiment is true nonetheless. Wherever you find yourself, you can rest assured you are there for a reason. And that's a lot, coming from a dyed-in-the-wool cynic like myself.*"

Six blocks to the motel. Six blocks and she'd know if crazy Ellen knew what the hell she was talking about.

* * *

Leaving the hospital proved harder than Jessie thought. The pull to remain close to her body was powerful, and it took tremendous effort to sever the tie. But once she set her sights firmly on the motel, each step became easier than the last until she was practically floating down the street.

Shit. I may actually be *floating.*

As she passed an old two-story house with a sagging porch roof, she was caught off guard by the appearance of a skeletal woman in a ratty bathrobe clutching a cigarette.

"Ree-ee! Get away! I din't do nothin'! Ee-ee!" screamed the woman through rotten teeth. Jessie moved along, but not before seeing that the woman's neck was twisted and black. "Ree-ee!"

She spotted two more such shadow people on her trip to Main Street. One was a weeping man in overalls who sat at the side of the road, an empty dog's leash in his hands. He barely stirred as she moved past. The second was a stern-looking young woman who glared at her as if *she* were the cause of the

245

woman's problems. Jessie simply ducked her head as she passed and whispered, "I'm sorry." Hoping that would keep the angry woman at bay.

Before her lay Main Street and the ramshackle motel she had put months of work into resurrecting. It looked like her motor lodge gone bad—as if a place could go to rot the same as the flesh.

She was just about to cross the street when a gunshot rang out.

"Death is just the beginning of a greater journey."

Jessie rushed across Main Street, midnight traffic passing through her like rain through a screen.

* * *

Steph unboxed the first of the nasal sprays and leaned in over Jessie's inert body.

"Not yet," Ellen warned, her eyes still closed, her thumb working overtime on the cow's head.

"I'm not waiting until she's a vegetable!"

"Not...yet."

CHAPTER 46

Michael gawked at the monstrosity before him, distorted and horrible in the parking lot lights. As before in the laundry room, to look at it directly brought terrible discomfort, and so he kept his head turned and eyeballed it sideways.

The man standing between him and the thing clutching the shooter momentarily lost all coherence, breaking into a chittering rush of black tendrils and smoke. With audible effort, his protector returned, taking control of his appearance so that he once more stood on two legs.

When the man finally spoke, it was with two separate, dissonant voices—his father's mixed with a guttural growl. "Leave."

Sister drew the man with the gun closer, setting her sharp chin on the crown of his head.

"Yes. We will leave. You will take us. Or we will take the boy. Take and eat."

Her skulking companion laughed at this, a dry rattling chuckle, and coughed a rough approximation of the word *eat*.

It was a standoff. Michael had experienced a similar scenario playing videogames with friends, and he was smart enough to recognize he and the man were being outflanked. As the creature holding the gunman stood her ground, the other was slowly making its way to their side. Soon, they'd be out of moves.

The commotion had drawn an audience of motel patrons, and Michael instantly feared for their wellbeing. He knew the term for these people in this type of situation: collateral damage. It came with the territory in videogames, but in real life it was horrifying.

He had to break the stalemate. And there was only one way he knew how.

Michael stepped from behind the man with the shifting face and addressed the smaller creature directly. "You hungry? You wanna eat? Well, come and get it!" He waved his translucent arms enticingly.

The effect on the smaller nightmare was instantaneous. Its jaw involuntarily cracked open wide, splitting its cheeks, tearing gristle. Michael and his father had once watched a nature program where a kingsnake unhinged its jaw to swallow an egg. That was bad—this was way worse.

The thing holding the gunman shrieked. "Back!"

But it was too late. Its gnashing companion was ravenous.

It happened in a rush. Michael bolted to the left, away from the row of motel rooms, away from the standoff, toward an outcropping of brambles at the motel's side—a cluster of garbage bins, discarded furniture and trash. Eager to reach the cover of the mess, Michael didn't even look back when he heard the sound of a shotgun blast.

* * *

Sister screamed for her companion to stop, but if his hunger was one hundredth the strength of her own, she knew her cries were in vain.

Seething, she turned back to the man in front of her. The figure was an impure mix—man bound to mist, Whisper intertwined with another—the two knitted together into one abomination.

Two could play at that game.

She set her multitude of fingertips on Butch's temple and willed her nails to *grow*. They complied, diving deep into the man's skull, seeking the warm, moistness of the grey, curling thought factory within. Killing the living was not allowed her, but anything up to that point was wide open, as was the now babbling gunman's mind.

She willed him to step forward, puppeteering him toward the man before her. The effort ripped her upper half free from her body, leaving her torso and legs behind to dance and die in a wreckage of bones and dust. She speared the man's spine with hers, clamping tight to his nerves.

Sister knew her new appearance must be gloriously abhorrent—riding astride the stumbling fat man—for the man before her retreated, unsure whether to pursue the boy or abandon the scene. She sensed an inner struggle, an impression borne out by the man's heated battle with himself.

"*Run!*"

"No!"

"*Fly!*"

"NO!"

A child's scream punctuated the scene, and Sister let loose a peal of laughter. Brother had taken his sup. Good. He would return to her with a full belly, and she would feed on him. She would return home strong and worthy...*if* she could secure passage.

Reaching forward with a sudden wealth of crab-like arms, she grasped the figure before her, capturing him as well as his attention. *Their* attention.

She drew the man close, limbs shattering and mending as she pulled him near. She raised the fat man's arms and thus the fat man's shotgun, placing the barrel beneath the other's chin.

"Home," she snarled, insisting with both her voice and Butch's.

Her prisoner wrestled to be free of her grip, agreeing and disagreeing to her demand at the same time. No matter. If she had to strip Whisper from his man, so be it. She pressed her cracked and oozing forehead to the man's skull and felt Whisper squirm beneath the surface.

"I see you," she crooned.

She was just about to dive her mind into his when the shotgun in Butch's hands went off, stunning her with its concussive blast.

"Get...off...of...me."

Sister felt Butch strain against her, felt him yearn to bring the gun to her head. Or his own.

* * *

As soon as Jessie reached the motel parking lot, she knew she was right where Ellen had meant her to be. A fact the strange woman's words seemed to confirm.

"Once you've resigned yourself to your lot in life (or in death, as the case would have it) you should see clearly where your next steps will take you. Could be toward the light; could be toward the dark."

Before her, darting in and out of shadow, was a struggle she couldn't quite get her mind around. Two mind-twisting figures were engaged in a heated skirmish. But she saw the scene as if through broken glass—at times there were two, then there were more.

Could be toward the light...

She scanned the grounds, looking in vain for any sign of the boy.

...could be toward the dark.

Her eyes lit upon a corner of the lot devoid of light and there she spied movement. Without a moment's hesitation, she broke for the spot, riding on instinct more than brains.

Because if I had even half a brain, I wouldn't be here. Wouldn't have taken those pills. Wouldn't have—

A twisted creature leapt from the shadows and planted itself squarely in her path. The thing was black and shiny, with hard-shell skin like a charred lobster. It stood snarling on all fours, angry at her intrusion. It lurched forward and she heard it snap and cry, as if every step pained it. Another step, another yelp—its accusing eyes blood-red, boring into her with carnivorous intent.

Behind the thing, a small shape popped up from behind a tangled pile of ruined pool furniture. It separated itself from its surroundings by giving off a soft, shimmering glow.

Michael!

The two locked eyes for a second as Ellen's words kicked back in, full volume.

"Once you have chosen to follow the path before for you, you will find—"

"I got it. Now shut the hell up!"

The voice in her head went silent. The thing rushed forward. And Jessie was there to meet it.

She heard the boy cry her name before the clatter of the beast's approach drowned him out. With splayed hands adorned with scores of claws, the creature pounced, barreling her over like the semi on the highway.

Jessie squeezed her eyes tight as the thing bore down on her and took its first bite.

CHAPTER 47

Peter took advantage of the struggle taking place before him to solidify his hold on reality. The demon to which he was bound wanted to run, *begged* to run, promising to shred his mind should he try to stop it.

It was the same brutal tug of war they'd waged since they'd become one, and the whole was threatening to shatter into fractions. And what would happen if it did? Peter imagined a fragmented hard drive, damaged beyond repair, eating up all its data. Garbling sound files, pixelating photos, upending carefully stored documents. In human terms, that meant the scattering of memories, all sense of himself, everything that was Peter Larson ground up and spat into the void.

Then what would become of his son? He corrected himself...what would become of Michael, the son of another Peter? Not his and yet so dear—in some ways even more so since *his* Michael was gone. Along with *his* Hannah and *his* life.

Gone.

His sorrow brought strength—the demon's days of calling the shots were over.

Concentrating all his being on the ground on which he stood, rooting himself in *this* moment, he wrestled control back from Whisper.

The response was immediate and furious.

"No! Go now! I rip!"

"Go on, do it! Rip. Rip all you want! Do what you're going to do or shut your trap."

"*I DO!*"

Peter felt the mental talons dig deep, slicing through the core of who he was. This was no idle threat—the demon meant to do it. No matter the consequences, it was prepared to tear itself free.

The outside world moved around him like an idea detached, untethered from anything of meaning. And yet, in it lived the only thing that had meaning. The boy in the brambles fighting for his very soul.

Peter turned inward and, with a ferocious abandon, sank his own angry talons into Whisper's mind.

As a child, he had once stuck a fork into an outlet at school. The resounding shock he received was but a gentle kiss compared to the jolt he received from the dark thing's head.

"*Mr. Tell gathers secrets! Whispers to her! To her, to her, for her alone!*"

The voice in his mind skittered along, howling with grief, as the claws in his brain cut deep in retaliation.

"*Gone, gone, gone, you, you, YOU!*"

The word caught in Peter's head.

Gone.

He seized on the dark thing's anguish and did something he hadn't before. He sought to soothe it.

"Stop fighting me and I'll help you. Let me take the wheel for five fucking minutes and you can have all of eternity."

"*Help? No!*"

"Yes."

With that, he dropped all defenses, relinquished all control. For the first time since their fateful melding, Peter was totally unguarded.

The demon at his side went silent.

"You see how it can be if I give up? Do you feel the peace?"

A single talon burrowed even deeper, striking alarmingly close to the nexus of all things Hannah, but Peter dared not flinch. Instead, he simply repeated his request.

"Five minutes. Let me be myself again for five minutes."

Dangling in the nothingness, his mind skewered like bait on a hook, Peter feared the answer would be ruin. Not only for him but for the boy.

The demon spoke so soft and low he almost didn't hear its response.

"*Two.*"

Peter nodded.

Focusing his concentration, Peter willed himself to become flesh. He felt no resistance from his companion—the truce was holding.

His heart came to life and blood rushed in his ears. Peter inhaled and stepped forward, feeling the sheer weight of being human once more. He made twin fists, knuckles cracking.

Two minutes.

Two would have to do.

CHAPTER 48

Jessie fought back, pummeling the beast that pressed her to the ground. But she knew her blows were in vain. Each time she struck the foul creature, her hands passed through it as if through brackish water.

The creature did not have this problem—it tore at her greedily with hands, teeth and claws. There was no physical pain. What the thing was inflicting was far worse. With each swipe, each bite, a searing sorrow raced through her entire being and she felt herself diminished.

Pain, she could endure, *had* endured, but the thing wasn't eating her body; it was devouring her soul.

Jessie tried to drag herself free but her hands could find no purchase. Soon she would be gone, erased, and the thought of it brought forth another screaming stab of grief, causing her to cry out in anguish. It was a woe so great, she thought it would consume her entirely, leaving the creature to starve.

She could hear Michael shouting at the thing to stop, but his voice came to her as if from across a long hall—muffled and incomprehensible. The boy should run. Leave her to her fate and run. She tried to tell him as much but found her strength was waning. Soon to be gone altogether.

She jolted at the sound of the child's laughter exploding in the air, and it wrenched her back into the world. When she opened her eyes she found the boy standing dangerously close, pointing at her tormentor and laughing his ass off.

"Look at you, you ugly puke! You puke stain! What a disgusting turd you are."

The beast snarled and clutched Jessie even tighter.

"You know what you look like to me, puke?" The boy launched into a taunting singsong, hopping up and down, fighting to lure the thing away. "Great green gobs of grimy greasy gopher guts, chopped up turtle feet, mutilated monkey meat."

The child's mocking unfortunately did the trick—the snapping monstrosity let go of Jessie and made a menacing advance. Jessie locked eyes with the boy, and absent her voice, she tried to warn him off with her eyes.

No, Michael!

The boy caught her meaning, knew she wanted him to run, but he stood firm, launching back into it, shouting into the ever-widening maw of the dark beast.

"Fifteen eyeballs rolling down the bowling alley and I forgot my spoon!"

New teeth sprouted in the thing's mouth, bursting through its inky black gums. Fresh teeth for a fresh kill. It turned its head, its neck bones splintering as it lined up for the attack.

She'd failed. She could barely think, let alone rise and protect the boy. She'd *failed*.

"*Jessie?*"

Her mind shifted into split-screen. She was watching the horror show before her while at the same time trying to focus in on a face only inches away.

"*I'm gonna give her another blast.*"

257

Jessie's heart sank as the situation became suddenly clear. They were bringing her back.

Don't do it, Steph. Not now!

The boy had well and truly hooked the beast, and it ripped open its side to accommodate more hungry mouths.

"Michael, listen to me," Jessie whispered. "I want you to very calmly move toward me."

Michael shook his head.

The thing snarled, unhappy with their communication. Still, Jessie had to risk it. She slowly held out her hand.

"I need you to take my hand. Can you do that? I need you to take my hand so I can bring you back."

The creature lunged first toward Michael, then back toward Jessie, torn between leaving a sure meal behind but tempted—oh, so tempted—by the delicious child before it.

"You come on back now, Jess. You hear?"

Time was up. Time to move.

The thing took another stutter-step forward, seeming to see Michael as the tastier of the two of them.

"Give me your hand! Now!"

The boy stood paralyzed with indecision.

"We're friends, aren't we? Trust me!"

At this, Michael bolted. A split second later, the creature did as well. The boy raced his heart out, running for Jessie like a baseball player heading for home. The dark thing made a grab for him and Michael ducked, his momentum sending him tumbling in Jessie's direction.

The beast yowled, angered at the boy's escape, and spun about in pursuit.

Michael scrambled toward Jessie.

"Come back!"

A wave of dizziness swept over Jessie, but the boy was almost to her now. She held out her hand praying to catch his hand, praying for Steph to hit her again with the naloxone spray, praying for Ellen's plan to work.

Michael made a mad leap toward her and his fingers brushed hers.

"Got you!"

And then, just like that, his fingers slipped out of reach and he tumbled to the ground at her feet.

"Michael!"

The boy looked back and she saw the creature's approach in his face.

Jessie clenched her fist. She placed all her thoughts, all her fears into her balled-up hand, making it the center of everything she had been and would ever be. The entire world disappeared, leaving behind nothing but her *fist*.

As the creature rushed past, Jessie swung back hard against one of the creature's many legs and felt her fist connect, felt bone crack. The thing shrieked in pain, spitting teeth and black spittle into the night sky. It whirled on her, its eyes swollen red.

"No!" the boy cried.

Jessie grinned at the thing and the thing grinned back.

Then…it pounced.

* * *

"Come on!"

Steph pumped the remains of the second nasal spray up Jessie's nose, willing the chemicals to do their job. And still her friend lay grey and still on the bed.

259

"You made me wait too long," she hissed.

Ellen ignored her, her eyes still closed, her thumb growing red from circling the cow's head.

"Do something."

"I am."

Steph stalked up to the concentrating woman. "Bring her back."

"Shut up, will you please? Shut up, just shut up!"

Steph grabbed Ellen by her black top, ripping the fabric. "Listen, you creepy little shit! You're going to bring her back or I'm going to send you where she is, you hear me?"

"Don't touch me!"

"Do you hear me?"

Behind them on the bed, Jessie suddenly took an enormous breath and all hell broke loose.

A dark, malignant stain spread across Jessie's sprawled body and through the blackness a wriggling, howling outrage was birthed, all jaws and ribs and nails. It landed on the bed next to her, a row of teeth still embedded in Jessie's thigh.

Jessie broke free from the thing, its teeth shattering like icicles. She rolled to the side of the bed and off, landing hard on the floor.

Ellen slipped out of Steph's grip and rushed to the bed. She raised a hand over the thing and began spouting an ancient language. Either that or she was speaking nonsense, Jessie thought, but she really wasn't in a position to analyze. She was cold and quaking and drugged to the gills.

The creature retreated from the woman in black, fearful of her words, fearful at being torn from its family. It grew weak in the separation, and each phrase the woman uttered was like a lash. It cowered beneath her incantations.

A horrid heat rose up its gullet, scorching its innards, boiling away its blood and bile. One eye popped, then the other. Blind and terrified, it worked its ruined jaw one last time as it forced a final cry for help.

"*Sis-ss-ster!*"

Then, it flew apart in a defiant swirl of ebony ash and was gone.

Steph scrambled over to Jessie and knelt by her side. "Are you back? Are you breathing? Talk to me."

"Lemme get a word in edgewise," Jessie croaked.

Steph wrapped her arms around her friend and hugged her tight.

Jessie gagged. "Toilet."

"Roger that."

Steph hoisted Jessie up and guided her toward the bathroom.

"I had him but I couldn't save him," Jessie said between labored breaths. "I tried, but I couldn't—"

"Easy, Jess."

"I *had* him, Steph. I could have pulled him out."

"If you could have, you would have."

"You did enough," Ellen said, slipping the cow into her pocket.

"Care to enlighten us, Spooky?" Steph asked.

Ellen didn't answer. Instead, she made a quick about-face and headed for the door.

"Where do you think you're going?" Steph asked.

The woman waved her off. "The kid isn't out of the woods yet, and you two are *way* too distracting."

"After what she's been through, my friend deserves a goddamn answer."

Ellen paused. "You did good," she said to Jessie. "But this isn't the path I thought we were going down. I'm going to have to improvise." With that, she unceremoniously opened the door and slipped outside.

Steph eased Jessie to the bathroom floor and pulled back her hair. "Honey, you've got a stomach full of poison and you gotta get that out of you."

"I'm trying, but…" Jessie strained until she coughed.

Her friend grimaced. "Don't say I never did anything for you."

She deftly slipped two fingers down Jessie's throat, eliciting a gush of Rexaphine-tainted spew.

* * *

Ellen raced down the stairs, taking two at a time until she reached the parking lot. Her heart pounded in her chest, upset at the unaccustomed effort.

"Come on, Ellen," she said, urging herself on. "Step to it."

She crossed to the office and threw open the door. A dead man stared at her, ogle-eyed from behind the desk as she passed, but she had no time for him. She had no time for any of them, the audience of the dead that had been watching her from the moment she arrived at this place.

The boy. The boy was all that mattered.

She hoofed it down the hallway to the cool of the restaurant space. She swept past her open portfolio and its years of collected notes and calculations. No more need for them now. Time to put up or shut up.

The plexiglass steer was waiting for her as it always had been. The toy was good in a pinch, but in the homestretch, she needed the real deal.

Pausing before the statue, she stared into its eyes which, to her mind, didn't look dull at all.

"I'm sorry," said a low voice, and for a moment Ellen thought the Angus had spoken.

She allowed herself a glance to where Wood now stood next to his empty, ashen clothes. He was changed in death and not for the better. He had a hollow aspect and a Stygian stench about him. Ellen had no doubt he was sorry. So many of the dead were sorry.

But that was none of her concern.

"If you're going to stay, then be quiet."

Ellen reached out and touched the cow's head.

She was six years old when she first realized she was sensitive. She was seven when she spoke to her first ghost. In the years that followed, she had experienced all manner of strange and wondrous things. But never had she seen or heard anything that caused her more than the slightest discomfort.

What she felt when she touched the cow's head was a fear so great it nearly brought her to her knees.

"Oh, God..." she gasped.

Tears poured down her face, and for the first time in her life, Ellen Marx wanted to run.

CHAPTER 49

Jessie's scream ripped through Michael's head and then she was gone. So was the creature that was savaging her. Both of them...gone.

Michael scrambled to his feet and rushed to the spot where Jessie had lain, taking the brunt of the brutal attack meant for him. Was she dead? Did the demon swallow her up? And itself as well? No answers came, only the sinking realization he was alone.

A commotion to his left belied that notion, for there, not fifty feet away, stood two figures squaring off. One was the shadow version of his father; the other was a horrible mix of man and nightmare. A black and rotting corpse of a creature riding piggyback atop the man with the gun.

The air had gone ice cold and the neon sign was having a hard time retaining its glow. It sputtered loudly like an enormous 4th of July sparkler, sections popping and blinking out entirely.

As Michael watched, the gunman brought the shotgun up to the thing on his back's chin. There was a bright flash and a loud report, and the demon's head snapped back, bits of bone scattering like dandelion seeds on the wind.

The thing screamed, and Michael felt its anger pierce his chest.

The blast brought still more guests running from their rooms. A shirtless young man was first, followed by Rosa's father. A woman wrapped in a towel stuck her head out her door and shouted, "Jesus, is someone shot?"

Grabbing at the air, the black monstrosity fell backward, dragging the gunman with it. They landed together, hard, the fall shattering the thing's spine and knocking the wind out of the man.

Michael took a step forward.

"Stay where you are!" shouted the shadow man, holding his hand out, traffic cop-style.

Michael put on the brakes and watched as the man with his father's face slowly approached the fallen pair.

"¿Papá?"

Horrified, Michael turned to see the diminutive Rosa rush to her father's side.

No! Get back inside!

* * *

The shotgun pellets had passed through Sister's head, ripping free the delicate, meaty network of thought.

No matter. She ground her teeth together, breaking some of them loose as she willed her body to rebuild. Muscle, bone and sinew—they were the painful consequence of forcing herself into the world. It was much easier to remain ethereal, to ride like breath on the air, but she had come to want more. To feel more, to *taste* more. More brought anguish and heartache and *PAIN*. And so, she endured the torment of her knitting tissues and her splitting skin. Endured them in order to *BE*.

She sank spiny fingers deep into the fat man's temples and he let out a surprised *ahh!* His eyes glazed over and his mouth went slack.

Her fingertips found the moist center of the man's mind and exploded in all directions, tiny bones branching out, exploring, eviscerating, lobotomizing. She felt the man's spirit untether from his body, and as it rose, she gulped it down greedily, taking pleasure as he streamed screaming into her gut.

Killing was forbidden, but now she had killed. And it felt so very *tasty.*

But his soul did not satisfy her. Withered and shrunk by his years at the bottle, her belly still roared after swallowing the man's spirit whole. She needed more. Without it, she was no match for Whisper.

No longer fettered by the fat man's resistance, she plunged herself into his pale, lifeless body. Her black blood poured through his veins and her eyes grew in his head, pushing out those he no longer had use for. With much agony and effort, she dove into the man's corpse—arms into arms, legs into legs. Charred ribs ripped into place, grey intestines devoured pink. She chewed her way from the back of his head to front until her battlefield of teeth poked from behind his torn and bloody lips.

Sister gripped the shotgun and rifled through the man's head, lighting upon the word *reload* and the means by which to accomplish this. How funny and small these meat men were! She let her borrowed hands do the work and then she rose on new legs, reveling in her horrible resplendence, knowing she would never bow down again.

* * *

266

As the thing rose before him, Peter felt Whisper's horror rise within him, but he held firm.

"Stay!"

Whisper didn't reply but receded to the back of his mind, shivering and angry and counting the seconds.

Peter stared up at the grotesque and growing thing, for it had added two to three feet to its height, straining the limits of dead Butch's body. He could hear cartilage pop and bones groan.

He took a step forward.

"What do you want of Whisper?"

The thing wrinkled its brow, splitting its forehead. "Not you. I speak to him."

"He's not here right now. Can I take a message?"

"Lie!"

An arm shot out and a swiftly lengthening finger pointed accusingly at Peter's head.

"In there. I see him."

"Lemme ask again. What do you want?"

The thing seemed on the verge of actually answering when it jerked its head around, eyes wide and focused behind Peter. He chanced a look and caught a streak of movement pass by, heading for the motel rooms.

Michael, what the hell are you doing?

The creature's gullet spasmed and it licked Butch's chops. "Eat," it snarled.

For a moment, Peter was transported back to their Manhattan apartment watching *Jaws* with Michael over a bowl of popcorn. For a month after, the boy had wakened screaming.

The thing before him was a shark, and Michael was the blood in the water.

Driven by the insanity of its hunger, the creature moved to pursue the boy.

Peter stepped in its path.

"Hey! I was talking to you..."

Without pausing, Sister raised Butch's arm as she passed, unleashing a flash of fire and shot, and Peter's chest exploded in a fountain of red.

CHAPTER 50

The gunshot startled Michael and he skidded to a stop.

He's not Dad. He might look like Dad, but he's not *Dad.*

Still, Michael screamed when he saw the man fall.

Unfortunately, Rosa screamed in kind, drawing the attention of the thing with the gun. It lurched forward on tortured legs.

As before, the little girl made a run for it, and Michael *knew* where this would end. Rosa trapped in the dryer, a gun blast echoing through the laundry room.

Because that's what happened before...

When he had first encountered the girl, she was a ghost. And if he didn't do something quick, she would be again.

The girl's father called after her, but the girl didn't stop. She ran on, escaping the scene, hands clasped over her ears.

Michael lit out after her. He had to divert her—but how?

You're a ghost.

The thought came to him as a flash of brilliance and as a surprise. He was a ghost. A ghost meant *dead.* Dead hadn't well and truly sunk into his mind until this point, and its repercussions were grave. He was a ghost—he was dead. Somewhere Mom and Dad were grieving over his body. *Mom and Dad!* He'd never see them again, and the weight of this ignited every emotion in the book—sorrow, confusion, fear.

But most of all he felt utterly *alone*. Is that what the dead felt? The crushing weight of loneliness?

The girl rounded the corner toward the laundry room, and Michael shoved all concern for himself aside.

Even as he heard the thundering footsteps of the approaching nightmare, he willed himself forward. Racing to beat the child to her destination. His feet flew down the sidewalk to the point he truly *was* flying. Tamping down his fear, he went with it, flowing mist-like through the air to block the child's way.

"Boo!" he said in his best ghost voice. And his boo did the trick. Rosa stopped dead and loosed a startled scream before darting left, away from the laundry room and the appointment she had with death.

To Michael's dismay, she headed for the lights of the office. Another dead end.

Michael glanced back. The thing rushed forward, leaving behind flaps of skin and discarded bone. It shrieked as it came, its long, matted hair splayed out and whipping behind it like anxious, eager fingers.

He took one look at the ravenous intent in its eyes and turned and raced toward the motel office.

* * *

With each of Peter's breaths came a sucking sound, indication he was in a bad way. He placed a trembling hand on his chest and felt nothing but wet meat.

Time.

"Please, no."

A promise.

"I've got to get up."

Two you said. Two is gone.

"Please!"

Peter felt the demon regain control, knowing he had no more say in the matter. For years they'd lived enmeshed, but now he was unspooling. Fading. Soon to be shrunk into a mere passenger as Whisper, as Mr. Tell roamed free.

A face appeared above him—a scrawny teenager with stringy black hair that hung about bare shoulders. He stank of weed. "You don't look good, man. You look…"

Messy.

"Help me up," Peter said.

A young woman in a bathrobe, her hair still wet from the shower, put a hand on his shoulder. "You *really* shouldn't move."

"I have to…I…"

"Holy crap," the teen cried, falling back. "Look at his face!"

Peter felt his features shift, felt the integrity of his form buckle. He tasted smoke on his tongue, and he knew his time was up.

Whisper burst forth, billowing upward, taking the last remnants of him along for the ride until they were hovering in a twisting, tangled mass of blackness above the heads of the astonished motel guests.

Messy! Whisper laughed. *MESSY!*

With that they shot upward, into the cold, dark bosom of the night.

* * *

Michael found the girl cowering behind the front desk. When he approached, she screamed again—a muted, strangled sound barely audible through terrified teeth.

He bent down close to her and held out his hand.

"Don't worry, it's just me," he said, adopting a calm tone. He had seen his father do this as well whenever a storm rolled in. As the thunder grew louder, his father grew calmer. Or at least, he acted the part well enough. "Shh. It's all right."

He had to quickly regain the girl's trust after scaring her, and while he racked his brain, the girl did his job for him. She reached out and waved her hand through his face, trying to dislodge his nose. She giggled at this and proceeded to flap both hands through his ethereal head.

"See? It's me. It's me, Michael. And you're Rosa. And *we*..." He tapped at her sternum with a single ghostly finger. "...we're going to go play hide and seek."

"¿Al escondite?"

"Si!" Michael didn't know if the girl understood, but it got her to her feet. "Come. Las esco...come on!"

* * *

Sister approached the glass door to the office and let loose with the shotgun.

Break it. Break it all.

The door exploded in a spray of glass shards, and Sister thrilled at the sight of it. She dug into Butch's dying brain, and it warned her that there might be someone within with a similar instrument of death. But as she stepped into the office, ducking

272

her head, she sniffed the air and caught wind of only one scent that interested her.

The boy! The feast!

She spied her silhouette on the office wall and noted she had grown viler than ever. She tittered at this, realizing how horrific she must appear and anticipating the moment she would corner the boy, breaking his mind with her hideous beauty before sinking her incisors into his soul.

But the boy was nowhere to be seen. He couldn't have escaped—the smell of him, the ever-loving *stink* of him permeated the office. Where...?

The thump of a falling box gave him away. She stepped past the front desk, leaving black, bloody footprints on the carpet, and pushed open the inner door.

A hallway.

Her face cracked as her nostrils doubled and tripled. She sniffed the air for the boy's scent.

He had fled down the hallway and into the abandoned restaurant.

Restaurant.

How apt.

* * *

Michael urged the girl to be quiet, but her entire body was a bundle of twitching nerves, excited at the 'game'. And when she scooted closer to him in their hiding place, her elbow caught on the edge of a cardboard box of napkins. The box tumbled, the girl giggled and Michael *knew* they'd been heard.

They were trapped. He could make a run for it, pass through the solid walls of this place and slip beyond the creature's reach. But the girl? She was flesh and blood and no match for a blast of shot. What to do?

Light appeared down the hallway along with a sinister chuckling. The thing in the man suit, the creature from the laundry had found them. It was too late.

Michael felt a tickle in his head. It was like the feeling he'd gotten when he'd been here with Jessie. But Jessie was gone and this wasn't her motel. Jessie was long gone. She was...

With a clarity that nearly bowled him over, the voice of the cow rang out in his mind.

"If you climb up, you can see the whole motel."

Michael almost laughed aloud.

Thank you, thank you, thank you!

In fear and confusion, he had forgotten something very, very special about this room.

The ladder!

CHAPTER 51

Ellen whirled about, swinging her fists wildly.
"Don't touch me!"

"Ease up, Spooky!" Steph shouted, stepping between Ellen and Jessie. "She's only trying to help."

The woman in black exhaled sharply, shaking off the shock of the contact. "You broke my concentration. You're ruining everything."

Jessie stumbled forward. Steph grabbed her arm and steadied her. "I felt him. *Right here.* I felt him through you."

Ellen was trembling. "I don't work with others. I'm solo. I don't…"

"Please." Jessie gripped the young woman's shoulders. She felt the resistance of her touch, and yet she held on. She locked eyes with the strange, diminutive Ellen and begged. "Please!"

"Yes or no, I don't care," Steph said firmly. "But make your decision quick because I'm getting this girl to the hospital ASAP."

Ellen stared into Jessie's dilated pupils. She hadn't sensed her arrival, hadn't felt her join the connection. Perhaps it would be okay—beneficial even. Perhaps…but every square inch of her body recoiled at the thought of her *touch.*

"One hand."

"Okay," Jessie said, nodding vigorously.

"And if I say 'let go'…"

"I let go."

None too pleased with the situation, Ellen turned back to the cow. Reluctantly, she yanked at her collar, exposing the nape of her neck.

"All right," she huffed. "Let's do this."

CHAPTER 52

The girl had gotten the gist of what he wanted—to climb and keep climbing to the top—but her execution left something to be desired.

"Keep going," Michael whispered, ever mindful of the hellish figure that had just entered the room. "Go, Rosa, go!"

"¡Me voy!"

The creature had moved to the center of the space and was sniffing about, stalking its prey. What did being eaten feel like? He tried to shove the thought from his mind, but an image of Jessie screaming, black teeth embedded in her side, rose up and refused to leave. It hurt, that was the plain and awful truth of it. Being eaten *hurt*.

"Estoy cansada," Rosa said.

It was one of the few phrases Michael understood, for it was his chemo friend Hervé's constant complaint. *I'm tired.*

"Keep going, keep going."

His insistence paid off, for the girl soon reached the top rung. They were in near total darkness, here at the ceiling, and he had to squint in order to see the outlines of the trapdoor to the roof.

"Push, Rosa!"

"¿Qué?"

Michael mimed pushing open the door with his hollow hands. "Push, push!"

The girl pushed with one small hand, pressing with all her strength. The door didn't budge. She pushed again. Nothing.

"¡Estoy cansado!"

What had he done? Saved her from being found out below only to be trapped here above? For the thing was circling now, down in the darkness, trying to lock in on their scent.

A low rumble of a laugh shook the creature's frame, and Michael could almost see it shiver with joy. Slowly, neck bones creaking and snapping, it raised its head toward him and smiled a barbed wire grin.

Gnarled and bloody hands lifted the shotgun and trained it at the ceiling.

Michael closed his eyes.

A metallic *click* sounded from below, followed by a ragged roar. Michael opened his eyes in time to see the creature fling the empty gun against the wall, its stock splintering.

With the need to whisper wiped away, Michael screamed at the girl, "Push...the...door!"

The darkness below reached the ladder and tested its limbs on the lower rungs. It shed itself of bulk, sloughing off flesh and excess bone. Its grin was gone—in its place was a frightful determination.

It learned the ladder quickly and ascended just as fast.

Michael thought to shout again at the girl, to get her moving, but the child was petrified.

That was it—they'd used up the last of their luck.

Unless I make a little luck of my own.

Gently slipping his arms into Rosa's, Michael attempted to pry her fingers from the rung. When that didn't work, he dove in fully, ducking inside her as he had with Butch. He felt the *click* as mind met mind, heard her astonishment and raised one small hand. He pressed it against the trapdoor and pushed—apologizing for the pain of the effort—but still he pushed.

"¡Abierta!" the girl laughed in his head.

Michael didn't need a translator to understand. A square piece of night sky had suddenly appeared above them, flickering with the hint of greater lightning to come.

The trapdoor was open.

"Go!"

The ladder shook wildly as the thing clambered up from below, and the girl hoisted herself up through the opening and to the roof.

Up and out!

The girl landed on the rain-dampened roof, and Michael rolled out and to her side. They had made it.

Their victory was short lived. A deformed and blackened hand reached through the hole and dug its nails into the tar paper. The thing had reached the top of the ladder and it was climbing through the trapdoor, bending, twisting and forcing itself through. Some bits had to be left behind, and when it emerged, crusty and bloodied, it was waving a new set of glistening stumps in the air, eager to grow fingers and claws anew to get down to the business of feeding.

Rosa retreated to the cover of the plexiglass cow, placing the statue between her and the rising, tangled horror. Michael joined her, though he had zero hope they'd remain hidden for long. The thing had a bead on them and would tear itself to pieces in order to get its prize.

The rain was coming harder now, and Rosa, shivering in the deluge, sneezed. The creature fell forward toward the cow before rising up on new haunches and lumbering their way.

It peered at the statue, regarding its painted eyes with ones that were coal black and bleeding. It leaned forward and placed a spidery hand on the cow's head.

The scream the creature let loose nearly ripped Michael's mind in two.

* * *

Ellen pulled back momentarily, as did Jessie, such was the jolt of malignancy that passed through them.

"What is that?" Jessie cried.

Ellen didn't have the words to explain to Jessie or herself, and so she settled for one.

"Ruin," she stammered.

But she would not remove her hand from the cow's head. Not even if it killed her.

* * *

As Peter and Whisper rose higher and higher, Peter frantically searched for any tactic, any move he could make to draw them back to earth, back to the boy. But he was wounded and weary, and Whisper's elation at running free was too much to counter.

It was over, and Peter resigned himself to the fact that the only choice left him was to give up.

A spark ignited inside him.

Give up.

When he had first proposed to Hannah, she had said no. He had gotten down on bended knee in the middle of the Met before Hannah's favorite painting, *Joan of Arc* by Jules Bastien-Lepage, and she had said no.

And so, he had given up on her. On her and the entire notion of marriage.

She told him later that by dropping his pursuit, he had drawn her nearer until at last she relinquished and two had become one.

Give up.

Yes, he would give up. Ever since he and the demon had been knitted together, he had kept it at arm's length, held it at bay, jealously guarding his soul. They were never truly one because Peter wouldn't let that happen. They were just a messy conglomeration of man and monster, of light and dark.

Yes, he'd give up. And maybe by losing he could eke out a win.

With the night wind rushing past like a freight train, Peter leaned back and let go. He split himself open, exposing all he ever was, letting go of his memories, letting them flow into the mix. Goodbye Hannah, the love of his life. Goodbye Michael, his wondrous child. Goodbye summers and winters and every recorded minute. He let it all go with a singular effort, and it streamed from him like blood from a razor's cut.

The demon caught wind of what had happened and it howled. *He* was Peter. *He* was Whisper. *He* was husband and demon and father and death.

The devil struggled in flight, but it was no match for the sheer weight of the purge. And as the last of the man flowed into him, Whisper knew he was beaten.

For he thought of the boy and the earth below. And he yearned to return to them both.

* * *

Sister withdrew her hand, leaving behind layers of grey-black skin. The unexpected connection was painful, and it felt as if someone was staring *into* her, sizing her up and spitting out judgment. It had made her feel small and weak and beholden.

She hadn't felt that way in so very long.

Her rage bubbled up along with her innards and she bashed the false beast, knocking it free from its moorings, toppling it over and revealing beneath…

Her prize!

"Mine," she hissed through the dead man's shredded face.

The two little ones lay helpless and sprawled on the wet roof, illuminated by the violent bursts of lightning overhead. Two prizes! One for the body and one for the soul.

The churning storm clouds dropped lower, adding majesty to the moment. She lurched forward, delirious with the duet of children's screams. Arms outspread, she bent to them, eager to gather them up and kiss them and squeeze them and rip them and eat them. It was time.

As she reached first for the boy, a shroud covered her eyes and she feared they'd gone to rot. She tore them from her head, making way for new growth, but no vision returned.

Panicked, she groped for the girl. She'd take the child's eyes for her own. But the air had grown thick and it caught in her throat, and instead of the girl, she reached for her neck. Sister clawed at her throat, ripping her windpipe free, desperately hungry for...

AIR!

But the world around her had congealed, solidifying into a heavy blanket of decay.

Gnashing her teeth and slashing blindly, she heard a familiar voice in her asphyxiated haze.

"I am Whisper..."

No.

"I am Mr. Tell..."

No!

"And I won't let you hurt the boy."

* * *

Michael urged the girl back from the swirling mass and she complied. They'd watched in wonder as the darkness descended from above, imitating the rolling anger of the storm, dropping onto the creature on the roof. It had surrounded the beast with its inky gloom and it now proceeded to squeeze.

The thing beneath fought back—he could see the black mist rise and fall with its flailing—but the darkness held firm, trapping the nightmare within.

It was the shadow man, come to call. The man with the shifting face. The Messy Man. But gone was any sense of the one who resembled his father. This was all rising smoke and roiling cloud, so like a storm cloud it threatened to let loose its own lightning.

A single tendril pulled loose and swept past Michael, brushing his cheek—a whip-sharp gesture of ferocious affection that left him with a solitary thought...

Goodbye.

And with that, the dark cloud drew inward and vanished with a howl.

A booming clap of thunder shook the two children, and Rosa commenced crying so loudly she nearly drowned out the storm itself.

Goodbye.

Michael heard the distant cries of Rosa's parents and he walked to the roof's edge. Below in the parking lot, the guests—the whole lot of them—were looking high and low for the girl. Strangers looking for a stranger's kid.

He called back and waved, unconcerned how a ghost on the roof might be perceived. As long as he got their attention.

Michael crouched at the girl's side where she lay clinging to the fallen cow—a tiny girl holding tight to the world's biggest toy.

"Don't worry," he said, placing his hand on hers. "Everything's going to be okay."

His hand passed through the child's and into the cow's plastic head.

"Come on, kid. Are you just going to sit there or are you going to go home?"

"What?"

"Michael. It's time to go home."

He heard a rhythm rise on the distant horizon—a wild and insistent beat like a rapidly approaching steam engine on a collision course. He saw light too, blinding and sharp, and he tried to shy away but found he could not. And when it seemed quite certain he would be dashed apart by the approaching doom, he opened his mouth and screamed.

"What's the matter, honey?"

Michael's eyes flew open and for a moment he couldn't make heads or tails out of his situation. Finally, the warmth of the sun on his face and the cool of the water brought him back to center.

He was in the pool. He was treading water in the deep end. And there was no need to fear something lurking beneath the surface, waiting to rob him of his breath. What lay below was simply more water, and perhaps a coin or two his mother had tossed.

"Michael?" Hannah Larson rose and stepped to the pool's edge. "You want to get out? Dad's bringing pizza."

The boy grinned and answered with an enthusiastic backstroke. "Nope! I think I'll swim until he gets here."

And so he swam—in the pool at the Intermission Motor Lodge where the only guests were the living.

CHAPTER 53

Ellen stepped back from the cow and brusquely brushed Jessie's hand from the back of her neck. "Okay, okay, that's enough."

Jessie shook off the connection, eager to clear her mind.

"What...just happened?"

"It's done," Ellen said, "The boy's out."

"Okay, but...*what happened?*"

Ellen sighed, tired and more than a little annoyed. "You're not going to understand it anyway, so why should I tell you and waste my time?"

Jessie slammed her hand so hard on the table Ellen felt the concussion in her molars. The woman in black shut up.

"Try me."

Ellen shrugged and turned to her open portfolio, calmly gathering together her papers. "Where's your friend?"

Jessie looked about the room. "She was...right here."

"And now she's not."

"No, she isn't."

Ellen rammed the last of the pages into the portfolio and closed it up, the thing looking like an oversized sandwich. Then she said, as if explaining to a particularly dim child, "And what does *that* tell you?"

Jessie felt the sudden urge to punch the little woman in the face, but instead, she worked her mind around the question being posed to her. Still on shaky footing, she replied, "That something's...changed?"

Ellen rolled her eyes and harrumphed. "Was that so hard?"

She turned and took off toward the hallway, seemingly finished with suffering fools. Jessie followed after her as quickly as her hip would permit.

"So, I'm right?" Jessie asked.

Ellen paused at the office door. "I'd give the boy most of the credit, but...I suspect we're going to find quite a few changes." The woman opened the door and stared at the parking lot. "Like the fact that I didn't drive here."

Jessie followed Ellen's glance. Gone was the little Geo Metro with the leaking radiator. Gone was Wood's crippled car. In fact, even her memory of the vehicles seemed to be fading.

"What's happening?"

"You sound like a broken record, you know that? I usually like repetition. I find it soothing. Like the drip from a faucet or clothes circling round in a dryer. But with you it's just—"

"I bought this motel two years after the shootings," Jessie said, more to herself than to the other woman. Said it to herself because that *too* was fading. Jessie trembled—her life was being ripped from her shred by shred. She clung to the office door. "I feel like I'm losing my mind."

"That's because you are. Or maybe you're finding it. Six of one, half a dozen of the other. You were in the mix with me and the boy and the dark. Might take a little while for you to line yourself up to the here and now, but—"

"How can you be so calm?"

Ellen saw the fear in Jessie's face and put a rare hand on the other woman's shoulder. "Imagine a guitar with a thousand strings," she said. "Each string is a tone. Most people only hear one tone—if they didn't they'd go nuts. Me? I hear *all the strings at once*. Makes for a terrible chord. But I'm me and you're you."

"Meaning?"

"You're not losing your mind. You're just moving over to another string. Might take a little while for you to line yourself up to the here and now, but—"

"Excuse me," Jessie said, shaking her head. "I must have spaced out there for a second. Can I help you?"

"Or not."

"I beg your pardon?"

"Nothing."

Jessie held the door open. "Are you looking for a room? Our grand opening's next week, but as you can see..." She gestured toward the pool where Peter Larson had just arrived with a pizza box in hand. "We're making a few exceptions."

Ellen waved her off. "Thanks but no thanks." She pulled out her phone and tapped an app. "No available cars? Are you kidding me? Do you people not know what ridesharing is?"

"Can I call you a cab?"

"Don't bother. I need an alcoholic beverage. Which way are the bars?"

Jessie pointed toward Main Street. "Take a left and go straight for twelve blocks. You'll hit the square, then keep on two more blocks. You'll find—"

Ellen waved her off yet again. "I get the gist of it. Take care." She started walking, paused and came back. She reached into her pocket and came out with a crumpled business card. "I may need you to sign a release. For my next book."

"Why?" Jessie asked, obviously talking to a crazy woman. "We've barely said two words to each other."

"I know," Ellen huffed. "But you'll have to do."

At that, she turned and stalked off down Main Street, an awkward vision in black toting her bulging portfolio.

Steph came up behind Jessie, her arms loaded down with towels. "Who was that?"

Jessie held up the card. "I don't know but she left this."

Steph gave the card a quick glance. "Hmm, spooky. These towels going to 201?"

"Not on their own, they're not."

"Har-har." Steph headed off across the parking lot.

Jessie was about to head back inside the office when she noticed the Larson boy standing at the fence, staring in her direction. The kid gave her a beckoning wave.

"How's the water?" she asked as she approached the boy.

"A little chilly, but I like it."

"Michael, I'm going to eat up all these mushrooms," his father teased.

"Gimme a second, will you, Dad?"

A quizzical frown formed on Jessie's brow. "What's up?"

The kid leaned in conspiratorially. "You're forgetting, aren't you?"

"Forgetting what?"

"Everything. The monsters, the man with the gun, the little girl."

"The monsters? Yes, I guess I am forgetting about those," she said, playing along.

"Me too! It's all going fuzzy in my head."

"You know, maybe you're just a little hungry. Maybe you need a slice of that pizza," she said, nodding toward where his folks hovered around the pie.

"I'm serious!"

"I can see that."

The boy searched her eyes but didn't find any spark of recognition.

"Well...I guess I just wanted to say thanks for saving me. I thought that thing ate you up for sure."

"You're welcome. And no..." She patted herself down, making a show of it. "I'm pretty sure I'm all here."

"Nom nom nom!" Michael's father said, biting into another slice.

"I'll be right there!" the boy cried.

Jessie bent to the boy's level. "I better get back to work. But if you see any more monsters around here, you just come find me and I'll..." She gave the air a swift karate chop, causing them both to laugh.

"Thanks," Michael said. He turned back to the pool, dove in and swam to the other side where his parents and pizza were waiting.

Jessie shook her head and headed back to the office. She was only one-fourth of the way through her to-do list and it was already nearly noon.

As she reached the office door, she stopped and backed up. She stared up at the restaurant's roof.

Maybe I should put that cow back up there.

The building looked rather empty without it. Steph had insisted they bring it down—a cow meant beef and beef meant a meal, something they were not yet prepared to offer. But the more she thought about it, the more she felt it was the right thing to do. It could be her watchcow, keeping an eye out over her place.

She'd make a call and have the thing back at its post in the next few days. Before the grand opening.

I bet the kid would like that.

The front desk phone rang, and Jessie hustled inside to catch it, making a mental note to add the cow to her to-do list.

"Intermission Motor Lodge, may I help you?"

CHAPTER 54

Riggs was busy wolfing down the first of four Gas-n-Grub burgers when the Blind Rock's front door swung open, breaking the bar's two-hour, no-patrons streak.

"Thank God," he said with a mouthful of beef. "I was starting to think I forgot to open up."

Ellen lumbered into the room, still hauling the cumbersome portfolio. She wrinkled her nose. The place reeked of sour, spilled beer. "Your bar smells like a frat house."

"Thank you."

Ellen picked her way through the crowd of mismatched tables and chairs and chose a stool at the bar, setting down her load before hoisting herself up onto the stool. Her hair was awake with static and her face was wet with sweat. She set her toy cow next to the napkin holder and raised her hand for service.

Amused, Riggs looked around the room. "Uh...school's out, missy. Can I get you anything?"

"What do you have that's hot?" Ellen snapped.

"Besides me?"

"Is that a joke?"

"I guess not."

"I don't do jokes."

"Neither do I, apparently."

Ellen shifted on her barstool, her legs an inch too short to reach the foot rest. "I'd like something hot. Damn hot."

Riggs set down the remains of burger one and sauntered over to where the woman in black sat, sucking the grease from his fingers.

"Are you talking food or drink? If it's food, I'm afraid you're outta luck—"

"Drink," Ellen spat, starting to get annoyed. "Why would I come to a place like this for food?"

Riggs bowed his head in agreement. "Fair enough. Let's see. I could make you a killer Bloody Mary."

"I hate vodka."

"A shot of Fireball?"

"Cinnamon makes me gag."

"Running outta options, I'm afraid."

Ellen took a quick inventory of the bottles behind the bartender, which was no easy thing, what with the distraction of his piss-yellow bowling shirt. Finally, she settled on her order.

"I want a Michelada."

Riggs frowned. "Not sure I know that one."

"Doesn't surprise me."

That elicited a chuckle from Riggs.

"What?"

"That's funny," the bartender said. "You're funny."

Ellen quirked her head. "Am I?"

She proceeded to run Riggs through his paces, gathering the makings of the drink: Mexican beer, lime juice, soy sauce and Worcestershire with a lime wedge as a garnish.

After he had all the ingredients lined up, Riggs rubbed his chin. "Yeah…not sure how all this adds up to what I'd call damn hot."

Ellen fished her miniature bottle of Boo-Hot from her purse and tossed it to him.

"Jeez," he said, examining the label. "One million on the Scoville scale. You must be having some kinda day if you wanna do this kinda damage."

"I have been. Yes."

Riggs waved the little bottle in front of the toy cow. "Looky here, Bessie. Mommy's about to get her heat on."

"Please don't talk to my cow."

"Sorry."

Ellen quickly gathered she had offended him—the man had the telltale signs of it on his face, and she had come to recognize those signs through much effort. And so, she picked up her cow and handed it to him.

"For me?"

"For the bar. It could use some character."

"Thank you kindly."

"Whoever decorated this dump put in absolutely *zero* effort."

Riggs snapped his fingers. "And you were doing so well."

He set the cow on the shelf between the Irish Cream and Crème de Menthe and stepped back to see if his patron approved. Ellen nodded, suddenly wistful at the thought of parting with her plastic friend.

In a minute, Riggs had mixed the drink and poured them both a pint of the brown mixture. He raised his glass high.

"What shall we toast to?"

"Do we have to toast to anything?"

"We must."

Ellen considered this for a moment before raising her glass skyward. "To finding your way home."

"To finding my way home."

"I wasn't toasting you."

"No? Cuz, the point of a toast is to—"

"Never mind."

Ellen brought the glass to her lips and proceeded to down the hellishly hot concoction in a single gulp.

CHAPTER 55

The darkness tastes like blood.

The thought traveled with the demon as it raced through the night, through a thousand nights. It helped cushion the blows and attacks of the other with which it rode. *Sister.* For sister she was. Vengeful and thrashing. She fought him every inch of the way—hate her only baggage, fear written down the length of her.

For years—for lifetimes, it seemed—Whisper had been anchored in unfamiliar places, tethered and bound to a fearful and fretful *man*. But the man had relinquished all to him. And in his acquiescence, Whisper had become *more*.

Saving the boy was inconsequential—a mere bump in the road. But the act had brought satisfaction and, yes, joy. It was not his joy, but the man's joy which ran through him. Of the *father* within. And, realizing this, Whisper wondered if the scales were truly tipped in his favor or not.

No matter.

He was untied.

He was heading where he had always wanted to go.

He was going home.

Sister bit and slashed and tore, but nothing could slow his progress. If he arrived in ribbons, so be it.

He was going home.

THE HUNGRY ONES

* * *

The barefoot girl in the homespun dress raised the maple twig and spun it once, spun it twice. The cold wind had kissed her cheeks pink and brought goosebumps to her skin. The snow covering the field was ankle deep, but she didn't feel it. And it was necessary—sole touching soil. Otherwise, the words wouldn't work. She would raise a whirlwind of snowflakes but nothing more.

She bent and brushed the snow from the blood-red keystone, centering herself and her thoughts.

The air snapped in anticipation but yielded nothing.

The girl took a deep breath, her lungs clenching against the cold, and she tried again.

"*Vu trah, nu klah, sey-tee, olan.*"

This time the air obeyed, hissing and popping like an eager fire. A ripple appeared before her, like the distorted eye of a great thing beyond her comprehension. She was out of bounds, tempting fate, but still she swirled the maple stick, cut from the branch of the lightning-kissed tree.

"*Vu trah, nu klah, sey-tee, olan.*"

The mingled sounds of a choir and an out-of-tune upright crossed the snow-covered field, the words of the song riding on the frigid breeze.

"*Bringing in the sheaves, bringing in the sheaves. We shall come rejoicing, bringing in the sheaves.*"

The tune came from the small, wooden church on the horizon. The girl's footprints led from there to here, to the circle of stone in the middle of the field where she rehearsed her incantations and practiced her art. Where she brought forth her friends.

"*Vu trah, nu klah…*"

Unlike her previous attempts, this time she knew she had hit the mark.

First, the tickle behind her ears—next, the weightless feeling within her gut. She never knew what she would draw forth, only hoped something familiar would rise from the mist.

For the mist *was* rising.

Bound by the circle of stone she had made while the others were not watching—they were *always* watching—those she lured from the Otherwhere brought many surprises. Some good, some bad, some which filled her dreams with dread.

A column of grey smoke spiraled at the center of the circle, violent in its aspect. Usually the conjuring was a peaceful event, a slow reveal like a birthday gift unwrapped. But this time…this was something different.

The column broke in two, the twin, turbid shafts spinning about each other like a double helix—twins angry and spitting in their dance. As the mist defined itself, she found she recognized both of the arrivals, and she called to them by name.

"Sister!"

The first swirling cloud stood at attention.

"Whisper!"

The second was not as compliant, content instead to jab and bite at the first.

"What's that you say?"

The second column darkened in response and the girl interpreted.

"Is this true? You've *killed*? Answer me, Sister."

The first column shuddered momentarily, roiling and guilty. And then Sister struck, lashing out at the girl, solidifying as she broke the barrier between circle and snow. The demon stood, arms outstretched before the girl, her dark and twisted body painfully contrasted against the field of white.

The girl was taken aback by Sister's boldness and stumbled. "Back!"

The demon stepped forward.

The girl responded in her secret tongue. "Vlel dai!" With a whip of the maple switch, the girl dispatched the offending thing. Sister went up in a flash of flame, ashes scattering in the wind and bones raining down about the stone circle.

The girl gathered herself.

"Whisper! Whisper, come to me."

The remaining column of smoke and fog drew inward, reshaping itself into the form of a man, devoid of feature and empty of expression.

This development further stirred the girl's interest and she brought up her switch once more. "Shadow, I draw you forth— you dare not resist. This is your charge. You must obey. This is your charge."

The mist split. The first plume rose up into the sky, rocketing upward with the elation of freed prey. And just when it seemed it would continue to the winter sun beyond, it spread its wings, flapping and crying with joy. And when she raised her arm as a perch, it dove, eager to sink its talons into the flesh of her arm.

The demon—now bird—lighted upon her forearm and held tight, nibbling her neck with its beak and relishing the reunion. And the girl replied in kind.

"Oh, my Whisper. My little Mr. Tell. What secrets have you brought me? What stories do you have to share?"

The crow leaned in, whispering and biting at her ear. The girl listened, amazed and enthralled.

And when the bird was done speaking, the girl looked back to the circle where smoke congealed into a man. He lay curled in on himself amidst the wreckage of Sister's scattered bones. The man was injured and horribly gaunt, but there was a familiarity to his face that kept her from running.

"Go," she said to the bird. "Bring help."

As the crow rose, winging its way toward the church, Willa knelt by Peter's side in the fresh, fallen snow.

A NOTE FROM ELLEN MARX

If you enjoyed this book, please consider writing a review.

If you found any typos in this edition and would like to celebrate your keen eye, send them to:

FoundATypoEllen@gmail.com

If you are looking to exercise a spirit or talk to the dead, please remember that I am a fictional character and have limited access to the internet or other forms of communication.

Finally, Chris would like to thank his wife Deborah, his mother JoAnne, Nick Sullivan, Stephanie Hilliard (the *real* Steph), Sondra Wolfer, Matthew Ballen, Tracy Robinson, John Bender, Gavin Kendall, James Cleveland, Gretchen Douglas and all the bloggers, reviewers and authors who have welcomed him into the indie horror world.

Ellen Marx
May 28, 2019

ABOUT THE AUTHOR

Chris Sorensen is the author of *The Nightmare Room, The Mad Scientists of New Jersey* and has written numerous screenplays including *Suckerville, Bee Tornado* and *The Roswell Project*. The Butte Theater and Thin Air Theatre Company of Cripple Creek, Colorado have produced dozens of his plays including *Dr. Jekyll's Medicine Show, Werewolves of Poverty Gulch,* and *The Vampire of Cripple Creek*. Chris has narrated over 200 audiobooks (including the award-winning *Missing* series by Margaret Peterson Haddix). He is the recipient of three AudioFile Earphone Awards, and AudioFile singled out his performance of *Sent* as one of the 'Best Audiobooks of 2010'.